TEA FOR TWO

Please be seated, Major Lyonbridge," Marian said in a voice that sounded too high to her own ears. "May I offer you some tea?"

He stepped forward quickly and took her shoulders in his big hands. When he spoke, his lips were inches from hers.

"I did not come for tea," he said huskily. Before even he knew what he was about, he had seized her about the waist and given her a whirl that threatened to sweep the teapot off the table. "Marian, I want to marry you."

"Do not be absurd," she scoffed. "Your father would never permit it. He wants you to marry an heiress, and he has every right to expect this of you."

"I can deal with my father. The question is not what he wants, but what you want. Will you marry me, Marian?"

Marian's lips worked, but nothing came out. . . .

Books by Kate Huntington

THE CAPTAIN'S COURTSHIP

THE LIEUTENANT'S LADY

LADY DIANA'S DARLINGS

MISTLETOE MAYHEM

A ROGUE FOR CHRISTMAS

THE MERCHANT PRINCE

TOWN BRONZE

HIS LORDSHIP'S HOLIDAY SURPRISE

THE GENERAL'S DAUGHTER

Published by Zebra Books

THE GENERAL'S DAUGHTER

Kate Huntington

ZEBRA BOOKS
Kensington Publishing Corp.
http://www.kensingtonbooks.com

ZEBRA BOOKS are published by

Kensington Publishing Corp.
850 Third Avenue
New York, NY 10022

All Kensington titles, imprints and distributed lines are available at special quantity discounts for bulk purchases for sales promotion, premiums, fund-raising, educational or institutional use.

Special book excerpts or customized printings can also be created to fit specific needs. For details, write or phone the office of the Kensington Special Sales Manager: Kensington Publishing Corp., 850 Third Avenue, New York, NY 10022. Attn. Special Sales Department. Phone: 1-800-221-2647.

First Printing: April 2004
10 9 8 7 6 5 4 3 2 1

Printed in the United States of America

For my writing chums
Jennifer Coleman, Jackie Schauer,
and Bob Rogers.

Chapter 1

July 1812
Salamanca, Spain

A haze of anger and gunpowder and black grit stung Major Adam Lyonbridge's eyes as he charged and slashed and took down frog after bloody frog. His horse had been shot out from under him after the first charge and, surrounded by enemies, he threw his head back and bared his teeth in defiance.

He was aware that his men called him The Berserker because of his ferocity and courage in battle, for, in truth, when the blood lust was upon him he felt no fear. His mind was consumed with war. It was his business, and he exulted in it.

It was a relief to be able to unleash the frustration that had been built up over three weeks of marching and countermarching by Lord Wellington's and the French General Marmont's well-matched troops while each wily commander waited for the other to make the first mistake.

The first to do so had been Marmont, and Wellington immediately sent the third division—of which Adam's regiment was a member—to shatter the French line.

Adam was aware of a weight hitting his thigh as the man next to him, a likable young soldier under his command named William Quarterhouse, called out a warning and deliberately took a bullet meant for Adam. The boy's mother had begged him with tears in her eyes at Portsmouth to take care of her precious son, while William looked on in acute embarrassment.

"Give them hell, sir," the boy shouted as he hit the muddy ground.

Adam fought on until his arms felt like lead and his legs were numb for Quarterhouse and the rest of his fallen countrymen, who would have been on their farms overseeing their crops, at their desks clerking, or in their own beds making love with their wives had it not been for this hellish war.

Adam threw back his head and shouted in savage exultation as another enemy hit the ground with his head half severed from his body.

The battle was over. A miasma of burning flesh, the screaming of dying horses, and horror hung over the battlefield as Adam searched for those of his fallen men who might have survived. He had returned to the place where he had seen young Quarterhouse fall, but the young man's body was gone.

Had he been taken for treatment to the regimental hospital, now housed in a convent, or had his corpse been removed for burial? And what of Adam's second in command and all the other men who had faced death on his orders?

There was only one way to find out. Adam ignored the invitations of some drunken soldiers to join them in their revelry and went to the regimental hospital.

He entered the hospital to find wounded men lying about, groaning. Those who were still in their right minds stood—or straightened, if they could not stand—at his entrance.

"As you were," he said mechanically as he looked around and recognized one of his men. The soldier's eyes lit up.

"Major Lyonbridge! Quarterhouse said the last time he saw you there was a saber poised at your head."

Adam grinned.

"So, he's still alive. He took a bullet meant for me."

"He's in there," the man said, indicating the room beyond.

As Adam turned away, one of the men said, "I told you it would take more than the French to cause The Berserker to stick his spoon in the wall!"

Adam strode in the doorway to see William lying on a cot, bare to the waist, and being ministered to by a—Adam blinked.

"You are a female," he said in shocked disbelief.

The tired, red-rimmed, green eyes of the said female narrowed. She had disheveled red hair and a trim figure clothed in a gray muslin gown streaked with blood and gore.

Her face was beautiful, with its firm jaw and delicate features, under the fatigue and sheen of perspiration. She looked like an angel of death.

"Oh, very good," she said sarcastically. "Now we know your eyesight is unimpaired. If you want attention for that arm, you will have to wait until I am finished here."

Adam frowned and looked down at the blood crusting his sleeve. He had not even known he was injured. It had happened before. When he was fighting, he was equally impervious to heat, cold, wet, and pain.

"But I—" he began.

The girl—for she could not have reached twenty—put her hands on her hips and scowled at him.

"Miss Randall, this is Major Lyonbridge," Quarterhouse said, sounding shocked.

"I do not care if he is Lord Wellington himself," Miss Randall snapped. "Two of his lot were already here and took my father away to coddle their hurts because the officers are so squeamish about being treated with the enlisted men, and this one can just wait his turn until I've got this bullet out of your shoulder."

"Major Lyonbridge led the charge," the private persisted. "He is a hero."

"Excellent," the girl said, turning to Adam. Her movement caused a surprisingly delicate fragrance to tease his nostrils for a moment.

Could it be . . . orange blossom? Suddenly he was reminded of moonlit gardens and pretty girls in white dresses with flowers in their hair right in the middle of all this stench and death.

"If you want to be useful, hero, you might hold down Private Quarterhouse, here, while I extract this ball," the girl said. "You're a big enough fellow that you should be able to do the job with one hand if your wounded arm bothers you."

"Have you any brandy?" Adam asked. The private was stone-cold sober and his face was dead white, not a good state to be in if some adder-tongued female was about to dig a bullet out of one's shoulder.

"Why? Do you turn faint at the sight of blood?" the girl asked.

He gave a snort of exasperation.

"If so, I am in the wrong profession, am I not?" he asked scornfully. "For Quarterhouse, of course."

"Oh. My apologies, Major," she said with a sigh as she reached back to rub the small of her back. "Watching their pain and knowing I am able to do so little to relieve it makes me snappish. I am sorry to say we had depleted our store of spirits an hour before the battle was over."

"Then brace yourself, Quarterhouse," Adam said grimly as he held down the man, and the girl competently extracted the bullet. It wasn't an easy process, and the pain in the private's eyes made Adam's gut clench. The whole time, Quarterhouse looked up at him with so much undeserved hero worship in his pain-filled eyes that Adam felt like an imposter.

"Thank you, sir," the young man said when the ordeal was over and the girl had wrapped his shoulder in clean bandages. "This is a rare honor. I must write to my family directly to tell them the hero of Salamanca personally held me down while the bullet was dug out."

"There were many heroes today at Salamanca," Adam said.

"Orderly, how many more are waiting outside?" the woman asked when the man who had been with the wounded in the outer room stuck his head in the doorway.

"None, Miss Randall," the man said. "The others must wait for the captain."

"It is your turn, then, Major," the girl said to Adam as he took Quarterhouse's arm and helped him get up from the cot. The boy groaned.

"Good lad," Adam said to him. "I'll help you to your quarters."

"Not until I see that arm," Miss Randall said. Her hands were on her hips again.

"It is nothing. Just a scratch," Adam said.

"It looks like more than a scratch," the girl said. "If I don't take care of it now, it could become infected. My father has more than enough demands on his time without being called away to treat you for it. Sit on the cot, if you please, Major. If you refuse, I will be forced to enlist Private Quarterhouse's assistance in holding you down."

The boy gave a surprised spurt of laughter.

"This is unnecessary," Adam said, frowning.

She gave a tired sigh.

"Major Lyonbridge, I know it isn't customary for officers to be treated in the hospital with the enlisted men, but I am the only person available to aid you. My knowledge is limited, but I am perfectly capable of cleaning and dressing your wound. Who knows when my father will return?

You might have a long wait in your quarters until he can be sent to you."

"Begging your pardon, sir, you should have your arm seen to," Private Quarterhouse said bashfully. The hero worship still shone in his eyes. "It would be a blow to the army if anything happened to you."

"On the other hand, if the Major is *afraid* to let a mere female dress his arm—" the girl began.

Adam gave a growl of exasperation.

"I am afraid of nothing, you impudent girl," he said, looking her straight in the eye. He sat on the cot and removed his coat, then his shirt.

Marian Randall barely kept herself from sighing. She had never seen such a superb specimen of manhood, but she was not about to gratify the famous Major Adam Lyonbridge's vanity by letting him catch her admiring the sculptured musculature of his well-developed chest.

Whatever was wrong with her? She had been looking at half-naked males all day without embarrassment, but now she felt a strong desire to blush.

How absolutely ridiculous.

Major Lyonbridge might have broad shoulders, a narrow waist, and muscular arms that would do justice to a warrior god, as well as compelling blue eyes that glinted at her alternately with annoyance and amusement, but he was hardly a young lady's dream of romance at the moment. His brown hair was matted to his head with sweat, and it was definitely wise if one refrained from inhaling in his vicinity.

"You were right," she said as she inspected the saber cut, which was long and crusted with blood, but looked relatively minor for all that. She started to clean it preparatory to probing it for bits of fabric and other foreign material that could cause an infection. "Just a scratch."

"Your father is Captain Randall, the surgeon, I presume. I am surprised he exposes you to such unpleasantness as this," the major said. Marian had to give him credit. He didn't even flinch when she probed the wound.

"My mother always accompanied Father on campaign, and I was old enough to leave school when she died, so I took her place," she said. "Ordinarily I would be with the officers' wives now, rolling lint for bandages and brewing tea, but Father was taken off to treat some officers and I had to do *something* to help these poor men. I am rather adept at patching up men's hurts when the situation arises. My mother and I both have had to dig out a bullet or two in an emergency situation."

"Does your father not hesitate to expose you to potential insult by permitting you to deal so directly with the men?" Major Lyonbridge asked.

She gave a snort of amusement.

"Hardly! He is a fair hand with a knife, my father," she said proudly. "Any man reckless enough to take unwelcome liberties with me would find himself at the wrong end of one of my father's extremely sharp surgical instruments, I promise you."

Marian finished securing the bandage and regarded her handiwork with satisfaction.

"There. If your arm gives you any trouble, send for my father tomorrow so he can have a look at it," Marian said in dismissal. "I am certain you have seen enough action to know you must keep it clean and have the bandages changed frequently."

"Yes. I thank you, Miss Randall, for your kind ministrations."

She gave him a sharp look to see if he had intended any sarcasm.

"You are most welcome, sir," she said after she decided he had not.

He winced as he shrugged his shoulders back into his shirt, and he left the room with his good hand on Private Quarterhouse's shoulder.

Marian took a deep, calming breath and stared after them.

So *that* was the celebrated Major Adam Lyonbridge, the one said to be such a devil in battle and the despair of all the infatuated ladies. After meeting him, she had no doubt it was true.

She felt her heart flutter with unwelcome feminine interest, and she quickly went back to her task of putting away her supplies.

Handsome, well-born cavalry officers were well above *her* touch. Especially this one.

Major Lyonbridge, she knew from listening to the officers' wives' gossip, was betrothed to the daughter of General Lord Grimsby, his commanding officer.

She smiled as she thought of what her late mother would have said if she were still alive.

Stop your mooning, girl. There's work to do.

"It was bad enough that you brought her on campaign with you against my expressed wishes! But to actually permit her to treat the men in the hospital? The *enlisted* men? Are you *insane*?" shouted General Lord Grimsby when Captain Lawrence Randall, the regimental surgeon, reported to his campaign office. The general had sent one of his aides to demand the surgeon attend him as soon as he had learned from Major Lyonbridge that the regimental surgeon's daughter—in reality *his* daughter—had made a tidy job of dressing his saber wound.

"Marian is a grown woman and she makes her own decisions," the surgeon said with a lift of his bushy white brows.

"It is too dangerous for her to be here! I told you she was to stay in London at school, and you disobeyed me."

They had been over this ground before. Apparently Captain Randall decided he might as well make himself comfortable if they were to hash over their old argument. Again.

"Sooner or later, a girl has to leave school," the surgeon said, sitting down uninvited. He stretched out his legs. "We agreed one-and-twenty years ago when I married Annie that you were to relinquish any interest in *my* daughter."

General Grimsby narrowed his eyes at the surgeon.

"Annie would be alive now if she hadn't married you. I would have taken care of her. You took advantage of her confusion to marry her behind my back, and you took her on campaign with you. It *killed* me to see her suffer deprivation and not be able to aid her."

The surgeon gave a snort of derision.

"All I did—and it was the best thing I've ever done—was offer her and her child the protection of my name. Don't come over the injured party with me, Lord Grimsby." There was nothing respectful in the way he spoke the general's title. "You were, and are, married. You should have told Annie the truth before you got her with child. You never should have *touched* her."

Knowing he had been in the wrong, the general returned to his original grievance.

"I have paid, and paid well, to have Annie's daughter kept at school, safe from harm," he said. "That was our agreement. I could not stop you from taking Annie on campaign, but my child was to remain in England."

The surgeon stood and leaned over the general's desk so he could glare directly into the superior officer's eyes.

"It shamed her mother and me to take your money for her schooling, but we took it for *her* sake. Beyond that I have never accepted a penny from you for her support. I have fed her and clothed her and sheltered her all these years. Do you think Annie or I, either one of us, wanted anything from you?"

No. Because you already had everything, you smug bastard.

"What if you die? She will be all alone unless you assign me as her guardian."

"You are assuming you will outlive me. In such a case you can come to Marian's rescue," the surgeon taunted him, "if you aren't too afraid of your lady wife's wrath to acknowledge her."

His lady wife. That was the crux of the matter.

The ambitious general owed his social position and the political preferment that got him a superior rank to the influence of his wife's powerful family, and well he knew it. She was aware of his little affairs. He suspected she had enjoyed a few of her own, although no whisper of scandal had ever been connected with her name. If she learned of his natural daughter, *he* would never hear the end of it. She was a petty woman, and her revenge would be terrible.

But he could hardly back down before the surgeon after declaring his interest in the girl.

"I would make sure she gets back to England," the general promised. "I would find her a husband to take care of her."

The surgeon sat down and passed a hand across his eyes. He looked exhausted and old. The general knew Captain Randall was only five years older than himself. Did *he* look so old?

"In truth, I have been much worried that I *would* die and leave her stranded on campaign without protection," the captain said ruefully. "I shall leave a letter with you for her, commending her into your care if I should die. In it, I will acknowledge the truth of her birth and state my wish that you become her guardian if I predecease you."

"Very well," the general said as he pushed paper and pen across the desk at him. The surgeon began to write.

"Until the day I die, she is not to know that I am not her natural father," the surgeon said, pausing for a moment in his writing.

The general nodded stiffly. The surgeon finished the letter and the general read it through. Then, satisfied, he dismissed the man. Captain Randall stood up with a stifled groan and made his weary way out of the room.

Little did the general suspect it would be the last time he would see his old rival alive.

Chapter 2

Marian slowly packed away her father's instruments and concentrated fiercely on what she would do with them now.

Should she give them to her father's assistant, who could no doubt put them to good use? Should she send them to England, to the university where he was educated, with the stipulation that they be given to a promising student of humble means? Should she sell them and hope they would bring enough money to feed and shelter her decently until she could find some respectable means of support?

And then there were his clothes to dispose of properly—a heavy coat, his practically new boots, the regimental headdress of which he was so proud. There weren't many of these objects, actually, certainly not enough to warrant her absorbed preoccupation with them. She touched the shirts and stockings that she, and her mother before her, had darned so carefully. The handkerchiefs. The smudged reading glasses.

She deliberately drew out the process of puzzling over what to do with them, for when her task was at an end she would have to accept the reality that her father, the alternately kind and irascible Captain Lawrence Randall, was dead of a fall from his horse as he returned from an evening of cards and drinking with the gentlemen of his regiment.

When she accepted that, she would have to give some thought to her own future, which was impossible.

But that, she thought, drawing herself up determinedly,

was utter nonsense. She was a healthy young woman possessed of some skill in nursing. Mrs. Pritchett, the wife of a clergyman, had invited her to live with her and her husband temporarily until she could sort out her affairs. She would continue to work at the hospital, as she always had done, to give succor to the wounded. She would write letters for the men, administer medicines and comforts, and help to keep the wards clean. Her father had devoted his life to healing the sick and wounded, and she would carry on his work as far as she was able.

With her father's death, the hospital would be in need of extra hands until his superiors assigned a replacement for him. There would be plenty of work to keep her mind distracted from her loss.

At that moment, an officer opened the door and walked in.

"Good morning, Miss Randall," he said, removing his hat and grinning at her. His hair was brushed to a fine gloss, and his coat was much decorated with gilt braid and lacing. *Yes, you think you are a fine fellow,* she thought cynically.

"Who are you?" she asked. "And how dare you enter my father's quarters without permission?"

"Captain Gerald Herbert, at your service, Miss Randall. This billet has been assigned to me," he said, still smiling.

Such efficiency, she thought bitterly. Her father was not buried two days, and already his billet had been assigned to another officer.

"I am ready to leave," she said, picking up the portmanteau that contained her own clothing. "May I trouble you to have someone remove my father's effects to the hospital?"

Effects. The property of the dead. It pained her to refer to her father's possessions in this manner, but she may as well become accustomed to it.

The officer moved so that he blocked her path to the door. She felt her jaw harden with distaste when he slowly drew his forefinger down her cheek. She quickly drew back from him.

"You need not be in such a hurry, Miss Randall. I am told you have nowhere to go, and no living relatives," he said. "Perhaps we may come to some sort of mutually beneficial arrangement."

"Highly unlikely," she snapped as she dropped her portmanteau and stepped back. While her father was alive, no man would have dared insult her so. "Have you no decency, sir? Get out of my way!"

"Do not be hasty, girl," he said. The smile was gone from his face now. "You cannot afford to be rash."

He moved closer to her and then gave a faint cry of surprise. He leaped away from her and nursed his injured hand. There was a streak of blood on it.

Marian hefted the knife in her hand. It had a graceful blade with a pretty mother of pearl handle, just the thing for a lady to carry in her reticule in the event she wished to peel a piece of fruit, cut a length of thread for embroidery or repulse the unwelcome advances of an impertinent officer who presumed too much.

"Why, you little termagant!" the man exclaimed, sucking the wound. He straightened, and the expression on his face was ugly. "It is time someone taught you some manners."

Marian grabbed her portmanteau and swung it at his midsection when he would have accosted her. Caught off guard, he dropped to his knees.

"Perhaps," she said as she retrieved her portmanteau and escaped through the door, "but it will not be you."

This was the sort of thing she could look forward to in the future, Marian thought with a long sigh as she made her way to Mr. and Mrs. Pritchett's quarters. Indeed, she had already received several such offers from men who assumed that a fatherless female should be eager to accept their advances.

She had only disdain for the sort of poor-spirited female

who would sell her body in exchange for the dubious security a male protector could offer her on campaign. Marian was not her mother's daughter for nothing—Annie Randall would have sent these lechers about their business with their ears ringing and their arms bloody stumps if they had dared trifle with *her*.

They were together now, her father and mother.

Marian smiled sadly at the thought. Her father's spirits had never quite recovered from her mother's death. There was a sadness that was with him always. Marian tried to be glad for these two devoted souls reunited at last, but all she felt was alone.

"You are to be congratulated, Adam," General Lord Grimsby said with false heartiness when Major Lyonbridge was shown into his presence. "You are going home." The general, for all his apparent joviality, could not quite meet Adam's eyes.

"Home? In the middle of a campaign?" Adam said quizzically. "I trust you are joking."

"It is time you did your duty by Isabella," the general said, blustering a little. "The wedding has been postponed twice, and she won't be able to hold her head up in Society if you do not marry this year."

The mention of Isabella Grimsby, his betrothed, would have been enough to depress his spirits if Adam had been in a *good* mood, which he most certainly was not. His best horse had been shot out from under him during the battle, and his spare horse was not performing to Adam's standards. His men, still suffering from the effects of their wounds and their celebratory drunkenness after the battle, had made a pitiful showing when he assembled them for inspection and drill. A preemptory summons from the general—which obliged him to make a trip to his billet for a wash and a more presentable uniform—was a nuisance he could have done very well without.

Adam *would* marry Isabella someday. Their mutual fathers had arranged the match between them before they were out of their cradles, and Adam was resigned to doing his duty by the wretched girl. He had just hoped that day was still several years away.

"Surely the demands of war preempt such personal matters," Adam said. "I could hardly rush off to enjoy my nuptials when my country had need of me."

Enjoy? Marriage to Isabella? Hardly. Adam wondered that his tongue did not turn black.

Isabella was a spoiled, selfish, headstrong little chit who reminded Adam painfully of her imperious mother, the general's wife. Certainly, he did not flatter himself that she was any more eager for the marriage than he. The last time they were compelled to endure one another's company, she had informed him he was a big, clumsy, uncouth barbarian, merely because he accidentally had trampled on the hem of her skirt during a dance at a ball. When he thought of their marriage at all, it was with the vague hope that after the deed was done he could continue serving with his regiment, and Isabella could stay in London flitting from one party to another, so they need not trouble one another overmuch.

The general stood and faced the window, clasping his hands behind him. The old fox was up to something.

"I am ordering you to go to England and marry Isabella," he said. "I have written to my wife to initiate the preparations. In addition, you will take the dispatches to the war office and personally make your report to the Government."

"*I* am to take the dispatches?" Adam asked, frowning. "Can you not find better use for an experienced field officer? Am I not needed here?"

The general turned at that and put both hands on his desk to lean forward.

"You are handsome, sir, and valiant in battle. The very flower of young English manhood. No one who is skeptical about the wisdom of continuing the war would persist in this notion after meeting you and listening to you recount your tales of personal bravery under fire."

"Spare my blushes, "Adam said, nonplussed. "If this be true, which I sincerely doubt, what is it to the point?"

"Lord Wellington is concerned about the strength of the new Government. It would be a disaster if it failed, and if the Whigs took over and refused to support his continued efforts in the Peninsula," the general said. "I have convinced him that sending a personable and much-decorated young officer as an emissary to London to create goodwill for Liverpool's Government would do much to help our cause. All the most important men in England will attend your wedding to Isabella."

"Politics," Adam said with a snort of distaste. "I am a soldier, not a diplomat. Is there no one else you can send to do the pretty in London?"

"No one who conveniently happens to be betrothed to my daughter," the general said dryly. He hesitated. "And there is one other commission you will discharge for me that must be carried out in absolute confidentiality."

Ah. Now we arrive at the crux of the matter, Adam thought. *The old fox wants me to do something that he dares not ask of anyone else.*

It wouldn't be the first time.

Adam, the son of the general's oldest friend, had benefited greatly from Lord Grimsby's patronage from the moment he joined the Army. Adam certainly could thank the general for his rapid advancement in rank and for bringing his valor to the attention of the right people. Now, unless he mistook the matter, it was time for Adam to repay the general for his generosity in promoting his career.

"I am at your service, of course," he said carefully.

The general gestured toward the chair in front of his

desk. Adam took it and leaned forward when the general indicated that he was to do so.

"You are acquainted with Miss Randall," the general said. "You told me she bandaged your wound for you after the battle."

"Yes," Adam said guardedly as he wondered what possible interest the general could have in the poor girl. Unless . . . Adam gave the general a sharp look. Had he been dallying with the surgeon's daughter? Lord Grimsby had quite a reputation as a womanizer, but Adam had assumed he confined his gallantries to more mature married ladies and females of a certain class. The old goat!

"The girl is my daughter. My natural daughter," the general said sharply, just as if he knew what Adam had been thinking. "I want you to take her to England, where she will be safe. You are to deliver her to my wife with a letter I will give to you."

Miss Randall. The general's daughter. Not the surgeon's.

"The letter to my wife will not disclose my real relationship with the girl," the general continued. Well, Adam rather surmised it would not! "Although Miss Randall herself will have to be told the truth."

"Not by me, I trust," Adam said, taken aback.

"No. Her father left a letter in my keeping in the event of his death. It commends her to my care. I will charge my wife with the task of arranging a marriage for her."

A marriage to some country squire or merchant, no doubt, who would keep her quite apart from Society, Adam supposed. He shuddered as he imagined Lady Grimsby's reception of this high-handed command from her spouse, even if she did not apprehend the whole truth of the matter.

"When am I to leave?" Adam asked.

The general's tense features relaxed.

"In three days' time. Now I wish you to go to Miss Randall and bring her here." He opened his desk drawer and placed a sealed missive on the desk. "It is the letter from her father. It is right that I should be the one to disclose its contents to her." The general straightened his spine. "That will be all, major," he said in dismissal.

That will be all, Adam thought in chagrin.

Poor Miss Randall. He had little pity to spare for her, however.

He was going to marry Isabella. Soon.

Heaven help him.

Chapter 3

Marian's hair had come partially undone in front, so she had to keep sweeping it out of her eyes with the back of one dirty hand as she exorcised all her sorrow and frustration in scrubbing the floor until the very paint was in danger of being stripped from the wood. Her face was damp with perspiration. Her gown was stained, for it was the old, faded one she wore for heavy work.

So it was inevitable that, in the irritating way of men, Major Adam Lyonbridge would appear in the doorway to the ward dressed in a meticulously pressed red uniform that made the most of his wide shoulders and imposing height, with every sun-streaked brown hair in place. She could have seen her face reflected in the sheen of his boots.

He bowed, and she had no choice but to scramble to her feet and do the same.

"Miss Randall, General Lord Grimsby requests your presence in his office. At once," he intoned. Then he frowned. "What are you doing?"

She frowned back at him and placed one hand to the small of her aching back.

"As you can see, I am scrubbing the floor," she said, annoyed at being found at a disadvantage.

"Surely it is not necessary for you to perform such menial labor."

"The floor was filthy, Major Lyonbridge," she said with a sigh. "And filth spreads the progress of disease."

He looked appalled.

"But this is hardly seemly so soon after your loss."

Her laugh sounded slightly hysterical, even to her own ears.

"What shall I do instead? Sit quietly in Mrs. Pritchett's parlor, dressed all in black, and weep for him? I have done so, I promise you, Major. I have cried and cried for him," she said. "It has not brought him back. I will go mad if I must have nothing to occupy my mind except the loss of the best of fathers."

Tears sprang to her eyes, and she impatiently wiped them away. It seemed she had some tears left, after all.

"You have my sympathy," he said, looking uncomfortable. "Captain Randall was a good man, and he will be sadly missed."

She gave a stiff inclination of her head in acknowledgment.

"You must come with me now," he said. "General Lord Grimsby has sent for you, and he is waiting."

Marian looked down in dismay at her soiled gown.

"May I not have time to make myself presentable?"

The major's handsome face softened.

"Of course," he said. "I will escort you to Mrs. Pritchett's house."

Marian nodded, and he extended his arm to her.

"Better not," she said ruefully. "My hands are filthy."

"I do not mind a little dirt," he said.

His blue eyes were . . . pitying, which made Marian wonder what unpleasantness awaited her in the general's office. She dismissed her feeling of disquiet. Perhaps Lord Grimsby merely wished to offer his condolences. It would have been more courteous of him to call on her at Mrs. Pritchett's house, but Marian supposed a general's convenience must always take precedence over that of a bereaved daughter.

"Your wound is healing well?" she asked Major Lyonbridge when they were outside and walking up the street to Mrs. Pritchett's house. People were staring, and Marian was not surprised. They must look very odd together, she in her creased and stained gown with her hair wildly disheveled and he in his spotless uniform.

"My wound," he repeated absently.

"Yes. The one I bandaged for you after the battle."

"Oh. Yes. Quite healed, I thank you. I had forgotten about it."

Then silence.

A man of few words, obviously, Marian thought, irrationally disgruntled.

Why should he exert himself to be civil to her? He was a decorated war hero and the general's golden-haired protégé. She was merely the surgeon's daughter, and not even that now.

At Mrs. Pritchett's house she quickly washed her face and hands, pinned up her hair, and donned her second-best gown. The woman who looked back at her from the glass had sad, red, tired eyes, but she'd do.

Now presentable, although nowhere near as gorgeous as her escort, Marian straightened her shoulders and lifted her chin. Then she went out to join the monosyllabic major, who conducted her into the general's presence.

"Come in, my dear, and sit down," the general said when the major motioned for her to precede him into the room.

My dear?

Uncertainly, she looked at the major, but he was looking straight ahead at the portion of the wall above the general's head. His face was impassive. He pulled out the chair the general indicated, and Marian had no choice but to seat herself.

The general stared at her as if he were attempting to memorize her features. It was quite unnerving.

"You are very like your mother," he said at last. Were those *tears* in his eyes?

"You knew my mother?" she asked in surprise.

"Yes. I knew her. My dear, what I have to tell you may come as a shock."

There it was again. *My dear*. What could he mean by it?

"My father has just died in a senseless accident," Marian said. "I rather doubt that anything you have to tell me could be more shocking than that."

"Captain Randall was not your father, Marian," he said. "*I* am your father."

"You lie!" Marian cried, jumping to her feet. "How *dare* you say such a thing to me?"

"I say it because it is true." He picked up a letter from his desk and extended it to her. "Here is a letter in your father's own hand, which will attest to it."

"But this is impossible!" she cried after she had quickly scanned the letter, even though she had recognized it instantly as her father's handwriting and the damning words were written clearly upon it. She let the letter flutter to the desk. "You and . . . my mother?"

The general bowed his head.

"I could not marry her, for I was already married."

"How very convenient. Major Lyonbridge," Marian said stonily. "Did you know this?"

"Yes," he said from behind her. He sounded uncomfortable, as well he might.

"And how many others know my mother played the whore for you, Lord Grimsby?"

"You will not speak of her in that way!" he snapped. "She was very young and innocent and virtuous."

"Virtuous!" Marian scoffed.

"She was! I will not have you think badly of her!"

"How can I not? You are telling me that she conceived a child with a married man."

"She did not know. I did not tell her. And when she learned that I was not free to marry her, she refused to have anything more to do with me. By then, it was too late. She was with child."

"And so she married my poor father. I wonder if he knew the truth."

"He knew, curse him," the general said bitterly. "He offered her the protection of his name. Except for that, all he could give her was a life of hardship."

"My father loved her," Marian said defiantly. "We were not rich, but we had enough. All that was important, at any rate."

The general gave a snort of distaste.

"You must believe that I would have taken better care of her than that. I intended to do so. I loved her. "

"You took advantage of her. You *lied* to her."

"I would have made it right," the general said bitterly, "but instead she married Captain Randall. And ever after, I had to watch, powerless, as she endured the hardship of campaigning without complaint. She was a saint, your mother. She should have come to me instead. I would have seen that she wanted for nothing."

"You would have bought a small, neat house for her, I suppose," Marian said.

"Yes. Certainly."

"With a pretty garden and perhaps her own carriage," Marian mused. "She was to be your little toy in a gilded toy chest, where you could keep her safe until you wished to take her out and play with her. And you are *surprised* she declined your generous offer. You say you knew my mother, but, I tell you, Lord Grimsby, that you did not know her at all."

"Oh, I knew her," he said bitterly. "She had pride and stubbornness like no other. She would not be my mistress, even though I begged her to let me take care of her. Instead, she married *him*."

Obviously, it still rankled, even though Marian's mother was dead these three years.

"What purpose is served now by telling me these things?" Marian asked.

The general leaned toward her.

"Because you are in an uncomfortable position, my dear. I feel it is my duty to make sure you are returned to England. It is out of the question for you to stay here."

Marian bowed her head in assent. He was right, much as she hated to admit it. Mrs. Pritchett and her husband had been all that was kind, but she certainly could not impose on their hospitality much longer. She had no money, for her father, a generous man, continually dipped into his own funds to make up the deficiencies of the medical supply chest.

All she had left was her mother's precious string of perfectly matched pearls . . .

She fingered them now. They were at her throat, for she often wore them when she needed courage. She had always assumed the string of pearls was a family heirloom, for Captain Randall's means, she knew, had not extended to such extravagance.

"My mother's pearls. Did *you* give them to her?" she asked.

"Yes."

"Then you shall have them back."

"Absolutely not," the general said, sounding appalled.

"I want *nothing* from you, sir!" she cried, standing up. She unclasped the pearls and flung them before the general on the desk. She would have fled from the room, but the major placed himself in her path and caught her shoulders to prevent her from doing so.

"Let me pass, sir!" she demanded.

"Sit down, Miss Randall," the major said. "Please."

"Miss *Randall?* Am I?" she said with a hysterical laugh.

"This has been a great shock to you," he said.

She laughed again at the extreme understatement.

"Yes, I suppose you might say so," she said as she stared pointedly at his hand on her arm. He released her, and she turned back to the general. She sat down, for her knees were shaking.

"It would be best," the general said, "that you continue to be known as Miss Randall. Your mother and Captain Randall would have wished it."

"He was my father," she said, looking the general straight in the eye, "in every sense of the word that mattered."

"I understand that," he said. "But it is my right and my duty to be of assistance to you now that he and your mother are deceased. If your circumstances were different, please be assured that I would have kept this secret to the grave."

"Are you offering me *money?*" she asked incredulously.

"I am offering you an opportunity to have a comfortable and respectable life," the general said. "Following the drum is no proper place for a female, especially one without male protection. Major Lyonbridge will escort you to England, where my wife will arrange a match for you."

He had a self-satisfied look on his face, as if he expected her to be grateful.

"And so the folly of my mother's youth is disposed of," she said dryly. "How neat. What if I do not wish to be married?"

The general blinked in surprise.

"Why should you not? You are young. You are pretty." He smiled benevolently, as if he were a fond uncle bestowing a treat upon her. "I shall arrange for you to have a new wardrobe. How will you like that? I cannot have my daughter wearing such rags."

It was the wrong thing to say. Marian felt her jaw harden.

"These *rags* were good enough for Captain Randall's daughter," she snapped. "They are certainly good enough for *yours*."

The benevolent smile was quite wiped from the general's face.

"You will leave in three days' time," he said. "That will be all."

When Marian would have continued to sit there like a block at the abrupt dismissal, Major Lyonbridge took her arm to assist her from her chair. She scrambled to her feet.

Major Lyonbridge bowed to the general, and, after a moment, Marian did so as well. Then the major quickly ushered her from the general's presence.

Once out in the hall, she stopped and leaned back against the wall with her eyes closed. Her heart was racing.

"Are you unwell?" Major Lyonbridge asked. "Shall I fetch Mrs. Pritchett?"

Marian's eyes snapped open.

"I am not so poor-spirited a creature," she said wryly, "as to be overcome with the vapors merely because I have just been informed that my father isn't truly my father, and I am to be carried off to England to make an expedient marriage so the general can salve his tender conscience by thus disposing of me."

"I stand corrected," he said, straight-faced.

Was that a glimmer of amusement in his eyes?

Surely not.

"And why have *you* been charged with the unenviable duty of escorting me there?"

"I am to marry General Grimsby's daughter, Isabella," he said.

"How nice. That would make us . . . brother- and sister-in-law, although not on the proper side of the blanket, so I daresay it does not count."

"Miss Randall," he said reproachfully.

"I am sorry. None of this is *your* fault."

"I am relieved to hear you say so. May I escort you to Mrs. Pritchett's house?"

"Unnecessary," she said. "I am not so overcome that I cannot find my own way."

With that, she set off briskly in the direction of her hostess's house, and Adam was left shaking his head in grudging admiration.

"What are *you* grinning about?" the general asked a moment later when he came upon Adam. He looked and sounded irritable.

"She is quite . . . unusual," he said. "Your daughter."

"My daughter," the general said with a sigh. "Heaven help us both."

Chapter 4

August 1812
At sea

Above deck, the sky was blue and the clouds resembled big, frisky woolly lambs. Quite a different scene from that below deck, where Marian had been nursing three miserably sick travelers.

One of the sufferers was Mrs. Pritchett, her supposed chaperon, who had agreed to accompany Marian on the voyage home for propriety's sake. The heat of Spain in summer had not agreed with the poor woman, and so she was glad for an opportunity to return to England for a visit with relatives at the general's expense.

Marian enjoyed a big gulp of blessedly clean, salty air and watched a pair of seagulls swoop down into the sea, presumably in search of fish.

Unfortunately, she was not destined to enjoy the refreshing solitude for long.

"Miss Randall. Well met," said Mr. Parker, one of the ship's officers, as he sidled up next to her at the rail. "Is the wind not too cold for you to be out here alone?"

He put his arm across her shoulders and leered suggestively. She could detect the sickly sweet smell of rum on his breath.

"Actually, I find the sea air quite bracing," she said as she moved away from him.

He would have taken her remark for coyness and followed, but he found his path blocked by a large, imposing body. The expression on the newcomer's face was stern enough to curl a man's liver.

Major Lyonbridge, Marian's loyal guard dog, right on schedule.

"Right, then," Mr. Parker said, smiling uneasily. "If you will excuse me, Miss Randall, I must return to my duties."

The major took an intimidating step in Mr. Parker's direction, and the man practically fled from his presence.

"You may stop flexing your muscles now," Marian said. "You've quite terrified the poor man."

Major Lyonbridge turned to face an amused Marian.

"How is Mrs. Pritchett faring?" he asked.

"Resting quietly at last, thank heaven," Marian said. "She is a brave woman. If I suffered as much from sea travel, I would not have had the courage to leave England."

"It has not been a pleasant crossing for you, either," he observed.

"Merely because I have had the nursing of several stricken travelers?" she asked. "Such is my lot in life. My father and I always found ourselves nursing our fellow travelers aboard ship, for we were both blessed with disgustingly sound stomachs and hard heads. I used to consider myself fortunate for having inherited this admirable characteristic from him, but I could not have, could I? It takes a great deal of getting accustomed to, this being a relative stranger's love child."

She turned back to the rail and looked out over the sea.

"People used to say I had his nose," she added wistfully.

"Nonsense," the major said. "The thing was as big as a battleship and all over his face."

Marian had to smile. Apparently the major was in no mood to indulge her lapse into sentimentality.

"His nose did not always look like that," she said. "It was broken some years ago when he was rash enough to come between a pair of drunken brawlers."

"That would explain it, then," he said, and lapsed into silence.

There was something oddly restful about Major Lyonbridge, Marian reflected. Possibly this was because he did not hasten to fill every lull in the conversation with his own words. Nor did he seem to expect his companion to entertain him.

Rather, he gave the impression that he would be content to stare out to sea for the next hour at her side in perfect contentment, with not a word spoken between them.

"What is she like, my half sister?" Marian found herself asking after a time.

He continued to stare over the waters, and for a moment she wondered if he had heard her.

"She has dark hair and brown eyes and is generally acknowledged to be a diamond of the first water. Talks incessantly." A muscle flexed in his jaw. "She more closely resembles her mother than her father, both in looks and in temperament."

"I have always wanted a sister," Marian said. "I never dreamed that someday I would have one—although I take it she is not to know the truth of my parentage."

"No."

"It will be exceedingly awkward, just the same."

"Yes."

Marian had to smile. Some gentlemen would be quick to offer reassurances. Not Major Lyonbridge.

"The ship's captain tells me the crew should sight land today," he said.

"Mrs. Pritchett will be glad to hear it," Marian said. "The poor woman has not been able to move from her cot for the whole of the journey."

To Marian's astonishment, at that moment Mrs. Pritchett herself came out onto the deck, staggering a bit at the movement of the ship. Major Lyonbridge hurried to steady her with a hand at her elbow. Her eyes were a bit sunken with fatigue and her cheeks were hollow, but she was smiling.

"Mrs. Pritchett!" cried Marian, going at once to put a supporting arm around the woman's shoulders as she guided her to the rail. "Surely you are not well enough to be out of bed!"

"My poor Miss Randall," Mrs. Pritchett said remorsefully. "I am sorry to have performed my responsibilities so ill. It is a useless sort of chaperon who lies sick below deck when her charge has need of her."

"Be assured that Major Lyonbridge has admirably filled your shoes in your absence," Marian said dryly. "The few men who have dared address a single word to me have been so thoroughly menaced by him that they invariably turn tail and run the moment I set foot on deck."

"Miss Randall exaggerates," the major said.

"I beg your pardon, major," Marian said archly. "I do *not* exaggerate."

"I am glad to hear it," Mrs. Pritchett said, although she cast an uneasy look between the two of them. Marian realized that to Mrs. Pritchett it must present a very off appearance for Marian and Major Lyonbridge to be conversing on deck without a chaperon. Marian found herself blushing.

On campaign, when she had thought herself merely the daughter of the regimental surgeon, she did not worry overmuch about propriety. Everyone knew that Captain Randall would unhesitatingly hack an ear off of anyone who dared to trifle with his little girl. His retribution would have been equally terrible against anyone who dared to imply that her virtue was less than perfect.

Marian had felt completely secure in her identity as the chaste daughter of devoted parents. The thought that anyone might regard her as anything else had not crossed her mind.

Little did Marian realize at the time that she was the natural daughter of an adulterer and a . . . but, even now, she could not think of her mother in that way. Annie Randall had been completely loyal to her husband once she was married. Marian had never been surer of anything in her life. Nor could any man have been a more loving and protective father to Marian than Captain Randall.

Now she was on the way back to England where many would think Marian no better than she should be merely because her parents had followed the drum and she herself had gone on campaign with Captain Randall when she was grown. If she were known to be the daughter of a woman who had been tempted into a liaison with a married man and bore his child, Marian's chances of making a respectable life for herself would be ruined.

The general was determined to see her married, and Marian supposed that in his mind it was the best solution. To that end she would be mixing at a level of Society that had been closed to Captain and Mrs. Randall.

Lady Grimsby would find a husband for Marian, and she would be expected to be grateful to this man for taking her off the general's hands. Marian had little interest or skill in the domestic arts, yet she would be expected to retire to the country with this stranger, to manage his household, to keep up appearances for the neighbors, to breed his children. And he would expect her to be *grateful* to him for the privilege, for he must, of course, be told the truth about her parentage.

Indeed, perhaps he would marry her *because* of the preferment that might come of placing the general under an obligation to him. The general was titled, he was rich, and his wife moved at the highest level of Society. Some men would find it useful to form such an alliance.

While some girls would regard the prospect of going to London to find a husband with delight, it merely made Marian feel like an unwanted milk cow destined for the auction block come market day.

Marian had hoped eventually to make a love match similar to the one her mother had made with Captain Randall.

Or so Marian had thought of their union before her eyes were opened to the sordid truth of her origins.

Now Marian knew her mother had married Captain Randall merely to give her child a name. Had they merely *pretended* to be a loving couple for Marian's sake? Had Captain Randall secretly resented his wife for not giving him his *own* children?

Marian suddenly was aware of a great deal of shouting and gesturing.

"What is it?" she asked, startled from her reverie.

"Land," Major Lyonbridge said, squinting toward the horizon. "Land has been sighted."

"Oh, thank heaven," said Mrs. Pritchett, who sniffed loudly with sudden emotion. "Soon we will be in blessed England."

Blessed England.

Marian had left England only a few years ago, giddy with excitement at the prospect of joining her father on campaign and being a help to him, as was her mother before her. She felt then that the world had been polished to a high gloss and laid at her feet. Her future was full of possibilities. And adventure. And excitement.

Now she was returning to England a woman of illegitimate birth, escorted by an officer charged with the responsibility of handing her over to her natural father's designated caretakers so that those strangers might arrange a marriage for her with a faceless stranger.

Marian smiled absently at Mrs. Pritchett's happiness. The older lady looked as if she would like to caper about the deck, but she remembered her dignity in time.

"I cannot wait to set foot on our familiar shore, can you, Miss Randall?" Mrs. Pritchett said gaily as she squeezed Marian's hand.

Marian made a murmur that might be construed as agreement, but in truth, she dreaded the ordeal that awaited her beyond that familiar shore.

Chapter 5

When the carriage stopped before the imposing town house in Mayfair, Marian's heart plummeted to the ankles of her dusty half boots.

"You cannot mean that *this* is the house?" she said to Major Lyonbridge, who was sitting across from her and Mrs. Pritchett.

Marian had been quite overawed by the huge houses they had passed as they progressed through London's most exclusive residential area.

This house made all the others resemble cottages.

"Oh, Miss Randall!" exclaimed Mrs. Pritchett. "Have you ever seen so elegant a house?"

Marian had to swallow, for her throat was so dry she found it hard to speak at first.

"No. Never," she said.

The general's house was a stately rose-colored brick mansion in the Palladian style, with marble columns and mullioned windows. The grounds were beautifully landscaped, and Marian could see masses of flowers in the gardens beyond. She was willing to wager the stables were larger than many of the churches the well-traveled Marian had seen in England and Europe.

She looked again at Major Lyonbridge to see if he was impressed by all this grandeur, but he was looking at her.

"Courage, my girl," Major Lyonbridge said softly.

Marian's heart clutched.

What was Annie Randall's daughter to say to the beings who resided in such a place as this?

As it turned out, it was unnecessary for Marian to say anything when she was ushered into the general's wife's august presence.

Lady Grimsby received them in her parlor, which seemed rather too full of people to Marian's dazzled eyes. In addition to Marian, the major, Mrs. Pritchett, and the general's wife, there was a pretty young lady present who strongly resembled Lady Grimsby, a neatly dressed older woman who was probably Lady Grimsby's maid or companion, two maids who had been in the process of laying refreshments on a tea table, and a conservatively dressed young gentleman who appeared to be some sort of secretary or upper servant.

Lady Grimsby ignored them all as she read her husband's letter. Then she looked up with a brittle smile on her face.

"Mrs. Pritchett, your responsibility of chaperoning this young person is completed, and no doubt you are eager to repair to . . . wherever you are staying," Lady Grimsby said to the older lady, who had been looking longingly at the tea tray. "I do not wish to keep you any longer. Mr. Stewart, kindly see Mrs. Pritchett to her carriage. If she has come with Major Lyonbridge in a hired carriage, you will pay the driver whatever fare he requires to take her wherever she wishes to go."

The young man bowed and offered his arm to Mrs. Pritchett, who was clearly confused by such an abrupt dismissal.

"If you will come with me, ma'am," the young man said.

Mrs. Pritchett looked at Marian in dismay, and Marian would have objected at such cavalier treatment of her companion, but Major Lyonbridge, who had been watching Lady Grimsby carefully, caught her arm and shook his head.

Still, Marian could not let Mrs. Pritchett go like this.

She moved forward and took Mrs. Pritchett's hands in both of hers.

"Thank you, Mrs. Pritchett, for accompanying me from Spain. I do appreciate your kindness."

"Fare you well, Miss Randall," Mrs. Pritchett said as she embraced Marian. She squared her ample shoulders and returned Lady Grimsby's frigid glare. "If you find yourself in some difficulty, my dear, do not hesitate to come to me. I will be staying at the parsonage at St. Luke's Church. My brother-in-law is pastor there."

"You are very kind," Marian said as the young man ushered Mrs. Pritchett from the room.

"Look at me, girl," Lady Grimsby commanded when Mrs. Pritchett was gone. Marian turned to comply, matching the woman stare for stare.

The general's wife might have been mistaken for a much younger woman had it not been for the pitiless afternoon sun that streamed through the lace curtains and illuminated the tiny lines around her eyes and lips. She had beautifully arranged dark hair with only a few strands of silver in it, piercing dark brown eyes, and a graceful figure. Her morning gown of soft ivory muslin trimmed with blond lace was sheer poetry.

The whole impression should have been one of elegance, but she rather reminded Marian of a hawk in the way she ignored Major Lyonbridge and the other people in the room and stared in that unnerving, unblinking manner at *her*.

"Go now, and take all of this away," she said to the two maids as she gestured toward the tea table. They quickly gathered up the crockery and fled the room with all the haste their dignity would allow. Marian noticed that the younger one's lips were trembling. Lady Grimsby made a dismissive gesture toward the elderly woman remaining, and she scurried from the room in the maid's wake.

Lady Grimsby tossed the general's letter to a small, highly polished table and made an angry gesture of silence when the young, dark-haired woman—presumably Isabella, Major Lyonbridge's fiancée, although no one had bothered to perform introductions—would have spoken.

"So you are the regimental surgeon's recently orphaned daughter, and my husband was so moved with pity by your plight that he has arranged for you to come to London and I am to find you a husband," she said with a sneer as she drew closer to Marian. "It appears my husband still thinks me a gullible fool, even after having been married to *him* for all these years."

"I beg your pardon, my lady?" Marian asked in consternation.

"My husband is not possessed of an altruistic disposition," Lady Grimsby said. "I do not believe for a moment that we can attribute his eagerness to provide for your future to some heretofore unplumbed reservoir of generosity in his nature. My husband has never felt a charitable impulse in his entire selfish existence."

"Captain Randall," Major Lyonbridge said in a tone of reproof, "was a much-valued member of our regiment. The general felt that he—that all of us—owed him a great debt."

"Did he, indeed?" Lady Grimsby said mockingly.

Marian gave an involuntary gasp as the older woman suddenly reached out and grabbed her chin to peer into her face. Her dainty fingers were stronger than they looked, and the pressure hurt.

"Tell me the truth, my girl! Are you my husband's whore or his bastard?" she spat out.

"Lady Grimsby!" exclaimed the major.

Marian reared back to break Lady Grimsby's grip on her chin and faced the general's wife with a scowl of defiance.

"His bastard," she said.

"His bastard," Lady Grimsby repeated. Her eyes narrowed as she continued to stare at Marian. "You are *her* daughter, aren't you? Annie . . . something. The little Irish piece with whom he was so infatuated."

"I will not speak of her to *you*," Marian snapped.

"Yes. You are *hers*, all right. Same blowzy red hair, same limpid green eyes. Lord, I hated her. I still fancied myself in love with my husband then. Although I knew he had gotten bastards by a handful of female servants and tenants' daughters, all of *those* had been made before our marriage. I thought he had mended his ways. Instead, I learned of *her*."

"You will *not* speak of her!" Marian cried.

"She did not know he was married," Lady Grimsby continued inexorably. "So I took some pleasure in telling her and watching the expression on her face when I did so. I offered her money to disappear, to go back to Ireland with her parents, but she would not. She was of good family—or what passed for such among the Irish. She found herself another husband. The regimental surgeon? How excessively convenient for the general. No doubt he enjoyed her at his whim on campaign with the surgeon's blessing. No wonder he feels a debt of gratitude to the man!"

Marian started forward with murder in her heart, but Major Lyonbridge caught her arms.

"It is untrue, and you know it," he said to Marian when she turned to look at him. His eyes were frigid chips of blue ice as he glared into Lady Grimsby's smug face. "She knows it herself."

"Do you think I do not know that? Get your hands *off* of me," Marian snarled through gritted teeth. He released her at once.

Lady Grimsby laughed.

"Good heavens. She looks positively *wild!* I am to find a husband for this *creature?*" she scoffed. "Where? Among the performing animals at Astley's Ampitheatre?"

"I want *nothing* from you," Marian cried. "*Nothing!*"

"Mother, for pity's sake," said the younger woman. "Stop baiting the poor thing. It has grown quite tiresome now, and it is not *her* fault Papa has a weakness for the ladies."

Miss Isabella Grimsby rather did resemble her mother, as Major Lyonbridge had said, only there was nothing of the termagant about her. She was all silky hair and long eyelashes and embroidered rose-colored muslin skirts. Her heart-shaped face was smooth and sweet in expression.

"You are not to know that creatures like her exist," Lady Grimsby said.

"Nonsense. I am to become a wife next month. I will know of their existence soon enough," she said cynically. "Besides, Miss Randall—or so I suppose we will continue to call her—is not, to our knowledge, a member of the sisterhood to which you refer."

"How dare your father insult me by sending her here?" Lady Grimsby said, but she seemed calmer now.

"Yes, yes, I know. It is too bad of him," Miss Grimsby said soothingly. "But he did not have anywhere else to send her, I suppose. Do not worry about it, Mother. We will find a husband for her, she will go off with him, and she will never bother us again. After all, it is not to *her* credit to be known as another of my father's little indiscretions."

Marian could have taken exception to being discussed as if she were not there, but her mind was reeling with too many revelations to make any objection.

"How many of . . . us are there?" she asked.

"Three that *I* know of, although there have been others, I assume," Miss Grimsby said. "I was quite grown up when my parents were obliged to make arrangements for them far enough from London to avoid causing the family embarrassment, so I could hardly avoid knowing about them."

"Three. What happened to them?" Marian asked.

"One was reared in Scotland by a couple there, and Papa bought him a pair of colors, anonymously of course, when he came of age. Unfortunately, he was killed in the war. Then there was the milkmaid's child. Mother found a husband for her, and she lives somewhere in the west with him and some outrageous number of children—seven, I think. And then there is you."

Marian had never been so shocked in her life.

"Fortunately, you are quite presentable, or you will be after we have furbished you up a little," Miss Grimsby said. "Remember the ordeal you had in finding a husband for poor little Lucy, Mother?" Miss Grimsby rolled her eyes. "The *nose* on that creature! And her eyes were crossed. And she chattered incessantly."

"None of this is to the point," Major Lyonbridge interjected.

"Oh, *you*," said Miss Grimsby. "Are *you* still here? Do you not have something that requires your urgent attention at this moment, Adam?"

"Several things," he said. "But I hesitate to leave poor Miss Randall to your tender mercies."

"Oh, go away, do," his fiancée said with a grimace. "No one is going to harm her." She put a friendly arm around Marian's shoulders and started to lead her away. "You will want to have a bath, of course, after all your travels, will you not, um, what is your name again?"

"Marian."

"Marian, as in Robin Hood's lady. Very well, Marian. We will just get you settled in the room next to mine. I hope you have a neat hand."

"A neat hand," Marian repeated blankly.

"You may as well make yourself useful, and we still have *hundreds* of wedding invitations to send to the post—oh, good heavens! You *can* write, can you not?"

"Of course I can write," Marian snapped.

"Well, that's all right, then," Miss Grimsby said sunnily. "Come along, now."

She looked back over her shoulder at Major Lyonbridge, who had been staring after them.

"*Go*, Adam! Come dine with us tonight, if you please. It will make a very odd appearance if you do not. And I suppose you must bring your father along with you."

"How could we, either of us, decline such a charming invitation?" he replied straight-faced.

But Miss Grimsby merely waved airily to him and walked on, herding Marian along ahead of her.

Adam was left with Lady Grimsby, and he did not know quite what to say to her.

"I suppose your whole regiment knows of this," she said.

Adam shook his head.

"I am sworn to secrecy by the general," he said. "No word of it will pass my lips to anyone, not even my father or brother."

Lady Grimsby nodded with satisfaction.

"Good. One thing I will say for you, Adam, you are no gabble-monger. How *could* he do this to me?" For all her snide unpleasantness, there was real sorrow in her eyes.

"The girl is blameless in this. She had no idea that Captain Randall was not truly her father. He and his wife were most devoted to one another."

"How charming for them," she said sarcastically. "And now, as usual, I am left to deal with my darling husband's mess."

She raised one eyebrow.

"I suppose my husband has made you feel responsible for the wretched girl's welfare, and so you hesitate to leave her here with us. He has a happy knack of surrounding himself with people willing to do his worrying for him. Do not concern yourself. She will come to no harm here. I *will* find her a husband. Somewhere. And, as you saw, Isabella is well on the way to making a pet of the creature, unless I am mistaken."

"I will take my leave of you then, Lady Grimsby," he said. "And if Isabella's dinner invitation was in earnest, I happily accept." Adam could make an assessment of the situation then. If Marian was unhappy or being mistreated, he would take her to Mrs. Pritchett himself.

"Come at eight o'clock, then," she said. "And do bring your father, if he is free, for we may as well take this opportunity to discuss the wedding arrangements."

Lady Grimsby gave a weary sigh, and Adam was moved to actually feel sorry for her, something he would have thought impossible a few moments ago, when she was taking out her bitterness on Miss Randall.

"It was bad enough when the general charged me with the task of putting on *one* wedding in a month. Now I must arrange another one for this girl he has foisted upon me."

She gave Adam a smile that did not reach her eyes.

"I hope when you are married, Adam, that you will be more considerate of my daughter than her father has been of me."

Chapter 6

Isabella's maid carefully arranged a dizzying number of evening gowns on the embroidered counterpane of the large, lavender-scented bed Marian was to occupy that night.

Well, actually there were four gowns, but this constituted a dizzying number for a woman who owned only three to her name, and one of them was fit only for mopping the floors and other heavy work.

"Green," Isabella mused when Marian had made her choice. "Yes. I do think I should like you very well in green, even though it is such an obvious choice for redheads. Unfortunately the gown is a bit out of style. No one wears sleeves like that this season. I could always have Betty try to do something with them."

"Oh, no! It is quite beautiful the way it is," Marian said as she touched the lace overskirt of the pretty muslin gown. The lace had been mended at the bottom, but so expertly that the repair was visible only if one examined it very closely. The gown had a square neckline with ivory silk roses embroidered all about the edge. The fitted sleeves were long and slightly puffed at the top, then closed with small pearl buttons at the wrist.

"Are you certain you do not want Betty to see what she can do? She is very good with a needle, my Betty."

Marian glanced at the maid, presumably Betty, although, naturally, Isabella had not introduced them. Not by a flicker of the eyelids did the girl indicate that she had heard the compliment. Isabella, as she had done earlier with Marian, was speaking of the girl as if she were not present, so perhaps it would have been a breach of etiquette on the servant's part to do so. Marian surmised she had a great deal to learn about how things were done in a nobleman's house.

"No, I would not want to cause any inconvenience."

She meant *Betty's* inconvenience, but did not correct Isabella's misapprehension when she said, "No inconvenience at all. I have no need of her until it is time to dress for dinner, and that will not be for hours yet."

"Even so," Marian said. "The dress is lovely as it is. They are all lovely."

"Very well, then," Isabella said, smiling. "You are certainly easy to please. If it fits well enough, the green certainly would be the best choice for your coloring. I had it made for a dinner party and ball held here a year ago in Adam's honor and mine, and I have not worn it since. The wedding itself was postponed—again—when Papa and Adam were abruptly ordered back to the Peninsula."

"Then I cannot wear this one," Marian exclaimed. "It is practically new."

"Nonsense. It was never one of my favorites. In fact, I will make you a present of it. If you are worried about it being recognized as one of my cast-offs, you need not. Adam will be the only one among our dinner guests tonight likely to remember it, and he never notices such things."

She picked up a ravishing blue gauze gown, and her eyes grew soft.

"*This* one, now," she said softly. "I would not mind lending it to you for an evening, but I could never part with it. I wore this two years ago when Adam was called away unexpectedly and his brother, Philip, escorted me to a ball on a summer night at the Castle Inn at Brighton. What a magical evening!"

"I did not know Major Lyonbridge had a brother."

"Philip is his elder brother, and the heir to their father's title." Her expression hardened. "He has just become betrothed to a grand heiress whose father owns the better part of six counties. She is said to have hands and feet as big as a man's and a mustache as well."

"What an unkind description," Marian remarked.

"It is Philip's," Isabella said, "and he should know the right of it. Their father is extremely ambitious for him. He wants him to go into politics, and so his wife must be an heiress with grand political connections."

She carefully laid the blue gown back on the bed and touched it delicately, as if it were the face of a beloved child.

"I wish her joy of him," she said, then turned to Marian with a brittle smile on her face. "Now," she said brightly. "What are we to do with your hair tonight? Right now it looks as if you have been drawn through a bush backward."

Marian drew back when Isabella reached out as if to take a strand of her hair between her fingers.

"Do not worry," she said with a laugh. "I am not given to initiating hair-pulling matches."

"Why are you being so kind to me?" Marian asked suspiciously. "Lending me your clothes, taking an interest in how I wear my hair, giving me this pretty room?"

"Well, you must sleep *somewhere*, and this room is as good as any. Further, I am not lending you any clothes that I cannot spare for one evening, and everyone knows an unattractive coiffure can ruin the appearance of any gown. It amuses me to have something to take my mind off the approaching ordeal, and the task of bringing you up to snuff will do as well as anything."

"The approaching ordeal?"

Isabella made a grimace that marred the perfection of her beautiful face.

"My wedding, of course. Adam Lyonbridge is a big, ill-mannered lout, and I would hardly look forward to being joined at the hip with him for the remainder of my natural life under the most ideal of circumstances, and this thrown-together wedding in *September,* of all the boring months, with nothing but stuffy political octogenarians in town to attend, is hardly the stuff of girlish dreams."

"Major Lyonbridge is not a big, ill-mannered lout, as you style him," Marian said. "I would rather have described him as a very imposing military gentleman."

"*You* did not know him as a youth," Isabella said bitterly. "He was clumsy and stupid, and he broke the head off my favorite doll once."

"It must have been an accident. I cannot imagine Major Lyonbridge doing anything so unkind on purpose."

"Well, of course it was an accident. Did I not say he was extremely clumsy? His arms and legs were so long and ungainly, and he was much bigger than any other child his age. His head seemed perched upon the whole structure like a walnut above a mountain. In adolescence he ran to fat, and had spots. You can imagine my joy when I learned that *this* was to be my husband! Our fathers determined on the match while we were still in our cradles, or while *I* was, at any rate. Adam is four years older than I."

"But that was when he was a youth. Do you not think the major very gallant and handsome now?" Marian asked in disbelief. Was Isabella *blind*? "All the ladies in the Peninsula were infatuated with him, I assure you. He is quite the dashing war hero, and the men admire him every bit as much as the ladies."

"I am aware of that," Isabella said glumly. "My friends think I am demented for not being delirious with joy at the prospect of marrying him, but when I look at Adam, all I can see is that awkward walking mountain of a boy who could not string three words together without stuttering, and who broke my new doll on my birthday less than five minutes after my parents had presented it to me. We had a nursery party, and all the children in the neighborhood were invited, including the Lyonbridge brothers, of course. I burst into tears, and Philip tried to put the doll back together again, but to no avail. Adam's father purchased a new doll for me a few days later by way of apology, but it was not as pretty as my Josette, and I never did play with it."

Isabella shuddered.

"How am I to anticipate my wedding night, if not with dread? If he could destroy my doll with one careless hand at the age of nine, *think* what the grown man could do to poor little me. He will crush me to powder—if he does not smother me to death first."

"Did your mother not talk to you about what to expect?" Marian asked delicately.

"I hardly think it appropriate for either of *my* parents to give *anyone* advice on marriage," Isabella said dryly. "They would say anything to make me go through with the wedding."

"If you find marriage to Major Lyonbridge so distasteful a prospect, why do you not tell your father you will not suit, and ask him to arrange a different match for you?"

"Cry off, do you mean? He would never permit me to do so, nor would *Adam's* father agree to it. This wedding is to be an important social event for the Tories, a sort of rallying point for the fledgling new Government. Lord Wellington, through my father, has been pleased to use my wedding as a propaganda device to garner support for his war against the French. Why else do you think Adam and I are ordered to marry in *September,* of all the unfashionable seasons? It will be just before Parliament reconvenes. Convenient, is it not? And because of the wedding, my mother and I are obliged to spend August, the most uncomfortable month imaginable, in London, while all of our friends are still at the seaside. We were to spend another month in Brighton. Philip was to escort us to a ball this week, but instead we had to return here."

"It sounds as if you are very fond of Major Lyonbridge's brother," Marian observed.

"Very fond," Isabella said with a sigh. "He is so charming and so handsome."

More handsome than Major Lyonbridge? Marian could not imagine how that would be possible.

"He has lodgings in London, so Mother and I have him to dine quite often when we are in the City," Isabella continued. "Only he is in Brighton now, like any sensible person."

"And he is to be married, you say?"

"Yes. Next spring. During the Season. At St. Paul's," Isabella said. "It is to be quite a splash. *Her* father, of course, could buy and sell mine ten times over. So Philip will be obliged to marry her, even if she is so fat that her father has to roll her down the aisle in a wheelbarrow."

Isabella gave a gusty sigh, like that of a disappointed child.

"*I* wanted to be married at St. Paul's, but it was not available for my wedding at such short notice. Instead, I will be married at St. James's, Piccadilly."

"I am certain your wedding will be lovely," Marian said. Even to her own ears, this sounded like thin comfort.

"Oh, it will," Isabella said as she pasted a determined smile on her face. "Do not mind me. Mother says *all* brides are nervous—and with good reason, I am persuaded."

Nervous? Poor Isabella seemed positively depressed by the prospect of marrying Major Lyonbridge.

"If you are truly unhappy in the match, would your father not take pity on you?" Marian asked.

"Hardly," she scoffed. "Moreover, he will not take pity on you, either, if you dislike the first man willing to take you off his hands."

Marian's mouth dropped open in dismay.

She was so weary and disoriented that she had completely forgotten that her entire future lay in the hands of Isabella's father and his less-than-friendly wife. If the general did not give a rap for the happiness of his legitimate daughter, he was unlikely to give even that much for Marian's.

Isabella gave a peal of laughter.

"Do not look so worried," she said. "We must simply make you look so pretty that none but the very most charming and dashing men will have the effrontery to offer for you. Now, I have ordered a bath for you. After that, we will see if Betty needs to make any alterations in the gown to fit you."

With that, Isabella gave Marian a fond little pat on the back, as if she were a new lapdog with which she was well pleased, and, with a little wave of her delicate fingers, she sailed out of the room, followed closely by her maid.

Marian let out all of her breath at once and lay down on the pristine counterpane despite the dirt of travel clinging to her outmoded gray traveling costume. It was a lovely room, with walls painted a delicate shade of violet, a big, lace-curtained window overlooking the gardens, and enough room to have contained Captain Randall's quarters several times over. The oval-shaped, rose-patterned carpet before the bed was so soft and thick, Marian was sure that if she took off her shoes and stood on it, she would sink to her ankles. The ceilings were so high, she knew she could jump up and down on the bed as wildly as she pleased, as she did when she was a child and her parents were not looking, and not bang her head on the ceiling. She did so once in their billet and almost knocked herself senseless.

"Well, Papa," Marian said aloud. "What do you think of this room? You can see everything from Heaven, I imagine. I'll wager Princess Charlotte does not have a bedchamber so fine."

Then she remembered that her father was not kindly Captain Randall, but the intimidating General Lord Grimsby, which quite spoiled her childish pleasure in all this unaccustomed luxury.

Chapter 7

Marian supposed she must become accustomed to walking into a room and having people stare at her. She had been under the impression that only a few of Lady Grimsby's neighbors were expected for dinner, but the elegant, well-proportioned drawing room seemed positively crowded.

Despite her fine new (to her) feathers, Marian felt exceedingly awkward. No one had accompanied her downstairs, and, since she was unacquainted with the house, the butler had shown her the way to this room. Marian told herself she had merely imagined the infinitesimal curl of disdain that had seemed to linger at the man's lips. It most probably was his habitual expression.

This seemed a singularly joyless house for all its fine trappings.

Coming suddenly upon a snake or bear in a forest held no terrors for so seasoned a campaigner as she, but deep inside Marian felt sure that Lady Grimsby's drawing room was fraught with even greater peril.

"Miss Randall," the butler intoned.

How silly. They can hardly skin me and eat me, Marian told herself in disgust. She held her head high as she moved into the room.

Lady Grimsby, who was positively glittering in gold brocade and diamonds, was at that moment making a fuss over a distinguished older man who was bowing over her hand.

Lord Liverpool, Marian realized at once. The prime minister. Marian doubted she would be singled out overmuch for his attention, so she forced herself to relax.

In fact, most of the guests in the room appeared to be distinguished older men and their wives. To her consternation, one of the women came to Marian at once and kissed her cheek.

"You are the very image of your poor mother," the woman said as she took Marian's hand. "I knew her well, and your father, too, some years ago."

Suddenly giddy, Marian fought a shocking impulse to giggle, something she *never* did as a rule.

Which father, she had almost asked. Then she recovered her wits. Her weariness was finally catching up with her. She really should have taken that nap after her bath, as Isabella had ordered her for fear her eyes would be red and puffy with fatigue before Lady Grimsby's guests, but Marian had been too restless then to lie down.

"I was so sorry to hear of your great loss, my dear," the middle-aged woman continued. "I remember Captain and Mrs. Randall as such young, energetic persons, full of wit and good humor. It is hard to believe they are gone."

"Thank you," Marian said as she returned the warm pressure of the woman's hand. Her eyes started to mist with tears, for this woman was the first person to offer genuine sympathy to her on the deaths of her parents since she came to this strange place.

Marian forced the tears back. She would not make a spectacle of herself before all of these strangers.

"I take it your father's death occurred some time ago," the woman said uncertainly as her eyes swept Marian's pretty borrowed green gown. Marian realized at once that she should be wearing black in mourning for her father, and the fact that she was not might be construed as disrespectful to his memory.

Fashionable persons in London adopted mourning even on the deaths of quite distantly related persons, Marian knew, although both of her parents had thought it a silly, ostentatious custom, and neither she nor her father had gone into mourning for her mother. At that time, Marian had been at school in Bath, and it had been impractical for her to dye her few decent clothes black and then be forced to buy new ones to replace them when the period of mourning was over.

Certainly it had not occurred to her to wear mourning in the Peninsula after her father's death. Events had transpired so quickly.

Rescue came from an unexpected source.

"Captain Randall died just after Salamanca," said Isabella. Marian had not seen her approach from behind her. "Marian does not wear mourning out of consideration for my family while she is our guest, since to do so would put a bit of a damper on the wedding festivities."

"I mourn him in my heart, of that you may be certain," Marian said.

"Quite right," the woman said approvingly.

"Marian, may I present you to Mrs. Colyer?" Isabella interjected.

"Where *are* my manners? I should have introduced myself at once, my dear. A pleasure to meet you, Miss Randall," Mrs. Colyer said. Marian realized she was the wife of one of the most famous and influential orators in Parliament. "Major Lyonbridge has been telling us about his role in the Battle of Salamanca. Such a stirring tale."

All the gentlemen, Marian could see, had clustered about Major Lyonbridge, and their faces reflected varying degrees of excitement and triumph as they vicariously shared in the danger of battle. At one point, they gave a spontaneous little cheer.

"Your fiancé is so modest, my dear Miss Grimsby," Mrs. Colyer said. "The dispatches were full of praise for his role at Salamanca, yet he takes none of the credit for himself. You must be very proud."

"Yes," Isabella said with a forced smile. "Quite proud."

With that, Isabella excused both herself and Marian.

"It is going to be an excruciatingly boring evening if Adam is going to prose on and on about that old battle all night long," Isabella said under her breath. "That gruesome accounts of such horrors *will* pass for polite conversation on social occasions these days never ceases to amaze me."

Marian looked at the girl in surprise. How could Isabella possibly find the telling of such military action boring when her own fiancé and his men heroically had risked death to win the day at Salamanca?

"Well, we *are* at war, Isabella," she said. "It is no surprise that the gentlemen wish to hear about the victory at Salamanca."

"I know," Isabella said with a sigh. "You are right, of course." She looked around the room. "My mother has managed to gather every important politician in London here tonight on only a few hours' notice, presumably so they may be impressed by Adam's stirring account of Wellington's triumph in Spain. She has a positive talent for this sort of thing, which is admirable, I suppose, but hardly conducive to the liveliest of parties."

"Ah, Miss Randall," said Lady Grimsby loudly when she caught sight of Marian. Marian forced herself not to flinch back when her hostess beckoned her forward and reached out to take her hand when she complied. Marian would not put it past Lady Grimsby to stab her with her fingernails or give her a hard pinch when she thought no one else was looking. The wide, insincere smile on the woman's face made her look like a bird of prey. "So glad you could join us, my dear."

"Thank you," Marian said warily.

"Everyone, this is Miss Randall. She has come to stay with us for a time, now that poor Captain Randall is dead of a fall from his horse. Such a pity," she said with false sympathy in her tone. "I depend upon you, my dear friends, to make her feel welcome in London."

There was a genial murmur in her direction. Marian acknowledged it with a polite inclination of her head and what she hoped was a small, dignified smile.

Lady Grimsby, in a move Marian had no doubt was deliberately calculated to embarrass her, lowered her voice to a level that still must have been audible to at least those persons closest to them.

"I am so pleased Isabella managed to find *something* for you to wear tonight, my dear."

Perfect. Now everyone knew she was wearing borrowed feathers.

Lady Grimsby obviously intended for Marian to be horribly embarrassed by this disclosure, and so she would have been had she cared for such things. Fortunately, after a few months on campaign she had become quite dead to vanity of any kind.

"Yes. It was very generous of Miss Grimsby to entrust this pretty gown to me for the evening," Marian said with a smile in Isabella's direction. "I shall take good care of it, I promise you."

Isabella gave an inclination of her head in acknowledgment.

"That was *not* well done of Mother," Isabella said to Marian after she had managed to extricate herself from Lady Grimsby's clutches without giving offense. "We shall punish her by going shopping for your new wardrobe tomorrow, shall we? We will spend Papa's money as if it were water. Since everyone knows the money is really Mother's, after all, it will vex her no end."

"I do not want your parents' charity," Marian said.

"Whyever not?" Isabella said with a shrug. "You must wear *something,* and I am sure Papa would agree that you are entitled to a few new clothes, at least. And hats and gloves and evening cloaks and fans, of course."

Marian felt herself weaken. It had been a long time since she had indulged in the luxury of new clothes. So long that she had forgotten how much she adored the swish of crisp, freshly pressed muslin skirts as she moved about a room that smelled of fresh-cut flowers instead of camphor.

"Well, maybe a few things," she conceded, and Isabella gave a little smirk of triumph. "But I do not wish to impose on your good nature, for you must be very busy with your wedding plans. I can go shopping alone."

"My *mother* is very busy with the wedding plans," Isabella said. "*I* have practically nothing to do but support the character of a happy bride in public, heaven help me. You need me to tell you where all the best shops are. From the look of that tired gray traveling costume you were wearing when you arrived, you have not the least idea!"

"Well, that's frank!"

"Sometimes, my dear Miss Randall, one must be cruel to be kind," Isabella said. Her eyes were dancing. "As for imposing on me, it would be no such thing. I have shockingly overspent my allowance this quarter, and Mama was obliged to deliver quite a stern lecture to me on the subject. She said I may have no more new clothing except what *she* chooses for my bride clothes until after the wedding, when presumably I will have to apply to Adam for the money to buy my bits and bobs. You may imagine how sympathetic *he* is likely to be to my entreaties. So while I am selflessly devoting myself to the cause of your adornment, it will be a simple thing to slip in a few trifling things for myself among the largess."

Marian had to laugh, and she soon realized she had done so a bit too loudly when several curious faces turned in her direction. It occurred to her that she had not been so amused in a long time, not since before Captain Randall died.

"I knew you would see it my way," said Isabella. "You may safely place yourself in my hands."

Isabella went on to detail the excellencies of the shops deserving of Marian's valuable custom and which items of clothing were to be found there, but she lapsed into a vexed silence when she saw that Marian was not paying any attention to her.

Marian was listening with rapt attention to Major Lyonbridge tell his audience about Salamanca. She could almost smell the acrid smoke from the cannon fire and see the miasma of death that lingered over the battleground. She remembered the faces of the poor wounded men as they patiently waited for the practiced ministrations of her bluff, good-natured father, for so he would always be in her heart.

She would give anything to be back there now, in the thick of the campaign with all its attendant horror and discomforts, if only Captain Randall could be restored to her.

Marian could hear about one word in three of Major Lyonbridge's narrative, and she found it strangely comforting to listen to him. As Mrs. Colyer had said, he was speaking of the heroism of others rather than himself. When one was coping with the day-to-day minutiae of living on campaign, one forgot one's role in the greater plan, that of keeping Mother England safe from those who would enslave her, as the Gallic monster had done to most of Europe.

Major Lyonbridge's words made her feel proud to have been part of such an enterprise, even in the modest supporting role of daughter to the regimental surgeon. Relegated now to the status of mere young lady in the civilian world, she doubted that she would ever feel so alive again.

The major's hair was brushed to a high gloss, his dress

uniform practically gleamed, and his shoulders were the widest in the room. With one notable exception, the face of every lady in the room positively gleamed with admiration at the sight of him.

"Will dinner *never* be announced?" Isabella asked with a false, sweet smile on her face for the benefit of her mother's guests. "Oh, weary me. There is not a single person under the age of forty here with the exception of you, myself and, though one can hardly count him for all the liveliness *he* ever displays, Adam."

Mercifully for Isabella's sake, the butler grandly made the anticipated announcement and the guests began filing into the dining room. Lady Grimsby went into dinner on the arm of Lord Revington, Major Lyonsbridge's father, as the most distinguished gentleman present, and Isabella, of course, was escorted by the major. Marian found herself paired with an elderly, mustachioed gentleman who needed the support of her arm much more than she needed his.

Chapter 8

Isabella Grimsby gave a long-suffering sigh at her fiancé's inattention.

"Adam, we have been separated for almost a year because of the war, and we are being married in less than a month," she said from between jaws fixed in a pleasant smile. "Do you think you could think of *some* remark to address to me?"

"Since from the time we were children, any chance remark I have foolishly cast in your direction has precipitated an argument, I thought to spare both of us," he said through a smile equally as fixed. "However, since you have a sudden longing for the sound of my voice . . . how are you, Isabella? I trust I find you in tolerable health and spirits."

"Quite tolerable, thank you, considering that you have just inflicted an unknown half-sister upon me," she said in a voice so soft and inaudible to others that they could fancy, if they chose, that the engaged couple whispered sweet nothings over the broken meats, "and you have been ignoring me completely to stare at her like a mooncalf these past five minutes."

This was utter nonsense, of course.

Adam had thought Marian Randall a remarkably pretty girl at the regimental hospital with dark circles of exhaustion under her eyes as she patched up the wounded, and later, on the journey, when she was liberally covered by the dirt of travel in her drab gown of gray. But dressed in a flattering gown and with her hair arranged becomingly, she was enchanting.

The transformation had merely surprised him, that was all, and this did prompt him to look at her closely at first. But Isabella was exaggerating, as usual, when she accused him of staring at her. Isabella was a female who thought herself ill-used if she did not have every male eye in a room fixed on her.

"The general ordered me to escort the girl, and so I did. And, because of this, I feel an interest in the girl's welfare. I *will* take her to Mrs. Pritchett if I have reason to think she is mistreated here."

"I have given her the clothes practically off my back," Isabella objected.

"Yes, I remember the gown," he said.

"You remember the gown I wore to our engagement party?" Isabella exclaimed in surprise.

"I remember the rare bear-garden jaw you gave me when I stepped upon the hem while we were dancing and tore it. Then you stomped off in high dudgeon to have your maid make repairs."

"Well, I *was* vexed," she admitted. "I was very proud of the gown, for the color was the very height of fashion then, and I *would* have it despite Mother's objections that green is not a particularly flattering color for me. She was right, of course, although I must say it looks very well on Marian."

"Indeed," he murmured as he made a conscious effort to tear his gaze from the girl in green. It was rude, however, to ignore his fiancée at a dinner in her own home, so he made an effort to look into Isabella's eyes.

"Would you really have taken Marian to Mrs. Pritchett if you thought she was ill-treated here?" Isabella asked.

"Certainly I would, my orders from your father notwithstanding. The girl is not to blame for her origins. She has been through a great ordeal and lost all the family she has ever known, besides. None of this has been easy for her."

"None of this has been easy for my mother and me," Isabella pointed out. "I think we are rising beautifully to the occasion when one considers that you and my father have thrust the girl upon us without a whisper of warning. I am to take her shopping tomorrow."

Adam could not help smiling at this flight of altruism.

"Shopping. Now *there* is a hardship for you," he remarked teasingly.

Another woman would have laughed.

Not Isabella.

"It pleases you to mock me, Major Lyonbridge," she said haughtily.

He supposed she thought she was being exciting and provocative by pretending to be insulted. He now was expected to apologize profusely and explain himself, which would precipitate a volley of flirtatious banter between them. The object, of course, was to call his attention to herself and keep it there. He had seen Isabella and other women adopt this style of conversation with men before, and, personally, he found it irritating in the extreme.

He was not in the mood tonight to play this silly game.

"I did no such thing, as you know very well," he said. He heard the testiness in his own voice and was nettled by it. It boded ill for the success of his mission.

General Lord Grimsby expected Adam to use his personal popularity and reputation as a war hero to foster goodwill for the new Government among the influential men of London, yet he could not maintain a civil conversation of several moments' duration with his own fiancée without having it degenerate into a skirmish of senseless bickering.

He was no diplomat, and so he had told the general.

Still, he was willing to try.

"Let us cry peace, Isabella," he said in an attempt to

forestall the inevitable barrage of complaints about his incivility. "After all, we are to be married in a month."

Lord help me.

"As you wish," she said coldly, and pointedly turned her back on him to converse with the gentleman on her other side.

This gentleman, obviously, was more appreciative of Isabella's coquettish wiles, and Adam tried not to be annoyed by her frequent trills of carefree laughter as she flattered the distinguished older man's vanity. The gentleman was an important and influential politician and Isabella, an ambitious general's daughter who could be perfectly charming when she chose to ingratiate herself with the right people, blossomed under his admiration.

Too bad she rarely chose to be charming with *him*.

Thus freed of her attention, Adam turned to the lady on his other side to engage her in polite conversation, as was his sacred duty as a guest. However, this lady was quite deaf and much more interested in consuming the excellent fish soup before her than she was in exchanging pleasantries with Adam, so he was free, once again, to glance at Marian Randall to see how she was faring.

Indeed, she appeared to be getting along swimmingly with her elderly male dinner companions. No doubt they thought her a heroine for having endured the hardships of campaign with her father, and so she was.

Adam was about to reluctantly return his attention to his fiancée when he surprised a startled look on Marian's face and a leer on her dining companion's. While the other gentleman had been hanging on Marian's every word with rapt attention, this man had been leaning sideways toward Marian, and his hand was no longer visible. From Marian's expression, Adam surmised that her dining companion had placed the delinquent hand where he ought not.

The bounder! Just because the poor girl was orphaned

and friendless did not mean he had the right to impose upon her.

Adam had half risen from his chair when he saw Marian whisper a remark to the man that made him straighten up and color with embarrassment.

No doubt she had threatened to gut him with her fruit knife if he would not keep his roaming hands to himself, Adam thought with satisfaction. Apparently the lady could take care of herself.

Adam could not stop a short burst of laughter from escaping his lips, and Isabella turned to him at once with a demand to know what he found so amusing.

"Miss Randall," he whispered. "Apparently the old court card on her right decided to put his hand on her knee, and she has left his ears burning for his impertinence."

"How vexatious! That is Mr. Dilhurst," Isabella said, looking displeased. "He is a widower, and on the lookout for a wife. Mama thought the two of them might suit, but nothing is going to come of it if Marian is going to cut up stiff every time a gentleman makes her the object of his gallantry."

"I hardly think that groping a lady under the table falls under the heading of gallantry," Adam said dryly.

"A female in her position cannot afford to be choosy. The sooner she is settled, the better."

"The better for you and your parents, you mean. The man is old enough to be her grandfather. Surely she is permitted to look about her a bit before she settles for *that*."

"You are taking an inordinate amount of interest in Marian's affairs," she said.

Adam raised one eyebrow.

"Jealous, my dear?"

"Hardly," she scoffed with a pretty toss of her head. She looked about her with a sigh. "Such a dull party. I could cry with vexation when I reflect that even now I could be in Brighton, dancing at the Castle Inn."

"I know just how you feel," Adam said with an answering sigh. "*I* could have been sleeping on a hard cot in a tent, and competing with the flies for my meager fare of stew made of stringy goat and onions."

"Why aren't you, then?" she demanded. "*I* did not ask you to come here."

"No, you did not. But your father did, with Lord Wellington's blessing. *He* thought he was granting me a huge favor by making it possible for me to embrace marriage sooner than would otherwise have been possible."

"Do try to remember you are not the only sufferer," she said, smiling through her clenched teeth again.

"Believe me, your manner makes it impossible for me to delude myself in this regard," he said, matching her tone.

"Mama says I will become accustomed to you in time," Isabella said sadly.

"And so you will. Happily, you will not be bothered with my offensive presence overmuch. I will return to the Peninsula almost before the vows have been uttered."

"What? You will abandon me before we are to have a proper honeymoon? How can you serve me such a turn? What will people *think?*"

"Consistency is not your strong suit, is it, Isabella?" Adam said with a sigh. "People will think that we are a brave and selfless couple to make such a noble sacrifice on behalf of our country."

"And I am to live with my *mother*, like the veriest schoolgirl, even though I would be a married woman."

"You could always follow the drum with me," he suggested. When she turned a look of utter horror and incredulity upon him, he muttered a dry, "I thought not."

"I suppose you haven't the means to make me a large enough allowance to set up my own household in London," she said.

"Sadly, no. But there is always the house in Derbyshire

that my uncle left to me," Adam said with a shrug. "You are welcome to live there, if you would prefer."

"The thing probably is falling to bits! It would take me *months* to make it habitable," she exclaimed. "Besides, it is a bit too close to your father's estate for my comfort. I can just see him poking his nose into my affairs and cutting up stiff over every little thing."

She cast a disparaging glance at Lord Revington, who was sitting at her mother's right hand and addressing some remark to her at that moment. Adam observed that even though there was a smile on his father's face, it was overshadowed by his habitually stern expression.

"Look on the bright side, my dear," Adam said. "With luck, I will fall in battle, and you will be free to look for a husband more to your liking."

Isabella gave him an injured look.

"Surely you do not think I am enough of a monster to wish for any such thing!" she said.

Adam saw that he had actually hurt her feelings.

"No, of course I do not," he said, mollified by her genuine distress at such an accusation. "Please forgive me. I am displeased, as well, by the speed with which events are progressing. All will be well. I shall not impose upon you overmuch as a husband, I promise you."

There. He had said in terms as blunt as he could that he would not be a frequent visitor to her bed. He expected her to be relieved. He was not stupid, and he knew that she anticipated the consummation of their marriage with distaste. She was a bit of a cold fish, for all her flirtatious ways. And, truly, Adam did not want to leave a pregnant bride behind if he fell in battle.

In typical Isabella fashion, however, she chose to put the worst possible interpretation on his well-meaning remark.

"You have a favorite little Spanish tart to warm your cot, no doubt," she said with a sniff. "I am hardly surprised, because it is obvious that some women quite fancy you." It was abundantly apparent that *she* had no idea why this should be so.

"Just take good care," she said in a low voice, "that twenty years from now *you* do not present me with a little surprise such as the one my father has inflicted upon my poor mother."

Her eye dwelt significantly on Marian, which put Adam so out of temper that it took all the discipline at his command not to rise from the table and stomp off to find a hackney to take him home.

To do so would give rise to gossip that would embarrass both his family and Isabella's, however, so he gritted his teeth through the next course and was relieved when Isabella did not address another word to him throughout the meal.

"I had not thought of mourning," Marian said when she brought the green gown to Isabella's room and started to hang it up in the wardrobe. She was wearing a dainty light blue dressing gown borrowed from Isabella. It was only slightly too tight in the breast and hips.

"Do not bother with that," Isabella said over her shoulder as her maid brushed her hair. "Just put it on the bed. Betty will take care of it. As for mourning, I suppose it might be best to have at least one good black gown for going out when we expect to be among the highest sticklers. Pity to waste good money on mourning weeds. Of course, black would flatter your coloring."

Marian had to laugh at her.

"There is that, of course."

"However, since the purpose of bringing you to London is to find you a husband, dressing you in black crepe would hardly be to your advantage. A likely gentleman might thus be reminded somewhat unpleasantly of his own mortality."

"I would not want people to think I do not mourn my father, for I do. Very much."

"I believe you," Isabella said. "That is enough, Betty." The maid put down the brush and went at once to hang up the green gown carefully in the wardrobe. Isabella waited until she had dismissed her maid before she continued. "But Captain Randall was not *really* your father, and it seems hard that you must wear mourning for him."

"My father . . . Captain Randall . . . did not approve of the custom of mourning. He thought it a waste of good clothes to be dyeing them black merely to avert gossip, when it is what is in one's heart that matters. Not what is on one's back."

"Marian, you clever girl! I knew if we put our heads together, we could think of something to get around the troublesome issue of mourning," Isabella said approvingly. "You need merely give *that* out to anyone who dares look askance at you for wearing colors. Say it in precisely that tone of voice, with the tears shimmering in your eyes, like you did just now. It will go down well, I think."

"I do not say this to be clever," Marian said, nettled. "I say it because it is true."

Isabella rose from the dressing table and surprised them both by clasping Marian in her arms.

"I am so sorry, my dear," she said with a suspicious sniff. "It must be sad to lose a parent one loves so devotedly."

"Well, it is," Marian said, finding her half sister's rose-water-scented embrace oddly comforting. She rested her head on Isabella's shoulder.

At that moment, both young women recalled their circumstances and sheepishly drew apart.

"I beg your pardon," Isabella said. "That was overly familiar when one considers our very short acquaintance. I had no wish to offend you, but you looked so sad."

"Indeed, I was not offended," Marian said, just as embarrassed as Isabella. "It was kind of you."

Almost sisterly, Marian nearly said.

"Thank you for everything, Isabella," she said instead. "I will be going to my room now. Good night."

Isabella gave a slight inclination of her head as Marian passed through the door.

"Sleep well, little sister," Isabella whispered to the empty room.

Chapter 9

"You said I could have any friends that I wished for my bridesmaids," Isabella complained. "It is little enough compensation, after all, for having to marry Adam."

Lady Grimsby's jaw hardened. She gave Marian a hateful glare, as if *she* were to blame for Isabella's stubbornness.

"It is unbecoming, Isabella, for you to refer to your future husband in such a disrespectful manner. I did say you could have any of your friends you wished for your bridesmaids, but your choice, in this instance, is inappropriate."

Marian cleared her throat. As usual, they had been talking about her as if she weren't present.

"Isabella, perhaps it would be best if—"

"No! You are to be one of my bridesmaids, and that is that," the girl snapped. "It is only right. Papa will approve, for it will bring you to the notice of all the gentlemen present."

Isabella appealed to her mother.

"Mother, was that not my father's purpose in sending Marian to us? To arrange a marriage for her? And have you not said that the sooner she is off our hands—no offense intended, Marian—the better you shall like it?"

"But what will people think?" Lady Grimsby asked. "She is the veriest nobody, quite apart from the true nature of her birth."

"What could make a better impression on Society than inviting the brave, bereaved daughter of my regimental surgeon to participate in my daughter's wedding to the glorious war hero?"

Lady Grimsby gave a long sigh of frustration. Angry with her husband she might be. But she was an ambitious, politically astute wife and hostess, and she could see at once the value of such a gesture to her husband's career and, therefore, to her own position in Society.

"I suppose, if you insist, you may have her. It is hard, indeed, that on my daughter's wedding day I must have my husband's love child thrust in my face at every turn."

"I shall take care not to put myself forward any more than is absolutely necessary," Marian interjected, which earned her another glare from her natural father's wife. In justice, she could not wholly blame Lady Grimsby for her hostility. Had Captain Randall played false with Marian's mother during their marriage, the good doctor most probably would have found himself bereft of a limb or two at the very least.

"Excellent," Isabella said in satisfaction at getting her own way. "We must go at once to purchase fabric for your costume, for there is not much time to have it made."

Lady Grimsby gave the two of them a look of glacial displeasure and strode regally through the door, as if she could not bear another moment in their company. Marian was surprised the room did not shake.

"She is very angry," Marian said. "Perhaps you should reconsider."

Isabella gave an expressive shrug.

"She is always angry over one thing or another," she said. "She is likely to be this way until you are married and out of her sight, so you may as well become accustomed to it. *I* certainly have done so."

"I am truly sorry to be the cause of so much strife in your household. I am certain that if I apply to Captain Randall's former colleague at Chelsea Hospital I can obtain a position as nurse. That should dispose of my future quite satisfactorily."

"What utter nonsense! You would work as a nurse in a hospital? Among a great, unwashed lot of enlisted men, where you would be subject to every insult?"

"Well, they would not be unwashed for long. Not once I got my hands on them," Marian said. "Uncleanliness breeds disease, you know."

This remark so shocked Isabella that Marian offered no more objection to serving as Isabella's bridesmaid.

"Oh, good heavens. What is *he* doing here?" Isabella whispered to Marian as she indicated her fiancé, who had just walked in the door of the shop where Marian was trying on hats.

Over the past three weeks, Isabella had already purchased so many clothes for Marian—with a few choice tidbits for herself, of course—that Marian did not know when she would wear the half of them. But, as Isabella had pointed out, a lady could not have too many becoming hats, and the blond straw trimmed in white silk roses was most becoming, indeed.

Major Lyonbridge drew every admiring female eye in the room as he lowered his head through the door to keep from smacking it against the upper frame.

"Isabella, Miss Randall," he said, bowing. The ladies bowed in return.

"Come to purchase a new military headdress, Adam?" Isabella asked humorously.

He gave a perfunctory smile.

"I have come looking for you," he said. "I wished to tell you, Isabella, that your father has arrived from Spain for the wedding, and your mother desires you and Miss Randall to return to the house at once. There is to be a dinner party in his honor tonight, and, of course, Lord Grimsby wishes to see you."

"We have not concluded our business here. What do you think of this hat for Marian?" Isabella said.

The major glanced in Marian's direction.

"It looks very well," he said, "although I am hardly a judge of such things. There does not seem to be much color to it."

Isabella pursed her lips.

"There is not supposed to be much color to it. It is elegant," she said. "With all that red hair and those green eyes, there is rather a lot of color to Marian already. We cannot be tricking her out in bright colors as well."

"I see nothing amiss with Miss Randall's coloring," the major said. To her annoyance, Marian found herself blushing at this tepid compliment, when all the lavish praise of Lady Grimsby's gentlemen guests over the past few weeks had left her unmoved. "How about that one?"

"A bright green hat with purple silk violets and rose-colored ribbons?" Isabella cried. "Are you *insane*? What a figure she should cut!"

"I never claimed to be an expert on feminine fashion," he said, looking a bit embarrassed. "After all, I wear a red coat every day of my life."

"True," Isabella conceded.

Although he bore it manfully, it was plain that he felt uncomfortable surrounded by so many laces and furbelows.

Marian found his consternation rather charming. It was quite the fashion for gentlemen to accompany their lady friends to the shops to advise them on the colors of their ribbons and whatnot. And, though young ladies were not supposed to know of such things, she was well aware that certain gentlemen often visited the shops without embarrassment to choose intimate attire for the females who enjoyed their protection.

The major, it was plain, was not of their number.

"Isabella, this hat is rather too dear," Marian said as she removed the charming confection and handed it to the shopgirl who had been assisting them. The girl had been mooning so intently over the major that she nearly dropped it.

"Nonsense," Isabella said mischievously. "My father would *want* you to have it—and for me to have that ravishing white chip hat trimmed in pink flowers."

She turned to the shopgirl.

"Have these conveyed to Lord Grimsby's house at once," she said.

"Very good, miss," the girl said.

"If you are *quite* ready, Isabella," the major said in an attempt to hurry the young ladies along.

"I am not," she said, although she permitted the major to escort her and Marian out of the shop. "We have one or two more errands to run before we leave the shops. I need a pair of evening gloves, and Marian must have some handkerchiefs. You may come along to carry our parcels, if you wish."

"I am in uniform," he said curtly. "A uniformed officer does not carry ladies' parcels."

"Do not be such a dull old stick," she said, indicating an officer walking along the street with a well-dressed matron and carrying several gaily colored bandboxes. "Come, Adam, it is time you supported the character of an infatuated swain."

"I have a better idea," the major said.

"Doubtful," Isabella murmured. "Extremely doubtful."

"Let us go instead to Gunter's, where I will treat you and Miss Randall to ices."

"A bribe! Most decidedly a bribe!" Isabella exclaimed in delight. "Adam, I am surprised at you! Clearly, you have been corrupted."

"And a very *welcome* bribe, Major Lyonbridge," Marian

interjected. “Isabella, my feet have blisters upon their blisters from walking from shop to shop over the past few weeks. An indefatigable infantryman was lost the day you were born a lady. I do not believe the troops walked so many miles during the retreat to Portugal.”

“I never took you for such a paltry creature,” Isabella said with mock scorn. “Very well, then. Ices, it is.”

“And then straight to your father’s house,” the major said.

“Oh, very well,” Isabella said with a pretty pout that was completely lost on the major because he was already scanning the cross street ahead and guiding them through the traffic.

Chapter 10

At Gunter's, Major Lyonbridge had not been quite the blockhead Isabella remembered. He had found a small table near the window so Isabella could look out at the passersby on the street, and he had managed to procure strawberry ices for her and for Marian without too much delay. He had conversed about *something* during the short interlude besides horses and the army, and he attracted a number of admiring glances from other young women when he rode beside their carriage on his horse to her father's house.

In short, she and Major Lyonbridge had exerted themselves so successfully in behaving well that Isabella had begun to think that this marriage would not be the horror that had loomed large in her nightmares.

Then she rushed into the parlor with a smile on her lips, expecting only a reunion with her father, and feeling quite charitable with him since she was becoming reconciled to the match he and Adam's father between them had wrought, only to stop so suddenly that Major Lyonbridge, who had been striding behind her, clumsily stepped on one of her heels.

He took her shoulders to steady her, but she merely shook him off.

No doubt she would have a prodigious bruise on her foot, but for now she could not feel the pain because her heart was beating so fast. She felt every drop of blood drain from her head.

She completely ignored her father, who had stood, smiling, and held his arms out to her, to stare at the handsome gentleman who sat conversing with her mother.

He was wearing a coat of blue superfine with canary pantaloons, riding boots, and a jaunty red carnation in his buttonhole. His attire was somewhat more casual than was strictly suitable for an afternoon call, as was the fashion among young men of their set, but the excellence of its tailoring clearly outshone the magnificence of the major's red uniform.

"Philip," she said faintly.

At that, her fiancé's brother stood and approached her, smiling, with one hand held out.

Isabella's hands curled into claws, and she wanted nothing more at this moment than to fly at him and tear out his beautiful eyes with her nails.

How could he do this to her?

His hair shone sleek and black as a raven's wing, and his mobile lips were smiling, even though the expression in his dark blue eyes was faintly anxious. He was some inches shorter than the major, and his physique was much more slender and elegant, but such was his presence that he rendered his brother's very existence utterly insignificant.

"Good afternoon, Miss Grimsby," he said as he took the trembling hand she automatically held out to him.

When she merely stared at him, too overcome to speak, her mother gave a mirthless little laugh that clearly indicated her displeasure at the spectacle Isabella no doubt was making of herself.

"It was quite civil of Mr. Lyonbridge to call, was it not, Isabella?" she said pointedly. "Such a delightful surprise for us all. But you must give his brother an opportunity to greet him as well."

"Yes, of course," Isabella said, recalling her company.

She would *not* make a fool of herself in front of this man, even though the earth had ceased its spin on its axis for a moment when she first beheld him.

She reclaimed her hand and pointedly turned away from him to smile at her father as the major and his brother shook hands.

"Papa," Isabella said, forcing air into her struggling lungs and cheer into her voice. Her father's face, which her entrance had surprised in quite grim lines because he had been conversing with Mother and that always put him out of temper, relaxed as he held out his arms for her. She walked into them and gave him a kiss on the cheek. "How delighted I am to see you! I began to fear you would not come to my wedding!"

"Nothing could keep me away," he assured her. "How pretty you look." He glanced at Marian, who had been standing silently beside the door, watching the little drama unfold with a look of uncertainty on her face. "And how is our Miss Randall faring?"

"Very well, sir," Marian said with a cool inclination of her head.

"You are much improved from when I saw you last."

"Thank you," she said, unsmiling. "I do not want to intrude upon your family's reunion, so if you will excuse me, sir, I will go to my room."

"No need to run off," the general said genially. "Miss Randall, may I present you to Mr. Lyonbridge, who has cut short his visit to Brighton in order to attend the wedding? He is Adam's brother, of course."

"Charmed, Miss Randall," Philip said as he gave Marian a polite smile and a slight bow. As was usual for him, he gave the lady he was addressing his complete attention regardless of what other undercurrents were awash in the room. This courteous attentiveness was one of the first of his many admirable qualities that had attracted Isabella to him.

Now it made her want to scream with frustration.

"Mr. Lyonbridge," Marian said, still unsmiling, as she returned his bow.

Isabella marveled that Marian did not appear in the least affected by Philip's smile or the singular grace of his bow. Her attention returned at once to the general.

"If I may be excused, sir?" she said pointedly. No doubt she sensed the unpleasant undercurrents in the room and wished to escape from them.

"Yes, do run along, Miss Randall," Lady Grimsby said with an impatient shooing motion of her hand. "My lord," she added, turning to the general, "I will leave you now, as well. I am afraid I have the headache."

Mother often had the headache when her husband was in residence, although, as a rule, she rarely suffered from them when he was gone.

"Of course, my dear. You must do as you wish," the general said absently as he watched Marian walk quickly out the door. Adam was watching her as well, and he nodded slightly as she passed him. She did not look at him. Lady Grimsby followed her from the room.

"Is she well?" the general said abruptly.

Isabella realized with a start that he was speaking to her.

"Mother seems quite well in general," she replied, "although, of course, she is very busy with the wedding in just a few days. Perhaps she is merely tired."

Her father made a slight gesture of impatience.

"I mean Miss Randall. Is she adjusting well to her new surroundings? Does she seem to take?"

"She seems content enough," Isabella said. "She has not gone out to many parties because of Captain Randall's recent death, of course, and it has taken some time for her new clothes to be made. She could not be *seen* in the clothing she brought with her, so it is early days to tell whether she will be popular with the gentlemen, if that is what you mean."

"Your mother tells me you have asked her to be a bridesmaid in your wedding," the general said. "I am pleased. That was well done of you, my dear."

"Well, Marian has been of enormous help to me these past weeks," she said. "To make a splash of a wedding, as you ordered, one must have a quantity of bridesmaids, and they do not grow on trees, particularly in London during the hottest part of summer, which is when I would have had to ask them."

"It was well done of you, just the same," the general said. He added for Philip's benefit, "Miss Randall's late father was our regimental surgeon. Her father named me her guardian in the event of his death."

"I see. It is most generous of you to take on the obligation," Philip said, but his eyes were on Isabella.

The general gave a nod of acknowledgment.

"Well, then," he said. "Adam, I would like to discuss a number of matters with you." He turned back to Philip. "Military matters, you understand," he said.

"I understand completely," Philip said, smiling briefly as the general ushered Adam from the room.

Philip turned to Isabella with a rueful smile on his face, and Isabella felt herself color with consternation. It was quite improper for her father to leave her alone with a gentleman caller. Her mother, she knew, never would have permitted it.

He held out his hand to her.

"Isabella—" he began, but she could contain herself no longer.

"How *could* you, Philip?" she blurted out. "I told you I wanted you to stay away."

"Isabella," he said reproachfully. He walked forward and held her shoulders in a gentle grasp. "When you marry my brother, we will be family. We must resign ourselves to seeing one another from time to time, and we may as well start now. My own wedding will occur in the spring, and you will attend as my brother's wife. We cannot invent excuses for the rest of our lives to avoid the sight of one another."

"I told myself I could do it—I *can* do it, but not if you are there, in the church, and I can feel your eyes upon me," she said.

"We are who we are, my dear," he said. "And we must do what we must. I cannot be absent from my brother's wedding. I offered my excuses, but my father is adamant. He is determined upon a political career for me, and so I am ordered to attend all the parties in your honor and the wedding itself so that I may ingratiate myself with the influential politicians who will attend those affairs."

"You *never* do what your father says," Isabella said, looking into those incredible blue eyes. "Why must you do so now?"

"Because until I see the deed done—until I see my brother take your hand in marriage with my own eyes—I cannot reconcile myself to losing you."

Angry as she was with him, her heart turned over and she gave an anguished sob.

Isabella could not help herself. She threw her arms around him and sighed as his arms came around her and held her to his chest. She could feel his heart beating under her ear. She could smell the crisp starch of his neckcloth and the faint, manly scent of bay rum with which he anointed his person.

His horrid brother always smelled of damp wool and horse.

"You cannot ask me to do this—marry your blockhead of a brother when it pains me to see the two of you together," she said. "The contrast between what might have been and what must be is too painful for my poor heart to bear."

"You *can* marry him, Isabella," he said as he gently extricated himself from her arms and squeezed her hands bracingly, "just as I can marry the gauche little heiress my father has chosen for me. You are who you are, and I am who I am. We can and will do what is expected of us."

"Blast you, Philip!" she cried, and fled from the room.

Chapter 11

"Well, it seems my brother has found the leisure to attend us at last," Major Lyonbridge said humorously as he gave a nod of his head in the direction of the doorway. Marian, with whom he was dancing at the time, turned to see Mr. Philip Lyonbridge lounge picturesquely in the doorway and scan the room with cool eyes.

"Such studied elegance," Marian mused. "It is so much easier to make a grand impression when one arrives after the receiving line has broken up, do you not agree?"

Adam threw his head back and laughed, which made the decorated war hero look quite boyish.

"For someone who has just met him, you have described the enigma that is my brother with quite astonishing accuracy," he said. "When he disappeared so abruptly two days ago, I began to wonder if he intended to brave my father's wrath after all and miss the wedding altogether."

As she admired the amused twinkle in the major's eye, Marian marveled again that Isabella would persist in describing her fiancé as humorless and monosyllabic. Marian had found him to be possessed of quite a keen sense of humor, the more refreshing for being rather more understated than that of most persons who prided themselves for their wit. As for being monosyllabic, he seemed to have no difficulty in expressing himself with *her*.

She supposed this was because he was one of the few persons who knew the truth about her parentage, so they could be frank with one another. By contrast, Major Lyonbridge and Isabella conversed with excruciating politeness in as few words as necessary in company, as if they both feared to upset the tenuous truce that existed between them as they approached their wedding day.

The wedding would be tomorrow, Marian thought as she enjoyed the bittersweet sensation of waltzing with Major Lyonbridge. He looked especially dashing tonight in a dress uniform lavishly trimmed with gold braid and a wealth of medals pinned to his chest. The sight of the wide-shouldered officer dancing with his ethereal, dark-haired bride had caused a positive whoosh of sentimental sighs to waft across the ballroom as the betrothed couple embarked upon the first dance of the evening.

If Isabella had not confided to Marian how much she dreaded the approach of the ceremony that would unite her in marriage with Major Lyonbridge, Marian might have shed a sentimental tear or two of her own at the sheer romance of it all. Instead, she was sorely tempted to grasp the little wretch by the shoulders and shake her until her pearly little teeth rattled.

How could Isabella be so blind, Marian wondered.

The major might not pay the most polished compliments of any gentleman in Society. He might not show to as great an advantage on the dance floor as he did on horseback. But Major Lyonbridge was an honest and intelligent man with little nonsense about him.

In addition to that, he was as handsome as a god.

Isabella, in her opinion, could do infinitely worse for a husband, and she would do well to desist in her pointless infatuation for a man she could not have.

Marian had no doubt that Mr. Philip Lyonbridge was a better hand at turning a clever compliment, and his tailoring, even to Marian's unsophisticated eye, was certainly superb. She had admired the grace of his dancing at previous balls. Who could not? He moved with the athletic ease of an acrobat upon the floor. But of what value were these qualities in contrast with Major Lyonbridge's brave heart and keen sense of duty?

If Isabella were to be believed, Major Lyonbridge did not wish for the match any more than she, but he had taken pains over the past few days to pay attention to his future bride.

He even had escorted Isabella and Marian on a number of afternoon excursions, such as to the British Museum and the Tower of London, pointing out the sights to both young women. Marian had enjoyed both of these outings, but Isabella had rewarded him for his kindness by practically yawning in his face when Major Lyonbridge described the historical significance of this artifact or that sculpture.

When Marian had taken Isabella to task for her utter indifference to the major's overtures of friendship, Isabella merely shrugged. The major, she insisted, escorted her about town not to please *her* but to gratify his superiors, who were eager for him to be seen in public with the influential General Lord Grimsby's daughter and thus foster goodwill for the fledgling Government and Lord Wellington's efforts in securing the Peninsula for the allies.

Marian sincerely doubted this. There was not a manipulative bone in the major's body. She was willing to stake her life on it. Never had she met a man so forthright. If he was making up to Isabella, it was because he hoped for a peaceful union.

And knowing Isabella—fond as Marian had grown of her half-sister—the poor man was not likely to get it.

Uh, oh. Here was trouble.

Marian almost missed a step in the pattern, and Major Lyonbridge was compelled to tighten his hold on her to keep her from tripping over her own feet.

"Steady, there," he said. "Is something wrong?"

"No, nothing at all," she said hastily as she deliberately steered him toward the other end of the floor. He arched a brow at her, for steering one's partner in the waltz was strictly a male prerogative. However, to her relief the major obliged her by following her course far away from the sight of Isabella standing pale and trembling not ten feet away from Philip Lyonbridge, who then hastened forward and took both her hands in his.

Isabella's expression of mingled elation and despair had been so revealing that the bride might as well have proclaimed her infatuation for her fiancé's brother at the top of her lungs.

It broke Marian's heart to see it. The least she could do was spare poor Major Lyonsbridge from the sight of his fiancée eating up another man with her eyes mere hours before he was to marry her.

Isabella felt her knees give way, but Philip was there to steady her.

"Good God, Isabella," he said under his breath. "You cannot go off in a swoon like some silly drama queen now."

"Certainly not," she said tartly as she reached inside herself and found her backbone. "It was just a shock to see you so suddenly, is all. You promised to stay away. When you disappeared so abruptly from town, I thought you meant to do it."

"I know. I'm sorry," he said. "I just could not. Dance with me."

The waltz had just ended, and sets were forming for a country dance.

Isabella swallowed hard when he placed his hand to rest lightly at the small of her back as he escorted her to the dance floor.

"For the last time," she said sadly.

"My sentimental darling," he said with a fond smile as he indicated a set lacking a couple ahead of them. "In point of fact, we will dance together often after the deed is done, for we will be family, and it will be expected of us. We may as well become resigned to it."

"I do not think I can bear it," she said. "To live with him, to *eat* with him." She shuddered. "To bear his children."

"And all the while, I will be living with *her,* eating with her, and begetting children upon her."

"Our children will be cousins," she mused. "I will look at the innocent faces of my children and see *him* instead of you. And I will look at yours and see *her*."

"When the family is together, I will be expected to greet you with a kiss on the cheek, as if we were brother and sister."

"I will live for those kisses," Isabella said as her eyes filled with tears, "and dread them at the same time."

"As will I," he said.

She halted in her tracks.

"I cannot do this now. I cannot stand up with you as if you were the merest social acquaintance. I cannot bow and smile and *think*."

"I will procure a glass of wine for you instead," he said as he changed direction and approached the small anteroom where refreshments were laid out.

"Yes. That would be better," she said.

"And several more glasses of wine for myself," he added with a wry smile that made her heart turn over. This was not going to be any easier for him, she realized. As a rule, he was so sophisticated and debonair and easy. It was why she loved him so much. But she could see the suffering in his eyes, and it both elated and saddened her.

She should be sorry to see his pain, but she was not.

And yet she was.

Isabella was so confused.

"Will this interminable night ever end?" she asked with a catch in her voice.

"Yes, it will end," Philip said, surprising Isabella by answering her rhetorical question. "Tonight we will part and we will meet again tomorrow morning. You will be in your wedding gown. I will be in my best morning coat. And we will smile and smile until our jaws ache because it is expected of us."

"We have no choice," she said glumly as they entered the refreshment room, and Philip procured a glass of wine for Isabella and for himself from the servant in attendance.

"Cheers," he said with one of those crooked smiles that so enchanted her as he touched his glass to hers.

Chapter 12

The day had dawned bright and beautiful and unusually warm for September—a good omen for a wedding.

What a mockery it was.

Marian, dressed in the fashionable ice blue gauze gown Isabella had chosen for her with such great care, and with her hair adorned with tiny white flowers, felt a lump grow in her throat as the morning advanced and there was no bride.

She had dressed early with the aid of one of the under maids and gone on ahead to the church with the other bridesmaids, for the bride and her parents would follow in state in the general's open carriage.

Or, at least, that was what was *supposed* to have happened.

Instead, the bride's parents arrived sans bride, and the hissing sound of four hundred wedding guests whispering to one another in consternation followed Lord and Lady Grimsby into the anteroom where Marian and the other five bridesmaids waited for their cue to appear.

Lady Grimsby was pale, and her eyes were red with weeping. The general's face was set in stern lines.

"What is it?" Marian cried. "Where is Isabella? Is she ill? Has something dreadful happened?"

"Did you know anything about this, missy?" Lady Grimsby demanded as she stalked up to Marian and grasped her arms in a grip that would probably leave bruises. "Were you in on this plot to disgrace the family out of some sort of petty revenge?"

"I do not know what you mean," Marian said as she extricated herself from the woman's clutches.

"Butter would not melt in your mouth, would it, my girl?" Lady Grimsby said with a sneer on her face. "She must have had some accomplice. She could not have done this alone."

"Isabella is gone," the general said bitterly. "She left a note on her pillow saying she could not bring herself to marry Adam."

"Oh, how could she do such a thing?" Marian said softly.

"This is what has become of your indulging your daughter, Madam," Lord Grimsby said as he glared at his wife.

"*Your* daughter, my husband," Lady Grimsby replied, glaring right back at him, "has proven as faithless and deceitful as her sire. What else could you have expected with *your* blood coursing through her veins?"

"Please. I do not understand," Marian interjected. "I saw her this morning. I went to her room after I was dressed so that she could see me in my gown. She even had her maid put more flowers in my hair. She was sipping her morning chocolate, and she appeared perfectly calm."

"When I went to her room to supervise the dressing of her, I found her maid there alone and this letter on her pillow," Lady Grimsby said. Marian snatched it from her hand and read it with growing dismay. Lady Grimsby poked her husband on the arm. "You must make an announcement."

"Stop," Marian said as the general nodded and turned to leave the room. "Have you told Major Lyonbridge?"

He positively blanched.

"No," he said, clearly dreading the prospect. His jaw hardened. "He will learn of it when I make the announcement."

"Oh, no! It would be too cruel!" Marian said. "You must tell him first. It is the only decent thing to do."

"I cannot," he said. "Adam is like the son I never had. How can I tell him that my daughter has jilted him at the very altar?"

Marian put her hands on her hips.

"For heaven's sake! You are a *general!*"

"And I know what Adam is like when he is angry," Lord Grimsby said. "They do not call him the Berserker for nothing."

"*I* will tell him, then, if you are afraid," she said contemptuously. "I will tell him outside, where no one can watch his face when he hears the news. Then you can make the announcement."

Marian then rushed off through the church, enduring the curious stares of the guests as the fragrance of the pink and white roses that were banked on both sides of the aisle mocked her. She found Adam in the vestibule, talking with several of his friends. One of them was looking at his timepiece when Marian stepped outside the inner door to the church.

"Major Lyonbridge," Marian said anxiously. "I must speak with you at once."

"Too late, girlie," one of the other men said jovially. "He is already taken."

Major Lyonbridge laughed along with his companions at this modest joke, but his smile faded when Marian continued to look grim.

"If you will excuse me," the major said to the other men. He took Marian's arm to lead her outside the church. His eyes were concerned and his touch was gentle. She could have wept. "What is it, Miss Randall? Has something happened?"

On the way through the church to find him, Marian had mentally composed various dignified ways of breaking the shocking news to him. Right now, she could not remember even one of them.

"Isabella is gone," she blurted out. She forced herself to

look him right in the eye. He deserved that much at least. "She has run off . . . with another man."

A red haze limned the edges of Adam's vision, just as it did when he engaged in battle. He thought his heart would burst from his chest for anger, but this time he could not release the tension by drawing his saber and slashing away at the vulnerable flesh of his enemies.

He took a deep breath, but it did nothing to dissipate his fury.

Marian was so beautiful in her blue dress with her auburn hair arranged in pretty ringlets with flowers strewn among them. Her big green eyes were moist with sympathy, and that was the most humiliating thing of all.

He did not want her pity. He did not want *anyone's* pity.

What Adam wanted was to wrap his hands around the throat of her faithless little jilt of a half sister and squeeze until her little pink tongue turned black.

He could not do that, more's the pity, but he *could* have satisfaction.

"Who is the man?" he demanded through clenched teeth. "Tell me who he is, so that I may kill him."

Marian hesitated just a bit too long, and he knew the truth.

The red mist of the battle rage thickened before his eyes. Through it, he could see that Marian's lips were white.

She was brave, the general's daughter. Seasoned soldiers ran in panic from his presence when this mood was upon him, yet she managed to stand her ground.

"It is my brother," he said slowly. "The little jilt has run off with my own brother! I am going after them."

"No, you must not," she said, catching his arm in both her hands when he would have run down the steps. "Not like this."

"Take your hands off me, Marian," he said, fighting for control. In his present mood, he was capable of flinging her away from him as if she were a bothersome insect, to leave her broken on the steps below them.

"At least *she* has the courage to avoid a marriage neither of you wanted!" Marian cried. "Admit it! It is only your pride that is hurt!"

"*Only* my pride . . ." he repeated in disbelief. For a moment, he could only stare at her in indignation. She was perfectly right, of course, but that did not make Isabella's betrayal any less painful.

"What do you think I would do to your precious sister that she does not deserve?" he asked.

"Beat her, in your present humor. Or strangle her," Marian said without hesitation. "I will not permit you to do so. If you are determined to go after them, I am going with you."

With a snarl of anger, he took Marian's face between his two hands and drew her close. Slowly and deliberately he traced the planes of her cheekbones with his thumbs, and her eyes fluttered closed as he bent his face close to hers.

He was frightening her, but he did not care.

"I could crush your skull between my two thumbs as easily as I could crush a walnut or an eggshell," he said harshly. "Your body is a twig I could break in my bare hands. Do you think if I truly wanted to kill Isabella that *you* could stop me?"

Incredibly, Marian opened her eyes and met his gaze fearlessly.

"Yes," she said with absolute conviction in her voice. "I could. And you know it."

He looked at her for a moment and then gave a growl of frustration.

"Very well, then," he said. He regarded the festive flower- and-ribbon-bedecked open carriage, which awaited in vain the emergence of the truant bride and her bridegroom, with contempt as he led the way to his father's sober black closed carriage.

"Off," Adam barked at the liveried coachman who was sitting on the box. The man scrambled away with such alacrity that he almost lost his powdered wig.

As Adam helped Marian onto the box of the carriage preparatory to taking the reins himself, the guests started pouring out of the double doors to the church. Several stopped in their tracks and stared at them.

"Excellent," Adam said sarcastically to Marian. "Perhaps now they will think that *we* are eloping."

Chapter 13

Marian knew she should be concerned for her reputation, for it was not *done* for an unmarried lady to travel alone with a gentleman unrelated to her.

A score of guests had seen the officer hand her onto the box of the carriage, but that could not be helped now. At any rate, she fancied she had few acquaintances on the Great North Road capable of recognizing her, although an officer driving a coach and four in full dress regalia and traveling with a lady dressed in a dainty blue gown with her hair shedding small wilted flowers were hardly inconspicuous.

Marian glanced at the major's face, which seemed to be set in stone.

"Running off to Scotland, are ye?" a toll booth custodian called gaily to the couple. "Good luck to ye!"

"Thank you," the major said through gritted teeth.

"Oh, do stop looking as if you were about to commit murder," Marian exhorted him after several miles further of being seated next to a fulminating basilisk. "We shall have the next one offering me his condolences. And is it quite necessary to drive so recklessly? I shall be surprised if I have an unloosened tooth left in my head by the time we catch up with them."

The major growled at her.

"The innkeeper at the last town said they are not above an hour ahead of us," he said. "Isabella apparently has been having the fellow stop at every posting inn for tea and little cakes."

"Perhaps your brother, too, is fond of tea and little cakes," Marian said.

"Bloody man-milliner," he growled under his breath.

"They are in love," she said.

"In love? *Philip?* Not bloody likely!" he scoffed. "The only person Philip loves is himself—and perhaps his tailor. Lord, I can't wait to bloody his nose for him."

"That's the spirit!" Marian said approvingly. He narrowed his eyes at her in suspicion.

"What are *you* so cheery about?" he demanded.

"I am pleased to see you are in a better temper."

"I just announced my intention of bloodying my brother's nose."

"I heard you," she said, "and it is a felicitous sign. I believe that you are much less dangerous when you are threatening merely to bloody your brother's nose than you are when you are driving in fulminating silence with a nerve twitching in your jaw. It is most discomfiting."

"I do *not* twitch," he snapped.

"You have come all the way from expressing a wish to murder poor Isabella to merely bloodying your brother's nose in the space of a mere four hours. I call that quite satisfactory progress for a gentleman of your reputed temper."

"Poor Isabella! Do not think I have altogether abandoned my resolve of murdering her. Has anyone ever told you, Miss Randall, that you are a most irritating woman?"

"Often. It is hardly *my* fault that unenlightened persons fail to appreciate my practical nature," she said. "Would you rather I entertained you with a fit of the vapors merely because my reputation is in shreds at having left London in the company of a gentleman and unchaperoned?"

He turned to stare at her. It was plain that he had been

so obsessed with catching up to his truant bride that this had not crossed his mind.

"Mind the horses," she cried out at his inattention to the task at hand.

"I refuse to marry you to preserve your precious reputation," he said bitterly, but he did return his gaze to the road in front of him. "You were the one who insisted upon accompanying me."

"The subject is moot if you manage to upset the carriage and break my neck!"

"You make that possibility look more attractive by the minute, I assure you," he snarled.

"Oh, do not return to glowering again. Of course, I do not expect you to marry me. In fact, you have done me a great favor in ruining me if it means the general will abandon his resolve of finding a husband for me and let me go to Chelsea Hospital to work as a nurse, as I originally intended to do."

"I have *not* ruined you! Spare me from all women and their fustian rubbish. As for working as a nurse, you may do so with my fervent goodwill, although the general may not be so easy to manage."

"I really do call this fine progress!" she said. "You have come all the way from murdering my sister through bloodying your brother's nose to deliberately oversetting your father's carriage to break my neck."

He gave a snort of what suspiciously sounded like amusement and lapsed into silence.

"There! Up ahead!" he called out after a half hour. "If there ever was such a gudgeon—Philip did not even have the wit to hire a carriage. No, he must take his fancy curricle with the blue body and the yellow wheels. Just the thing for a discreet flight to the border."

When they pulled abreast of the couple, Mr. Lyonbridge whipped up the horses and tried to pull away from them, but the major, in a maneuver that caused both ladies to let out shrill screams, cut him off and forced the curricle to the side of the road.

"I have you now," the major growled as he jumped off the box and stalked off to confront his brother.

"Oh, do stop sneering like one of those overblown villains from a Minerva Press novel," Marian said in disgust. "Isabella, dear. You look shaken to bits."

"Traitoress," Isabella, looking stricken, said to Marian.

"Such ingratitude," Marian said. "I have come to keep the major from wringing your neck. Oh, dear!"

The major had in the meantime neatly plucked his more slender brother off the box of his carriage and planted him a facer. He gave a savage grunt of satisfaction as the blood ran down Mr. Lyonbridge's nose, and that gentleman whipped a white handkerchief out of his pocket to staunch it.

"Brute!" cried Isabella, scrambling down from her seat on the box at the risk of breaking her neck to run to the aid of her wounded hero. She bared her teeth at the major. "Beast! I am *glad* I jilted you."

The major knotted his fists and loomed over her.

"Be glad you are not worth the effort of killing, Isabella," he snarled.

Isabella's eyes rolled back in her head and she would have fallen in the dirt of the road if Mr. Lyonbridge had not caught her about the waist with one arm. His other hand he kept pressed to his nose with his handkerchief as he gazed at the fainting woman in concern.

"Now, look what you've done!" Marian shouted in frustration. "Do stop glowering at the poor things in that sinister fashion and help me down from the box."

With a sigh of exasperation, the major walked over to the carriage, reached up to grasp Marian by the waist, and set her down none too gently on the ground. Her feet were in motion, carrying her to her unconscious sister, before they touched solid earth.

"Carry her to your father's carriage, if you please, Mr. Lyonbridge, so that I may take care of her," Marian said. "Have you any water in your carriage?"

"No," he said as he lifted Isabella into his arms. She had opened her eyes and begun to moan softly.

"It is all right now, my dear," Marian said soothingly to Isabella. "Come quickly, Mr. Lyonbridge. You must get her out of this hot sun."

The man roused himself to carry Isabella to the carriage and lay her full length on the seat at Marian's direction. At Marian's prodding against his back, he withdrew to let Marian kneel next to Isabella. Then he got back in and bent over to place a fleeting caress on her cheek.

"Philip," Isabella whispered.

He squeezed her hand.

"Rest yourself, my dear," he said. He stood and would have withdrawn from the carriage, but Isabella clutched his hand.

"Do not go out there," she said fearfully. "That brute will kill you."

"Major Lyonbridge will do nothing of the kind, Isabella," Marian assured her.

"Noooo!" Isabella refused to release Mr. Lyonbridge's hand.

"Isabella, be sensible," Marian said. "He must face him sooner or later. I will go out with him to make sure he comes to no harm."

"I do not need to hide behind your skirts, Miss Randall," Mr. Lyonbridge said in indignation.

"Men!" huffed Marian. "Lie still, Isabella. I will be back in a trice."

She got up in a half crouch from the floor of the coach and herded Mr. Lyonbridge out the door.

Major Lyonbridge approached them with a purposeful glare on his face. Before he could open his mouth, though, Marian forestalled him.

"Major, I would be obliged to you if you would drive Isabella and me to the next inn. She needs water and some respite from the heat of the sun. Mr. Lyonbridge," she added crisply, turning to his brother, "you will drive your curricle. Once there, one of you—I care not which—will arrange for a private parlor so that you may air whatever grievances you feel compelled to deliver to one another without providing the entire population of the Great North Road with entertainment."

"Are you mad?" Major Lyonbridge exclaimed. "The coward is likely to run off if we allow him to drive the curricle."

"Well, *I* am not about to drive it," Marian shouted back at him. She put her hands on her hips.

Mr. Lyonbridge glared at his brother.

"I am *not* a coward!" he said. "I should call you out for that."

"Do," the major said, showing all his teeth in a frighteningly avid smile. "Nothing would give me greater pleasure than to put a bullet through you right now."

"Oh, for pity's sake," Marian snapped. "Save it for the inn. Mr. Lyonbridge, get up on your curricle and drive on to the inn. Go on, now," she added when he balked. "The major will not prevent you."

She grabbed the major's arm when he made a threatening movement in his brother's direction.

"Enough!" she barked at him. "You may assist me into the carriage, if you please, major."

He glared at her for a moment. She glared right back at him.

"Very well, then," he said curtly, and opened the door to the carriage so he could hand her in.

Chapter 14

"Oh, good God. There she goes again," Adam said in disgust after Isabella alighted from the coach with her sister's assistance and, finding herself face to face with Adam, rolled her eyes up in her head and keeled over.

Marian staggered a few steps under her sister's unexpected weight.

"You did that on purpose," she said to the major.

"All I did was *look* at her."

"Ha! You *glared* at her. You deliberately frightened her. Do not stand there like a block," she said impatiently as she continued to struggle with the fainting woman. "Help me with her! I cannot hold her up by myself for much longer."

"Let her fall, then," he said, crossing his arms. He would be dashed if he was going to run to the little drama queen's side like some overwrought hero out of a bad novel and sweep her up into his arms.

Happily for the condition of Isabella's traveling costume, Philip rushed to them from up ahead, where he had been directing a postboy in the disposition of his curricle, and relieved Marian of Isabella's weight.

"There, my girl," Philip said to Isabella, who had revived sufficiently to open her eyes and whisper his name as he lifted her carefully into his arms. "We will have you in bed in a moment."

He carried her ahead of them into the inn. The innkeeper's

wife came out from behind the counter with her brow furrowed in concern at the sight of the prostrate woman being borne into her establishment.

"I need a bedchamber for this lady," Philip said.

"At once, sir," the woman said with a slight curtsy. "If you will follow me."

"I will arrange for a private parlor," Adam said to his brother with a compelling stare. "Join me there when you are done."

Philip nodded in agreement, but Isabella clutched at his coat with trembling fingers.

"No, you must not meet him," she said. Her eyes were frightened.

Adam gave a snort of disdain and turned his back on them as he went off to find the innkeeper.

"You do not know what he is capable of doing to you."

"I have a fair idea," Philip said wryly. "My nose still hurts like the very devil. I shall endeavor not to bleed on you, my dear."

"We can escape," she said. "There must be a back way to this place."

"No," he said. "To do so would be the act of a coward. You demean me, Isabella, to suggest such a thing."

Her face crumpled.

"He is going to challenge you to a duel and kill you. I just know it."

"Your faith in my prowess is touching," he said. "Did it not occur to you that *I* might be the victor in such a contest?"

Her look of sheer incredulity caused him to give a sour smile.

"Apparently not," he murmured as they passed into the bedchamber.

He lowered Isabella to the bed, and the bossy Miss Randall rushed forward to remove Isabella's hat and slip off her shoes.

"I will take care of her now, Mr. Lyonbridge," Miss Randall said in firm dismissal. Isabella's beautiful, troubled face was a reproach to him. "You are free to join the major."

"Or to run away like a coward," he said bitterly, and left them.

Philip's younger brother looked every inch the hero, standing at parade rest before the fireplace in his dress uniform, the one he had donned for his wedding to a young woman who should have been accepting the congratulations of all her friends at this moment, but instead would never be able to hold her head up in Society again because of Philip.

Adam never fidgeted. He never paced. But his stance suggested that of a panther ready to attack just the same.

His brother. His rival. His nemesis.

Blast his eyes.

Philip had expected to be hundreds of miles away in Scotland by the time his brother and father found out what he had done, and by then the old man would have to accept the runaway marriage as a fait accompli. He had not thought much on the matter beyond that, for he had been blinded by his desire for Isabella.

Isabella had begged him to save her from entering into a loveless marriage with a man she despised. Quite apart from Philip's lust for Isabella, he had been gratified to encounter *one* female who preferred him to his magnificent brother.

Heaven knew it seldom happened.

Philip might be the elder, but in the eyes of the world, Lord Revington's heir was merely a pale copy of the brave, the stalwart, the muscular and athletic Major Lyonbridge. At the age of two, Adam had outstripped Philip in both size and girth and thereafter, new acquaintances had routinely assumed that the bigger, stronger brother was the elder. In his heart of hearts, Philip had to admit that one of the attractions of going along with this elopement had been to embarrass his disgustingly superior brother.

Instead, though, here was Adam, looking like a hero about to chastise a recalcitrant recruit.

Philip was merely the contemptible cur who had disrupted the hero's wedding by ignominiously stealing his bride.

As usual, he had failed.

"And so it comes to this," Adam said contemptuously.

"Isabella is innocent. I alone am to blame," Philip said.

Adam's lip curled.

"Unless you bound her hand and foot and bore her off against her will, she is no innocent. But you hardly need fear that I will retaliate against *her*. The vain, selfish little chit is beneath contempt after this day's work. I would not soil my hands on her."

"You will not speak of her in this way," Philip said, finding courage despite the deadly coldness in his brother's eye.

"I will speak of her in any way I choose, and *you* are hardly in any position to prevent me."

"Leave her out of this. I am at your disposal. Under the circumstances, I trust we can dispense with the convention of seconds."

Adam cocked one sardonic eyebrow at him.

"Are you actually challenging me to a duel? Over *Isabella's* honor?" He gave a mirthless snort of laughter. "She has none."

Philip's fists knotted.

Adam crossed his arms and gave him a wolfish smile.

"I could crush you with one fist."

"You could *try,*" Philip said, but his heart wasn't in it. His brother was going to pound him to a bloody pulp. And when Isabella emerged from her bedchamber, she was going to know him for the paltry fellow he truly was. She had already watched Adam bloody Philip's nose for him.

"Lord, what a figure I should cut," Adam said. "I outweigh you by at least three stone. It would be no contest."

"Even so," Philip said, gritting his teeth in defiance at his bigger, stronger brother. He almost welcomed the pain, for it would put an end to this wretched suspense. And, if Philip were very, very fortunate, perhaps he could pop a hit over Adam's guard and darken his daylights for him before Adam broke him in two.

It would be *some* consolation for his bloody nose.

Adam merely gave a snort of disgust.

"Do not flatter yourself. Like Isabella, you are beneath my contempt. I would not soil my hands on you, either."

Philip positively hated the feeling of relief that surged through his body. He actually felt his knees go a little weak.

"You are wrong," Philip said, striving for a cool tone. He even managed to give his brother a smile of sheer bravado. "Oh, not about me. I am every bit as despicable as you think. You are wrong about Isabella."

"It is a bit too late to defend your lady fair," Adam scoffed. "You are a coward, Philip. You sought this means of disgracing me because you aren't brave enough to fight me man to man. You aren't brave enough to fight *anyone* man to man."

Philip knew exactly what his brother meant by that.

"Father refused to buy me a commission," Philip snarled, "and you bloody well know it."

"It makes for a convenient excuse . . . coward," Adam snarled right back. "You have that legacy from our mother's brother quite apart from your allowance as heir. You could have purchased your own commission at any time these three years after our uncle stuck his spoon in the wall."

It was true. Absolutely true. Philip *could* have purchased a commission at any time and his father could have done nothing to prevent it, but he had been reluctant to go to war in his brother's shadow and invite the inevitable comparisons between them that were sure to be in his disfavor.

Instead, he squandered his allowance on horses and drink, and supported the character of a sophisticated fashionable fribble about town while he grew green with jealousy every time he read one of the newspaper accounts of Adam's bravery in action and watched his father's face glow with pride when acquaintances congratulated him on Adam's latest promotion on the field of battle.

"I think your cowardice makes you a prime match for the fair Isabella," Adam continued. "She could have broken our betrothal at any time by informing me that she wished to do so. All the girl had to say was no. *I* could not do so, for I was bound by our father's honor. No, Isabella did not merely wish to escape from the marriage. She wanted to humiliate me. And my own brother was her willing accomplice."

He made it sound so cold. So sordid.

Philip wanted to protest, to tell Adam that he had been powerless to resist Isabella's blandishments when she had begged him to save her from this marriage, but he could not, for he knew there was no acceptable excuse for what he had done.

He should have encouraged Isabella to tell Adam the truth and cry off from the wedding if she did not wish to go through with it, even if it was the very night before the ceremony. It would have been a nine-day wonder, but she could have emerged with her reputation intact, more or less.

Isabella had pledged her undying love for Philip with an eloquence no man could have resisted. She had *begged* him to take her to Scotland and marry her. But what if she merely had been suffering from bridal nerves, and he had taken advantage of her momentary confusion to steal her away because he *wanted* to believe that his brother's lovely fiancée might in truth prefer him to Adam?

What a joke! How *could* she?

She was desperate and confused, but as her childhood friend and future brother-in-law, he should have encouraged her to withdraw from the betrothal with some degree of honor instead of taking her off with him before she could change her mind.

Or, more to the point, he could have encouraged her to marry the better man by extolling his brother's superior qualities. It was what any man of honor would have done.

Instead, he had taken the ignominious path of not only preventing her marriage to his brother, but also of putting an end to his own unwanted betrothal to the influential heiress.

The ugly truth was that he had used Isabella's infatuation with him to settle an old score against Adam and to escape his responsibility to his own fiancée, and when disillusionment set in—which it must—she would realize it.

Philip could not marry her now, much as he wanted to. She would grow to despise him if he did. All the world would despise him—Isabella, his father, all the influential members of Parliament and the ornaments of Society who had gathered at St. James's Church for Isabella's wedding to the glorious war hero only to find that the bride had been ignominiously stolen away.

By him. The coward.

He squared his shoulders.

"Take Isabella back to London with you," he said to Adam. "You and Miss Randall between you can make up some tale. Make me the villain of the piece. Say I took her against her will. Say . . . I care not what you say as long as you minimize the damage to her reputation and self-esteem."

"Oh, I see. You are running away from the consequences of your actions," Adam said.

"No. I am running *toward* them," Philip said. "It is inadequate I know, but tell Isabella I regret all this. Tell her . . . tell her I wish her well."

"See here! You are not going to put a period to your existence, are you? For if you are entertaining any such ridiculous notion—"

Incredibly, he sounded genuinely alarmed.

"Spare me your expressions of brotherly concern," Philip said wryly. "We both know I haven't the courage to put a bullet through my brain."

With that, he left the room to go in search of his carriage and his destiny.

"Where is he? What have you done with him?" Isabella cried hysterically when she burst into the parlor to find Adam its sole occupant. Her clothing was disheveled. Her hair was hanging in damp wisps below her crushed bonnet.

She looked like a madwoman.

Isabella ran to Adam and pounded his chest with her fists. He caught her elbows to hold her away from him.

"Control yourself, Isabella," he said coldly. "I have done *nothing* to him."

"You lie," she cried, baring her teeth at him. "You have murdered him. I *know* it."

"Hardly! He has run away," he said bitterly. "And, might I add, I am not surprised. It follows a familiar pattern."

"Here, now, Isabella," Marian said, entering the room at that moment and rushing forward to catch her sister's shoulders when she would have flown at Adam's eyes with her nails. She looked daggers at Adam, who merely raised a sardonic eyebrow at her. "Calm yourself."

"Run away," Isabella repeated dully. She sat down abruptly on a chair. "No. He could not have done such a thing to me."

"Oh, good lord," Adam said, rolling his eyes at Marian, who was now fussing over her half sister, "if she is going off in a swoon again, I will wait for you in the carriage."

"Do not be an idiot," Marian snapped as she chafed Isabella's wrists.

Isabella pushed Marian's hands away. She did not want to look at Marian. She did not want to look at *him*. They had ruined everything. And Philip—his desertion had been the worst betrayal of all.

"I am perfectly all right," she said, sticking out her chin.

She would not cry.

She *refused* to cry.

Her Philip, her savior, had abandoned her. She was beyond tears.

At that moment, Isabella's tender, hope-filled heart turned to stone and her limbs became steady.

She rose to her feet.

Marian made a motion to assist her, but Isabella waved her away.

She would have to face the disgrace alone. She might as well begin the way she meant to go on.

"I am ready to go home now," she said in a voice not her own.

Chapter 15

The return of the truant to her father's house was every bit as terrible as Adam had expected.

"There you are, you dreadful girl!" screeched Lady Grimsby as soon as he, Isabella, and Marian had entered the house. Adam's father clasped his arm. He looked . . . old and frail for the first time in Adam's memory.

"What did you do to him?" he asked fiercely. "Tell me! Is he dead or alive?"

"Your heir is intact, sir, as far as I know," Adam said. He should have known the well-being of his firstborn son would be Lord Revington's first concern. "Surely you did not think I would put a bullet through my own brother over *her*."

He gave Isabella a look of contempt that she missed entirely because her mother was shrieking at her, and Isabella was meeting her abuse with her chin thrust stubbornly forward.

Adam winced, as always, at the resemblance between them.

"Where is he, then?" Lord Revington asked.

"I neither know nor care, Father," Adam said as he briefly returned the pressure of his father's hand. "He went off when I refused to fight a duel with him and he left Isabella with us."

"Come along, Isabella," said Marian as she attempted to

wrest her half-sister from her mother's grip on her arm. "Isabella must rest now. She was unwell on the journey."

"True," Adam said without the least attempt at hiding his contempt for her. "She fainted dead away at the sight of me when I caught up with them. Quite the heroine, our Isabella."

"Just so," Marian said with a quelling look at him. "If you will excuse us."

She would have taken her sister from the room, but the general blocked their path.

"You will marry Adam as you are bid," he said to Isabella. "Quietly. No bridesmaids. No flowers. No wedding breakfast. I am extremely displeased with you!"

Adam could not believe his ears! Surely not even the general could expect him to marry Isabella now.

Before he could disabuse the general of this absurd notion, Isabella drew herself up to her full height and turned on Adam with a look of utter loathing.

"I will not!" Isabella said. "*Nothing* would induce me to marry the man who has ruined my future happiness."

"Yes, you will, my girl," her father shouted. "And you will stay confined in your room until you are willing to see reason."

"It is rather too late for sending her off to her room to punish her as if she were a naughty child!" Lady Grimsby said. "Perhaps if you had been more the disciplinarian with your daughter when she was eleven instead of rushing off at every opportunity to play at soldiers, she would not be so headstrong now."

"I know nothing of girls. It is a mother's responsibility to rear her daughter properly," the general snapped. "And an excellent job you have made of it, madam!"

Isabella gave a brittle laugh.

"A word with you, Isabella," Adam interjected before the hostilities could escalate into a full-blown melee. He glanced at the others. "In private, if you do not mind."

Lady Grimsby, the general and Marian all opened their mouths to object, but Lord Revington cut them off.

"I am sure you will agree my son is owed that much satisfaction, at least," he said with a forbidding scowl on his face.

The general looked his old friend in the eye and gave a curt nod.

"You may use the library, Adam," he said.

"Major Lyonbridge," Marian blurted out. "No good purpose will be served by—"

"I will not lay a hand on her, I promise you," he said to Marian, who appeared to be the only person present who actually seemed concerned for Isabella's well-being. She looked indomitable despite the crushed blue gown and the windblown ringlets with a few wilted flowers clinging stubbornly to her ruined coiffure. "I merely want to *talk* to her."

Marian looked searchingly into his eyes and must have been satisfied with what she saw there, because she gave a nod of reluctant acquiescence and stepped back just as General Grimsby said heartily, "Tell the girl what's what, lad. We can have the wedding tonight. I'll send for the parson."

The major favored his commanding officer with a stare he suspected would have earned him a severe reprimand for insubordination if they had been in their army encampment. Then he ushered Isabella into the library and firmly shut the door.

Even so, the sounds of a vicious row clearly permeated it. Lord Grimsby and Lord Revington were shouting at one another, but Lady Grimsby's strident shrieks clearly sailed over their voices. The murmur of Marian's voice was heard briefly, then silenced as she was shouted down.

Isabella closed her eyes for a moment and shuddered.

"Please believe," Isabella said calmly to Adam once she had seated herself on the sofa, "that nothing would induce me to marry you, no matter how much pressure you and my father bring to bear on me."

Adam stood by the fireplace and crossed his arms over his broad chest.

"You relieve my mind," he said dryly. "I merely wished to make plain to you that no matter how much coercion our respective fathers employ against us, I will not marry *you.* I am not unwilling to concede that you may have done me a favor in the end by refusing to go through with the ceremony, but you can have no idea how humiliating this was for me."

"I would suspect this was as humiliating for you as it will be for me to be singled out as the heartless jade who left the valiant Major Lyonbridge, war hero, at the altar to run off with his brother, and then was abandoned, in turn, by him," she said. "It was quite unnecessary for my father to threaten to imprison me in my room. I will have no wish to leave it for at least a year, I promise you."

"If only I, too, could closet myself in a room and not come out for a year," he said with a sigh. "*Why*, Isabella? Why did you not simply tell me you did not wish to marry me?"

"Because you would not have listened! My father is your god. He often enough says you are the son he never had. Do you think I am fool enough to believe you would have defied him and your own father in the matter of our betrothal merely because I *asked* you to?"

"In this case, you are mistaken. At the risk of wounding your vanity, I was hardly so infatuated by your beauty and sweet disposition that I could not have been persuaded to withdraw my suit."

"If you despise me so much, why did *you* not break off the betrothal?" she scoffed.

"You know better than that. The betrothal had been puffed off in the papers. A man of honor could not withdraw at that point. We have never been friends, but I had no reason to think we would not suit well enough."

"Suit well enough! What you mean is, you would have gone back to battle with my father to play the war hero, and I would have been left here, cooling my heels in my mother's house until the time you had need of me to set up a household and bear your children."

"What else do you want from marriage?" he asked, genuinely perplexed. "Did you think it was going to be all fancy dress balls and house parties?"

"I want to be married to a man I choose for myself!" she said with gritted teeth. "Listen to our parents out there! Those are the people who arranged for this match between us. Do you have any reason to believe they chose any better for us than they did for themselves? Is *that* the kind of marriage you wanted? Do you want a home like this one, in which every word spoken between husband and wife is a harsh one?"

Adam shrugged.

"All marriages seem to deteriorate into that sort of thing sooner or later. One does one's duty to one's name and makes an attempt to maintain civil relations with one's spouse. If both parties are willing to be reasonable, it need not be unpleasant."

"I would rather die," Isabella said with a shudder, "than enter into a marriage like that."

"Do you think it would have been any different with Philip?" he asked.

He really seemed to want to know. Strangely, Isabella thought that this, perhaps, was the first real conversation she and Adam ever had between them.

So she returned an honest answer.

"I love him," she said. "I have loved him since we were children. I do not expect *you* to understand."

"What I understand is that we had a long-standing betrothal that you could have broken at any time these three years by merely saying the word. But you chose not to do so."

Isabella gave a long sigh.

"I thought I could go through with it. Right up until last night, I expected to go through with it. And if Philip had not shown up so unexpectedly at the ball, I could have done the thing. But seeing him again—he was so handsome in full ball dress, and—"

Adam held up one hand in disgust.

"Please spare me your girlish rapture over the excellence of my exquisite brother's tailoring," he said dryly. "I haven't the stomach for it."

"Very well," she said. "Tell me instead what you said to him that would make him leave me without a fight."

"Not a pleasant feeling, is it, that of being abandoned by a person one expected to marry?" he said sardonically.

"The cases are entirely different," she said, but she could not meet his eyes. "Philip *loves* me. He never would have abandoned me unless you did something terrible to him."

"I told him the truth. That it was the act of a coward to abscond with my bride on the day of my wedding. Do not flatter yourself that his actions had anything to do with you. His object was to humiliate me. He admitted as much."

"You *lie!*" she cried.

"I do not, Isabella. The truth is, when he had achieved his object, he had no need to go through with the elopement. We have *both* been betrayed by him."

"Why did you have to interfere? If you had not come after us, I would be married to Philip by now."

"Perhaps I did it to save *him* from a fate worse than death," he said with a cold smile.

"Villain," she spat.

"Oh, sheathe your claws," Adam said, unimpressed by her show of spirit. "My brother is not known for his steadfastness. He would have tired of you within a twelvemonth, and turned his attention back to his horses and his gambling companions. Or one of the other silly women who fancy themselves in love with him. There are many such, I assure you."

"I hate you," she said softly.

"I know," he said with a sigh. "I hate you, too. That's it, then. Come along."

He held the door open for her and she sailed through the doorway with chin held high to fall alive into her mother's clutches. She knew she would wear the bruises on her arm from Lady Grimsby's cruel grip for weeks, but she hardly cared.

"Miss Grimsby and I have agreed we would not suit," the major said formally to his father and hers.

The general looked daggers at him.

"I can make her obey me," he said, rounding on Isabella. She flinched back. "You *will* marry him! Do you hear me, girl?"

"But you cannot make *me* obey you," Adam said. "Not in this matter, at least. Please believe, my lord, that *nothing* will induce me to marry your daughter. Not now."

"See what you've done, girl!" shouted the general.

"I think it would be best, under the circumstances, for the two of us to return to the Peninsula without delay," Adam said.

"I agree," the general said. He almost looked relieved.

"Yes, do run off to your horrid old war and leave *me* to deal with the scandal," Lady Grimsby jeered. "And with *her*," she added with a contemptuous look at Marian. "She probably put Isabella up to this, the sly creature."

"Marian had nothing to do with it," Isabella said. "Nothing at all. I will go to my room now."

"And you are to have no supper," snapped the general.

Isabella gave a high-pitched burst of laughter that had Marian bundling her out of the room with a look at the general that should have made him burst into flames.

* * *

Adam was waiting for Marian in the parlor when she emerged from Isabella's bedchamber.

"You wished to speak with me, Major Lyonbridge?" she asked when she joined him.

"I wished to take my leave of you," he said. "The general and I will leave for the Peninsula on tomorrow's tide. Thank you for your good office today, Miss Randall. I was so enraged that without your presence I might have done something I would have regretted for the rest of my life."

Marian cocked her head at him.

"I do not think, now, that your famous temper is so bad as all that," she said. "I am persuaded that, left to your own devices, you could have restrained yourself from murdering your brother."

"Perhaps, but I might have inflicted a bit more damage on him than a bloody nose."

"I must admit I was rather tempted to snatch Isabella's head bald for her at first," Marian said. "What she did to you was unforgivable. I think you have behaved beautifully under the circumstances."

"I have behaved beautifully," he repeated in disbelief. "I am sure Isabella does not share your opinion."

Marian gave a long sigh of exasperation.

"Isabella is a romantic who chose to see a knight errant in your irresponsible rogue of a brother. But she has a good heart. I am persuaded she did not set out deliberately to humiliate you."

"You are a remarkable woman," he said slowly.

She gave him a quizzical look.

"Remarkable? I?"

"You met Isabella less than a month ago, but you care for her. Another woman in your place would feel only spite and jealousy toward her natural father's legitimate daughter. In my recriminations against her, I have forgotten that Isabella is your half-sister, and that you are fond of her."

Marian's face softened.

"But she is a faithless jade, just the same," he added, which caused her to compress her lips in disapproval. He laughed at her expression and caught himself up short. Indeed, he had not expected to laugh in genuine amusement at all this day.

Adam sobered and took Marian's hand. She looked down at their clasped hands in surprise.

"Miss Randall . . . Marian." She raised one eyebrow at his use of her Christian name. "Someday the war will be over and I will return. Unless you are married in the meantime, will you be at home if I call on you?"

Her eyes widened as she took in the significance of his words.

One of the things Adam admired most about Marian Randall was her lack of coyness when a person was asking her a question that hinted at a deeper meaning. That she comprehended this meaning, and his interest in her, was obvious.

"I will be at home," she whispered, and he kissed her hand.

"Be safe," she added as he turned to leave the house.

Chapter 16

November, 1812
Portugal

It had been three months since Isabella had left Major Lyonbridge cooling his heels at the altar while she absconded with his rogue of an elder brother. The scandal had died down as much as it was going to, but still she remained secluded in her father's country house.

Marian, meanwhile, had been sent to friends of Lady Grimsby's in Tunbridge Wells to proceed with the all-important task of getting a husband so that the general's wife need never set eyes on the wretched girl again, which is how she described the situation both in and out of Marian's hearing.

The ladies parted with polite, if insincere, expressions of goodwill and mutual relief when her accommodating hosts came to take her away. Marian wondered what inducement Lady Grimsby had provided for them to perform this service, but she never did find out. Marian knew only that she was to masquerade as a distant relative of the couple.

Her hosts were quite elderly, and the circle they frequented was well outside the highest in that unfashionable but respectable watering hole. The prospective husbands Marian met were all elderly widowers with country properties situated well away from London, or city professionals in remote cities, the better to ensure that the fact of Marian's continued existence would no longer be an embarrassment to her father, the general, once she married.

The summer visitors had long since departed from the resort, but her hosts assured Marian that she would continue to be their guest until she somehow snabbled a husband—although she was at a loss how to do so when all that remained in Tunbridge Wells was a nice collection of invalids, mostly deaf, and she had shouted herself nearly hoarse attempting to carry on civil conversations with them.

Marian was bored to tears. The previous year on campaign, she had daydreamed about how wonderful it would be to have no work to do, only to find that when this state of affairs actually came about, she was heartily wishing herself on campaign again.

"There is a letter for you, my dear," her hostess said gaily when her man returned one morning with the post.

A letter! Marian almost knocked the poor lady down in her zeal to see who had written to her. The receipt of a letter entailed the delightful occupations of actually sitting down to read the letter, of sharing its contents with her hosts and explaining how she knew the writer, of mentally composing a reply, then sitting down at her hostess's writing desk to actually write it.

Marian's brow furrowed in concern as she read her letter. Her hostess waited impatiently for her to share its contents.

Marian,

I am Desperate. You must find some way to come to me at Papa's estate in the country. I have nowhere else to turn.

Isabella

Marian carefully folded the letter and, when she could avoid doing so no longer, smiled into her hostess's expectant face.

"Who is the letter from, my dear?" asked that good woman, who thought the receipt of a letter for her guest almost as exciting as the receipt of a letter for herself. "Not bad news, I trust."

"No," Marian said. "At least, I hope not. It is from Miss Grimsby, who, as you know, is staying in the country." Her hostess's expression became neutral, which told Marian she knew perfectly well why the general's daughter was rusticating alone in the country while her mother visited her relations in Dorset. "She has taken ill, and has asked me to visit her there."

"Oh?" her hostess said in surprise.

"Yes, well, we became quite good friends when I was staying with her family after my father's death. I must make preparations for the journey immediately."

"I am so sorry that you must leave," the woman said, and it was apparent she meant it.

Marian smiled at her.

"Thank you for your hospitality. I had a wonderful time. Now I must go pack my things."

"I hope you will return as soon as you may," her kindly hostess said with a twinkle in her eye. "Your beau will be so disappointed that you have left."

Her beau. How ridiculous!

The most persistent of her admirers had actually written to ask Lady Grimsby, the general's deputy and therefore Marian's substitute guardian, for permission to marry her, and Lady Grimsby had returned a positive reply. Marian had been searching about in her head for the most humane way of telling the frisky septuagenarian that they would not suit.

Marian knew her hostess was looking forward to the wedding. In fact, she had advised haste, for none of them, she pointed out, was getting any younger.

Well, Marian was determined that both her hostess and the septuagenarian were going to be disappointed. Perhaps in her absence her admirer would find another lady to lavish his attentions upon.

She would meet with him briefly before she left and tell him as gently as possible that her heart belonged to another.

It was probably the most effective way of discouraging him.

A vision of Major Lyonbridge in full dress uniform appeared before her mind's eye, and she gave a long sigh of self-recrimination.

Alas, it was also the truth.

When a very weary Marian arrived at General Lord Grimsby's country house, Isabella ran down the steps, threw herself into her half sister's arms and burst into tears.

Marian held her away from her for a moment and looked into her bloated, tear-stained face.

These were not fresh tears.

Isabella's gown strained at the seams, for she had gained weight. Her formerly lustrous dark hair was dank and obviously would have benefited from a good wash some time this past fortnight. The house was dark even at midday, for all the heavy draperies were drawn.

"You should be in bed," Marian said, frowning. "You look dreadful."

Isabella burst into fresh tears.

"Come along, then," Marian said, not even bothering to remove her own hat and gloves. She took Isabella's elbow and guided her upstairs. "Which room is yours?"

Isabella indicated a room to their left and sank upon the wrinkled linens of the unmade bed.

"Where is your maid?" Marian demanded.

Isabella bit her lip.

"I sent her away. I sent all of them away," Isabella said as she buried her face in her shaking hands. "Oh, for the lord's sake, do not tell Mother. *Please* do not tell Mother or Father."

"Tell them what," Marian cried. "What is it? Are you truly ill, then? Are you dying?"

"I *wish* I were dying," Isabella whispered. "I am pregnant."

General Lord Grimsby sent his aide for Major Lyonbridge and looked straight ahead, focusing on nothing as he rehearsed the words he must say in his mind.

The damning letter from his former friend, Lord Revington, lay on the desk.

Would this terrible business never end?

At that moment, Major Lyonbridge strode into the office and stood at attention before his commanding officer's desk.

Lord Grimsby loved Adam like a son. Indeed, he had once hoped to call him son in truth, if only by marriage. He did not want to tell him what he must, but better he should learn it from him than from a stranger.

"Your brother is dead," he said, paying Adam the tribute of giving him the branch with no bark on it. "Your father requires your presence in London at once."

Adam's face was like flint. He had known his brother was missing in action. He had been informed immediately. But he had hoped he would be recovered alive.

"There is no possibility of mistake?"

"We had made inquiries in the event that he was being held prisoner and ransom could be arranged. But a cache of bodies has been found. Apparently they were taken prisoner and executed. Several were identified as being those gone missing with Captain Lyonbridge. The other bodies were unrecognizable, but enough of them were found to compel the war department to count your brother as among the official dead. I am sorry, lad."

Adam nodded in acknowledgment because the lump in his throat was so big he could not speak.

The last time Adam had seen Philip was when he paid a call upon Adam at his regiment's encampment. Philip had been resplendent in the uniform of his new cavalry regiment, for, to Adam's astonishment, he had bought himself a commission as a captain.

Apparently Adam had pricked his pride, and the stupid gudgeon had chosen this means of proving he was not a coward, after all.

Adam had surprised himself very much by being filled with concern for his heretofore pampered brother, but he had squashed this emotion down immediately and adopted a scornful tone. Adam now regretted that instead of shaking his brother's hand and wishing him well, he had laughed in his face and told him he would not last three days on campaign.

He heard news of Philip from time to time, and he was surprised and secretly proud to learn that his superiors and his men thought well of him.

Any thoughts of reconciling with his brother ended at the Siege of Burgos in October, during which Philip and several other members of his regiment had gone missing. And now, it seemed, their bodies had been found.

"You are ordered to return to London to take up your responsibilities as your father's heir," the general continued. "I have Lord Revington's letter here. You are to resign your commission and leave at once. Therefore, I hereby relieve you of your command. That is all."

"You relieve me of my command," Adam repeated dully. "Just like that."

"You know I do not want to do it," Lord Grimsby said fiercely. "You are my best officer, and you will be sorely missed. But your duty is clear. It is Lord Revington's right to demand your return."

"I will return to London," Adam said. "It is, as you say,

my duty. But nothing will induce me to resign my commission and stay there. My brother was an absentee heir, and my father's holdings have survived perfectly well in spite of that. I cannot imagine that my presence would do him or them any good. I know nothing of planting fields or reaping crops."

"Your father had political ambitions for your brother."

Adam's heart sank.

"Of course. He thinks he is going to mold me into a bloody politician. I should have known." He gave a harsh laugh. "I can see it now. I am to garner sympathy as the brother of the fallen war hero, for I have no doubt Father is even now exaggerating my brother's role in the action that resulted in his death."

"Waste of a bloody good soldier to make a bloody politician of you, if you ask me," the general said with a scowl.

"I heartily agree with you, my lord," Adam said with a sigh. "Do I have your permission to leave?"

In spite of everything, he almost laughed at the look of relief on the general's face. Lord Grimsby might not want to lose one of his most competent cavalry officers, but he very much wanted an end to this uncomfortable interview.

"Permission granted," the general said brusquely. He extended his hand and the gentlemen shook heartily. "I look forward to your return if you can make your father see reason, and I wish you health and good fortune in civilian life, if you cannot."

"I *will* return," Adam said grimly as he saluted smartly and strode out of the room.

Chapter 17

"I cannot tell them," Isabella cried. "I cannot!"

"They will find out sooner or later, love," Marian said. "Meanwhile, you cannot go on like this. You will injure your baby if you stay here in these dark rooms with no one to talk to, and eat practically nothing."

"I thought if I did not eat much, my stomach would not grow so very large."

"Isabella! Your baby needs nourishment. *You* need nourishment!"

"I am ruined. Completely ruined. When I refused to marry Adam, and Philip abandoned me, I *thought* I was ruined. But that was nothing compared to *this*."

"You are not the first woman to have a child out of wedlock," Marian told her. "I promise you, the world will not end."

"You should know," Isabella said waspishly. "Oh, forgive me," she cried, instantly contrite. "How could I say such a thing to you?"

Marian grew very still, and not only because of the reference to her mother's indiscretion with the general. Isabella had given her an idea that might be a solution to both their dilemmas.

She did not want to marry any of the gentlemen the general's wife and her well-meaning accomplices in Tunbridge Wells were throwing at her. If they believed she had conceived an illegitimate child, their efforts at matchmaking would cease immediately.

"What is it?" Isabella asked, narrowing her eyes.

"We will tell your mother that *I* am the one who has conceived. It was something that happened while I was still on campaign. The father of my child, of course, is dead."

Isabella's mouth dropped open.

"Your parents will be eager to keep me out of the way of Society," Marian continued, "and where better than here? From what you've told me, neither of your parents have a taste for the country and rarely come here. I will stay with you and take care of you. We will receive no company. No one need know which of us is pregnant. When I go out, I will be heavily padded."

Isabella's eyes shone.

"You would do this for me, Marian?" she asked hopefully.

"I would do it for both of us," Marian said. "I am running out of excuses for not marrying any of the suitors your mother and her friends have found for me."

"Oh, it will not work! We will have to have a midwife to deliver the baby, and she will tell. They *always* tell. This is too good a secret to expect anyone bred in the country to keep."

"*I* will be your midwife," Marian said, patting Isabella on the shoulder. "I delivered several babies on campaign when no one else was available to do so. Believe me, I intend to take excellent care of you and my little niece or nephew."

"You are truly my sister," Isabella said, practically falling on Marian's neck with gratitude.

Marian hugged Isabella back and hoped she was equal to the trust being placed in her.

"Now comes the hard part," she said grimly. "You must write to your mother."

* * *

Lady Grimsby was filled with sour satisfaction when she read Isabella's letter about the little hussy who called herself Marian Randall and the predicament in which she found herself.

Hadn't she known the minute she set her eyes on the girl that she was no better than she should be?

Well, she made her bed. Now she could lie in it.

So Isabella had agreed to keep her company at the country manor until she gave birth, had she?

Over Lady Grimsby's dead body!

She was not going to house the little strumpet in her country house with her own daughter. Not even her husband could expect her to condone such a thing.

It was time Isabella rejoined Society. Three months was long enough for her to be exiled from everyone who mattered. The gossips had moved on to new scandals.

Her impressionable daughter merely had been led astray by a practiced seducer, but no harm, after all, had been done. She had been returned to her father's house before she spent the night in his company. It was unfortunate that the man she had jilted was practically a national treasure, but he had gone back to war and was not around to remind the gossips of Isabella's folly.

Lady Grimsby ordered her maid to pack at once.

She would go to the country to fetch her daughter.

And she would throw her husband's round-heeled love child into the gutter where she could starve for all she cared.

But first, she decided with absolute glee, she would write a letter to her husband to tell him that his precious natural daughter was going to have an illegitimate child, and Lady Grimsby considered her obligation to put a roof over the little wanton's head discharged.

* * *

"Father," said Adam when he was shown into Lord Revington's study. The look of grief in his father's eyes almost unmanned him.

He had turned into an old, old man virtually overnight. His hair was more gray. Adam was sure of it.

Lord Revington stood, and instead of taking the hand Adam held out to him, he enveloped his much taller son in a hug, which Adam could not remember him doing since the day he turned twelve.

"You are all I have left," Lord Revington said sadly. "I am glad I wrote to the war department in time to have you restored to me before they killed you, too."

He gave a long sigh.

"He died a hero," Lord Revington said. "We can be proud of him."

As far as Adam knew, his brother was merely one of several men captured by the enemy, probably because they had been stupid enough to relax their vigilance.

"Indeed," he offered.

His father gave him a sharp look.

"You never liked each other."

"*He* never liked *me*," Adam corrected him.

"You thought he was a coward. You taxed him with it after he ran off with that wretched girl of Grimsby's. He came to take leave of me after he had purchased his commission. He told me he had something to prove to you. I hope you are satisfied."

Adam held on to his temper with an effort.

"No. I am grieved that my brother is dead. I wish we could have been friends instead of rivals, for the rivalry was of his making, not mine. I regret that I did not make my peace with him before he died. But he chose to fight for his country. I honor him for his decision, but I take no blame for it. Indeed, I never knew my brother to do anything he did not want to do. Do you think that a word from me would have stopped him?"

Lord Revington gave a long sigh.

"He was stubborn as bedamned," he said gruffly.

"He was that," Adam agreed wholeheartedly.

After a short silence, Lord Revington waved Adam to a chair.

"I see you are still in uniform, sir," he observed. "I believe I made it clear in my letter to Grimsby that you were to resign your commission at once."

"Yes, you did. But I am not ready to leave the Army. In fact, I have informed Lord Grimsby that after I help you put my brother's affairs in order, I will return to the Peninsula. Bonaparte is far from beaten, Father."

"You are my heir. My sole heir. I will not risk you, too."

"You have been risking me, as you put it, for years. I am no more likely to die now than I was then. Less likely, in fact. I am rather better at soldiering now than I was as a mere lieutenant."

"I am proud of your war record, boy. The proper people, no doubt, have taken notice. Now is the time to capitalize on it to launch a new career."

"Politics," Adam said in distaste. "I am not cut out for it."

"You will be by the time I am finished with you. I saw the great men of Parliament hanging on your every word at that ill-conceived betrothal party. A bit of good luck, that business with Grimsby's girl," he said.

"A bit of good luck," Adam repeated incredulously. "What do you mean?"

"If Philip hadn't lost his head and run off with the flighty little baggage, you would be shackled to her now." He shook his head. "One would think a general's daughter would have more in her brain-box, but I assure you she would have done you no credit in a political career."

"On that, at least, we may agree," said Adam, relieved that apparently his father was not going to suggest that

Adam honor the betrothal that Lord Revington and Lord Grimsby between them had arranged for their children.

"Excellent! I have taken the trouble to make some inquiries, and I have drafted a list of the most suitable young ladies for you to consider."

"For me to consider . . ." Adam repeated.

"Do not be dense, boy. As a wife, of course."

"Surely there is no urgency in that," Adam said, taken aback.

"No urgency! You are my sole heir. I have no brothers whose sons might inherit my title and my lands if something should happen to you. I have no other sons. Who but you will give me grandchildren to carry on our name?"

Adam leaned across the desk to put his hand over his father's.

"I promise you I shall do so in time," he said. "But first it is my duty to return to the Peninsula and do whatever I can to stop Bonaparte from sacking the rest of Europe and invading England. If he isn't stopped, you will not have anything to leave to future generations, I assure you."

"I am an old man," Lord Revington said sadly as he bowed his head. "I do not know how much longer I have in this world. I would like to see you settled before I die."

"What utter rot!" exclaimed Adam. "You are a mere fifty years old, and a more vigorous fifty I have never met. You have many years ahead of you in which to be plagued by me and your future grandchildren, whom I cannot but think will be every bit the handful that Philip and I were to you."

There were tears in Lord Revington's eyes when he looked up at Adam.

"You were a joy to me. Both of you," he said in a husky voice. "A positive joy."

"A joy!" Adam said with affectionate scorn. "Now there's a clanker if I ever heard one."

"Be that as it may, I need you now."

"I know, Father," he said contritely. "And here I remain

for the present." He stood. "Now I must take leave of you. I have several calls to make."

They stared at each other for an awkward moment. Adam wondered if his father was going to hug him again. The thought filled him with an odd mixture of pleasure and consternation.

Instead, though, Lord Revington stood up from his desk and shook hands with his son.

"You will stay with me at the town house, I trust, instead of seeking lodgings," he said.

"As you wish," Adam said, although he rarely did so, for he found the air of formality in the house and its huge, cavernous, perfectly decorated rooms filled with fragile treasures intimidating in a way that a charging line of Boney's best cavalry would never be.

"Tonight there is a musicale that I want you to attend with me. Lots of eligible young women will be there. I should warn you that Miss Grimsby is back in London after her rustication, but you will have to meet her in company eventually, so you might as well get the thing over with."

"And Miss Randall?"

Lord Revington gave him a straight look.

"And what, may I ask, is your interest in Miss Randall?"

Adam strove for an indifferent tone.

"She is the daughter of the regiment's late surgeon, and I escorted her to England," Adam said. "It behooves me to take some interest in her welfare. Lord Grimsby will want a report on the matter."

"You will be taking no interest in that girl's welfare from now on, and Lord Grimsby—not that I give a hang about his wishes—will have washed his hands of her himself by now," he said grimly. "The ungrateful little hoyden is breeding, and Lady Grimsby has cast her out, as any decent woman would do. I thought Miss Randall had too bold a look about her."

"Where is she now?" Adam asked, disconcerted.

"I neither know nor care, sir, and neither should you."

"We shall see about that," Adam muttered.

"See here!" Lord Revington called after Adam as he stalked from the room. "I forbid you to have anything to do with that girl!"

Chapter 18

As it turned out, Adam went to the musicale after all, even though he had resolved to find some excuse not to attend. When he had called at General Lord Grimsby's town house earlier in the day, Adam, a former intimate of the family, found the massive oak door firmly closed to him.

Lady Grimsby and Miss Grimsby were not at home, the butler said. It may or may not have been true. Therefore, if he wanted to find out what had happened to Marian Randall, he had to approach them during a social occasion that would make it impossible for them to avoid him without causing a scene.

"Good evening, Miss Grimsby," Adam said as he gave the pretty fellow sitting next to Isabella a commanding look that had him scurrying away so he could sit next to her.

"Major Lyonbridge," she said as she put one lily-white hand to her throat.

"None of your airs and graces, if you please," he said softly, conscious that every eye in the place was trained upon the interesting spectacle of Miss Grimsby being accosted by the gentleman whom she had left cooling his heels at the altar several months before. Adam knew her mother had insisted to all her acquaintance that Isabella had become suddenly ill on her wedding day and thus could not help doing so, and the *ton,* at least to Lady

Grimsby's face, seemed to accept this fiction. "I am not here to berate you."

"I have nothing to say to you," she said with a toss of her dark curls.

"No doubt. And I have nothing to say to you. That precious little drama, thank God, has been played out between us. I do want to know where Miss Randall is, however."

Was that remorse in the girl's eyes?

Probably a trick of the light.

The Isabella he knew of old would be eager to disassociate herself from a disgraced connection now that she apparently had weathered her own scandal and was accepted into Society. Never mind that the young woman had become her friend.

"I tried to stop Mother from casting her from the house," she said with a sigh, "but she was adamant." Her lower lip started to quiver.

"None of that," he said brusquely. "Everyone will think I am abusing you, and we shall have the hostess calling her footmen to throw me out."

"What a lovely idea. You always knew how to cheer me up," she said sarcastically.

"That's my girl," he said, matching her tone. "Where is she?"

"I do not know where she is living, but she said she would seek employment as a nurse at Chelsea Hospital, caring for the wounded soldiers."

"Of course," Adam said slowly. "It is where she wished me to take her instead of to your father's house. She had some notion about carrying on Captain Randall's work."

"I intended to go to the hospital to see her, but Mother would not permit it," she said. "She watches me like a hawk these days."

Her eyes shifted over to where her mother was sitting, making no pretense of listening to the concert as she watched Adam and Isabella with a brittle smile on her face.

"She does not have any illusions that we are still going to make a match of it, does she?" he asked.

Isabella rolled her eyes.

"Of course, she does. Especially now that . . . he . . ." She appeared to be overcome, and Adam felt the ever-present lump in his throat grow harder. He knew perfectly well she was talking about Philip and did not quite dare to mention his name in Adam's presence. "She believes it would be the neatest solution all around. Have no fear, Major Lyonbridge. I have done all I can to disabuse her of this idea."

Incredibly, she reached over to touch his hand.

"Please believe you have my sincere condolences on his death," she said. "I suppose there could be no mistake? The first news listed him as missing rather than killed."

"The bodies were found," Adam said, looking straight ahead. "There is no mistake."

"No. I suppose not."

The musical selection ended at that moment, and the guests were invited to file into the refreshment room for fortification after the long program of music.

Adam offered Isabella his arm.

"You are only building up her hopes," she warned him with an anxious look toward her mother.

"I am certain you will find a way to tear them down again," he said dryly.

Marian felt ill when she awoke in her small, musty smelling room at the lodging house near the hospital, but she attributed that to the cold and the fact that since becoming Lord Grimsby's ward she had become unaccustomed to sleeping on hard, lumpy beds. She had not slept well, but that was no excuse for not reporting for duty.

Fortunately, her lodgings were cheap and located close to the hospital. It was just dawn when she arrived.

"You are late, Miss Randall," the head nurse said sternly. "Do not let it happen again, or you will be dismissed."

"I am sorry," she murmured as she hurried to the ward where she was assigned to work with the poor, broken bits of men that the army had sent home to recover or to die.

Which it was to be in many cases depended upon her, she told herself sternly when she could have gladly curled up on the floor in a ball and gone to sleep. It was a measure of how unwell she felt that she would even *consider* lying down on such a dirty surface. It was part of her responsibility to keep this ward clean, so she must scrub the floor as soon as she checked on her patients.

One man, to her regret, had died during the night, and she covered his face with a sheet until his body could be taken away. She had hopes yesterday that he might recover.

Others were somewhat improved, she was glad to see, but the presence of a corpse in the ward definitely dampened everyone's spirits. It was a relief when the men came to take it away. Marian made a mental note to write to the poor dead soldier's relations, for none of them lived in London.

"New one for you, Miss Randall," a breathless hospital worker called out while she was changing a bandage on a man's arm.

"I will be with you in a moment," she called out pleasantly.

"Bit restive, miss," the worker said warningly as he and another man wrestled the struggling new patient into the room and tried to get him to lie on the bed.

"You won't take me alive!" the man cried out as he fought his captors. "If I die, I'll take a dozen of you with me!"

He was big and brawny and had a head wound with a bandage on it that was encrusted with dried blood. Marian turned to approach him.

"Careful, miss," one of the men said. "He nearly broke my arm for me."

"Hold him down," she said. "That bandage needs changing. I need to see if the wound is infected."

"No! No!" the man cried, looking at Marian with fear in his eyes.

"He's off his head," one of the men explained. "We will have to strap him down."

Marian tried to help them by holding down the man's shoulders, but he suddenly broke free and had his hands around her throat. He pushed her down to the floor and punched one of the men who sought to restrain him in the face. He was about to strike the other one when a vision appeared in the doorway.

Marian blinked. It couldn't be . . .

"Major Lyonbridge?" she whispered in disbelief. There was not a mark on him that she could see. What was he doing here? Whatever reason he had for coming, she was heartily glad to see him.

"Stop him!" she called out as the patient ran for the doorway.

"Halt!" the major barked. He had sized up the situation immediately.

"Major Lyonbridge," the man said with awe in his voice. Apparently the sight of the tall, erect, uniformed major was enough to jolt the poor man into momentary sanity. Then his face crumpled. "I tried to escape," he said. "I tried, sir."

"Well done," the major said heartily as he buffeted the man's shoulder. "These good people are only trying to help you. Do come along, then."

He started to go quite tamely with the major toward the bed that Marian indicated, but then the insanity overcame him again.

"It's a trick!" he screamed. "It's a trick to break me! You aren't real."

With that, he tried to go out the door again.

The major grabbed him and dragged him to the bed. The men attempted to strap him down.

"Do not hurt him," Marian croaked. Her throat hurt.

Marian moved in too close, and the patient managed to get one hand free and push her down to the floor again. The major half turned in her direction, but a cry from one of the hospital workers recalled his attention to the task at hand.

Marian could only be grateful. Suddenly it was too much of an effort for her to get up again. Instead, she gave a sigh of relief and let the weariness overtake her.

"Marian. Marian!"

The major's voice dispelled the slight stupor she had fallen into. She was so weary she could have slept despite the cold, hard floor if every bone in her body wasn't aching. Her eyes were running, and her nose was so plugged up she could hardly breathe. Her ears seemed to be full of cotton wool, for she could hear his voice only dimly.

"Just leave me here," she said as he grasped her by the shoulders and pulled her upright. He bent, and she realized he was about to lift her into his arms.

"Do not be ridiculous," she snapped, and gave him a half-hearted shove. He straightened and peered into her eyes.

"You are ill," he said.

"What nonsense. I am never ill," she said. She moved toward the patient, who had subsided and was sobbing softly. "I must see to this man's head wound."

She stooped over the patient and carefully unwrapped the bandage to find the wound infected. It took all of her strength to clean and rebandage it. When she finished, she wearily held her hand to the small of her back and was annoyed to see the room spin slightly.

The major, who had been standing at alert in case the

poor man should somehow escape his bonds, peered into her eyes.

"That is enough for you, I think," he said as he ushered her out of the room.

"I have work," she protested.

"Not until after you see a doctor."

"*I* see a doctor? Whatever are you talking about?"

"You are ill."

"I am not—" She stopped in confusion. She felt so wretched. Of course she was ill.

It did not take long for the major to find a doctor who was thrilled to meet the war hero in person.

If Marian had not been so miserable, she would have enjoyed the look of polite impatience on the major's face as he endured the man's gushing compliments.

"I would appreciate it if you would examine this young lady," the major said when he could get a word in. "She appears to be ill."

"Certainly, Major Lyonbridge," the doctor said. "If you please, Miss Randall."

She seated herself in a chair, and the doctor made only the most cursory examination before he arrived at a diagnosis.

"You have the influenza," he told her. "You must go home at once. It will get worse before it gets better."

"But, doctor!" she said. "I cannot go home. I must work."

He shook his head slowly.

"Now, Miss Randall. Your father was a medical man. You know I cannot have you working in the wards, spreading the contagion to the patients. There already have been several cases of influenza here. No doubt that is how you contracted it."

Marian closed her eyes and leaned back against the chair. Suddenly, it was too much trouble to protest any longer.

It was too much trouble, even, to open her eyes.

"That's it, then," the major said gruffly as he pulled her to her feet. She sagged slightly, and he put a supporting arm around her. "I shall see her home."

Once outside the hospital, he called a hackney carriage.

"I always walk. It is not far," she protested, even though she knew the major was too much the gentleman to make her pay the fare.

"Not today. Does the doctor know about your condition?"

"My condition?" Then she remembered. *Oh. That.* "No. Else I do not believe I would have been hired. Major Lyonbridge, I do appreciate your concern, but I *must* work, else I cannot pay for my room and I will have nowhere to live. As it is, my landlady might very well turn me out if she thinks I am about to spread the contagion to her house."

"You will not be staying there. We are only going to your room to fetch your clothing."

"But I—" Her head was spinning. "I have nowhere else to live."

"Yes, you do," he said. "If Lady Grimsby will not take you back into her house and take care of you, I am going to take you to live at my house in Derbyshire until your child is born."

Chapter 19

The poor girl stared at Adam as if he had taken leave of his senses, as well she might!

The solution to her dilemma had come to him so suddenly the words were out of his mouth before he was aware of their existence in his brain.

"I have a small house left to me by a maternal uncle," he said slowly. "It is in the country, not far from my father's primary residence. I have a housekeeper and a caretaker living in the place, a married couple, although I will not deceive you. I go there occasionally to make sure the walls are still standing, but I have not been there in some time. It may not be what you are accustomed to."

She gave a snort of pained mirth that ended in a cough. "Until a few months ago, I was accustomed to a tent in the middle of a lake of mud. I cannot accept this charity from you," she said. She gave him a straight look. "It *is* charity you are offering, is it not?"

He gave a bark of laughter.

"Only charity, my poor girl," he said sympathetically.

"Why? I am not your responsibility."

"No, but you are alone and ill. You should be *someone's* responsibility."

"I cannot accept your generous offer," she said, leaning back against the cushions of the carriage. "But I thank you for making it." She closed her eyes.

"Miss Randall? Marian?" He heard the panic in his own

voice. Influenza could be fatal. What if she just went to sleep and never woke up?

To his relief, her eyes opened. She even managed the ghost of a smile.

"Present, Major Lyonbridge. I am not about to expire, like that poor soldier I found dead in his bed this morning."

"You should not be subjected to such sights as those in your condition," he said, appalled that the poor woman had endured such hardship.

"My condition?" She looked at him blankly for a moment. Then an expression of comprehension came into her eyes. "Oh, yes. My condition," she said. "I had forgotten about that for a moment."

Adam gave her an incredulous look.

She had *forgotten* she was pregnant? Was her mind disordered by her illness?

Another solution to her dilemma occurred to him. He found it repugnant, but it had to be voiced.

"Who is the man?" Adam demanded. By God, the fellow had much to answer for! "If you wish, I shall seek him out and force him to marry you."

"You are too late. He is dead."

A soldier then, while she was still in Spain. He had suspected as much.

"I am sorry," he said, although it was hardly true. The fellow *deserved* to be dead. "But he must have family. Someone who will take responsibility for you and the child."

"There is no one," she said. Her voice was the merest thread. "You need not worry about me. I am a grown woman. I can take care of myself. Here. This is the place. I thank you for your escort, but I need no further assistance from you."

"I will see you inside."

"Quite unnecessary, I assure you," she said, giving the lie to this by staggering a bit when he handed her out of the carriage. He got a firm grip on her arm. "All right," she admitted ruefully. "It is necessary. I must ask you not to tell the landlady that I am ailing. I cannot afford to be thrown out of my room."

As it happened, it wouldn't have mattered whether or not the landlady knew Marian was ill.

"Here are your things," the grim-faced woman said with a disparaging poke of her shoe at a battered black portmanteau. "Take them and get out."

"But . . . why?" Marian asked in dismay.

"I run a respectable house! I won't have a pregnant girl with no husband staying here!"

"But, how did—" Marian began.

"Do not come over all innocent with *me*, missy! One of the boarders is related to a servant in Lord Grimsby's house, so I know Lady Grimsby threw you out for your lewd behavior. You have been sick the past two mornings. The other boarders heard you and complained to me, so I know it is true." The landlady looked Adam up and down. "I suppose this is your fancy man. How *dare* you bring him here!"

"Never mind him! I paid you for a month in advance!"

"You entered my home under false pretenses!"

"That will do, madam," Adam said stiffly. "I believe Miss Randall is due the return of a portion of whatever rent she has paid you. And the sooner you discharge this obligation, the sooner Miss Randall will be gone."

She pursed her lips in disapproval, but she absented herself for a moment. When she returned, she slapped a bank note into Adam's hand.

"Here! Now, begone!"

"With pleasure, madam," Adam said. When Marian would have remonstrated further, he snatched up the portmanteau, took her elbow and ushered her outside. He had to stop and let her lean against him for a moment so she could get her breath.

"Now what am I going to do?" she asked plaintively.

"If the general's wife won't take you back, you are going to accept my offer of the use of my house, of course," he said. "At the very least, I am going to make Lady Grimsby give you the rest of your clothes. This cannot be all of them."

"This is what I brought from Spain," she said in a slightly stronger voice. They moved forward and he helped her into the carriage. "I would not take any of the clothes that dreadful woman provided for me."

"Admirable, but foolish," he said, although he shared her opinion of the general's wife.

It was a measure of the degree of her illness that Marian merely sagged back against the cushions and closed her eyes instead of arguing with him. At one point, her throat worked convulsively, and he hastily ordered the carriage to stop. After a moment, however, she waved him on, and he signaled for the coachman to proceed.

"I shall be just a moment," he told her with a squeeze of her hand after he alighted from the carriage at the general's house. She did not give any indication that she heard him.

He hesitated. The day was bitterly cold, and her slightly threadbare coat gave her little protection from it. She was shivering so hard, her teeth were chattering. He hated to leave her alone in the cold, damp, musty carriage for even a moment. Coming to a sudden decision, he reached through the open door and scooped her up in his arms.

Marian merely rested her head on his shoulder and tried to stifle a groan.

When the butler opened the door, Adam barged right past him.

"How dare you bring that little hussy into my house, Major Lyonbridge?" Lady Grimsby demanded regally from the top of the stairway. She apparently was on the point of going out, for she wore a hat and gloves. "Remove her from here at once!"

Her face was a grimace of hostility. Adam decided he could not leave poor Marian to the mercy of this harpy, even if Lady Grimsby would agree to have her back.

"I have come for her clothes, madam," he said, not at all intimidated. "I am taking her away to someone who will take better care of her than you have done."

"Oh, Adam! You have found her!" cried Isabella from just behind her mother. She ran down the stairs to them. "What is wrong with her?" she asked Adam in an accusing voice.

"She is ill. With the influenza."

Lady Grimsby gave a loud screech.

"Get her out of here! Get her out!" She signaled for two footmen, who had been summoned by her shrieks, to cast Adam and his burden from the house.

Isabella turned and stared up at her mother in defiance.

"If she goes, I go with her!"

Adam was so surprised, he nearly dropped Marian.

"Now, see here—" he began.

Lady Grimsby compressed her lips in displeasure.

"If you do, I will never speak to you again. And I will see that your father does not, either."

"Father never does anything you say," Isabella shot back. "Come," Isabella added to Adam, "bring her up to my room. She can rest on my bed while I have my maid pack my things and hers."

"You go too fast," Adam said, taken aback. "I intended to take her to my house in Derbyshire, but—"

"Shameless!" cried Lady Grimsby. "Positively shameless!"

Adam gave her a look of exasperation.

"I am not going to stay with her!" he snapped.

"In that case, I definitely am going with you. You will need someone to take care of her," Isabella said.

"*You?*" he scoffed. "You need the assistance of a maid to put on your shoes."

"You need me, Adam," Isabella persisted. "Her reputation will be damaged even further if you take her into the country without another woman along to play propriety, regardless of whether you stay there with her or not. I am going with you. It is settled," Isabella said calmly. "Stop dawdling, now, and bring her upstairs."

With that, she set a spanking pace up the steps, and Adam followed in her wake with Marian in his arms. Isabella confronted Lady Grimsby at the top of the stairs. She stared her mother down when she tried to bar her way. Then the elder lady gave a snarl of indignation and retreated from the stairs to huff off down the hall, presumably for her own room.

For the first time in his life, Adam caught himself actually admiring Isabella Grimsby.

Naturally this state of affairs was not destined to continue.

By the time he had lowered Marian to the embroidered counterpane in Isabella's virginal white room and cooled his heels while Isabella ordered her maid to pack enough luggage for Marian and herself to sustain an army on campaign and informed him that *of course* she must take her maid along, he was ready to strangle her. It was some time before the carriage was set in motion again, and by then the afternoon was well advanced.

To Adam's irritation, Marian roused herself from her sickened state to plump a pillow behind Isabella's back in the carriage and ask her if she had eaten.

"I did not agree to bring you along so Miss Randall could take care of *you,*" he said witheringly when Isabella did admit she could use a little something in the way of sustenance.

"Do not shout at her," Marian said weakly.

"Why? *She* is not the one who is increasing," he said baldly.

The sisters looked at one another.

"It makes my head hurt," Marian said.

"I am sorry," he said at once. "I did not think."

"You rarely do," Isabella snapped.

"We will stop at my father's house to borrow my father's traveling coach for the journey into the country," he said, ignoring this ill-natured remark. "It will be more comfortable than a hired carriage, for then Miss Randall can lie at full length on the seat, and I will ride on horseback alongside to give the two of you more room."

When they stopped at Lord Revington's mansion and Adam made as if to get out of the carriage, Marian caught his hand.

"I thank you for your kindness, Major Lyonbridge," she said.

"It is nothing," he said as he lifted her into his arms to carry her inside. Isabella scrambled down with the help of a footman who had come from the house to meet the carriage. He lowered his voice. "You do not have to have Isabella with you in the country if you would rather not."

"I want her," she said with a tremulous smile.

"See here! What is the meaning of this?" blustered the scandalized Lord Revington when he observed his heir carrying a limp young woman over his threshold with that shameless little jilt, Isabella Grimsby, on his heels and a girl he assumed was her maid following them.

"Strictly temporary, I assure you, Father," he said as he breezed on by the old man and met the housekeeper at the top of the steps. "Where may this lady rest for a time?" he asked her.

"The blue room is readied, Mr. Adam," the well-trained servant told him. By her serene expression, one would have thought the master's son brought semiconscious young women into the house every day of the week and expected her to supply vacant beds for them.

"That will do," he said gratefully as he followed the housekeeper to the blue room with his entourage of females. "We will set off for the country within the hour, and my guests will require a meal. Bread and cheese will do. And soup, if you have it."

"Very good, sir," the housekeeper said, rising to the occasion.

"I did not know what to do," Marian told Isabella after the maid had put a cloth dampened in rosewater to her throbbing temples. "It is wrong to accept Major Lyonbridge's kind offer under false pretenses."

"But this is perfect! I will stay with you, and when I have my baby, no one need know it is not yours. Meanwhile, we will look about us for a kind married couple to take care of it." She closed her eyes for a moment. "Then I can return to London and forget this happened."

Marian's eyes slid to the maid.

"Betty knows everything," Isabella said. "I could not hope to hide my condition from the maid who dresses me every morning."

The maid gave a little dip of her head in acknowledgment.

"It is essentially our original plan," Isabella continued, "only instead of staying at my father's country house, we will be at Adam's house. I never thought to be *grateful* to the dreadful man."

"Major Lyonbridge has been all that is kind and considerate," Marian pointed out. "Without his assistance, I would have found myself in dire straits, indeed."

"True," Isabella said thoughtfully. "I wonder what he means to gain by it? Perhaps he has conceived an infatuation for you."

"Hardly!" Marian scoffed. "If so, he is thoroughly cured of it by now. The man has definitely seen me at my worst today." She sneezed—again—and the maid handed her a clean handkerchief. Marian's own and Adam's had been soiled beyond use some time hence. She emerged from this operation with her nose reddened and her feverish eyes red and running with tears.

"And he is likely to see you at it a while longer, poor dear," Isabella said sympathetically. "Imagine Adam being so thoughtful. He probably intends to set you up as his mistress, but never fear! *I* shall put a stop to that at once if he has the effrontery to suggest any such thing!"

Marian gave a brittle laugh.

"Unnecessary. If he announces his full purpose, I have only to *sneeze* on him to exact my revenge." She sobered at once. "Oh, my poor Isabella. What if I give *you* the influenza? It could be very dangerous in your condition."

"If that happens, I shall have the best of nurses to look after me," she said with a coy little smile.

Chapter 20

"If she is sick one more time," Adam said through clenched teeth as he watched Isabella scamper in haste to the shelter of the trees, "I am going to leave her at the side of the road."

"Isabella is not a good traveler," Marian said from the open door of the coach. She started to get down and Adam ran to assist her. "Thank you. I do believe I feel a bit better."

"*You* are the one who is sick, yet you and that maid keep cosseting *her*. I brought my father's traveling coach so *you* could lie down on the journey, not Isabella. And should you be outside the carriage? The air is cold."

"Stop fussing, please, Major Lyonbridge. Isabella and Betty are taking splendid care of me, I promise you," she said, looking up at him through swollen eyes. As for her nose, it was painful merely to look at it. From the look of her flushed skin, the fever was upon her again, for all of her optimistic words. "I only want a breath of fresh air. You have caused so many hot bricks and blankets to be placed in the carriage with us that I am in no danger of becoming chilled."

"We will be another day on the road," he said. "I had hoped to travel a while longer today before seeking an inn, but perhaps we had better stop for the night."

"I would be grateful," she said with obvious relief.

With that, Isabella came back onto the road with her maid in anxious attendance.

"If you are ready, Miss Grimsby," Adam said disapprovingly.

"Quite, Major Lyonbridge," Isabella said haughtily as she accepted his assistance into the carriage.

Adam looked about him in dismay when he showed the two young ladies into his house. His caretakers were so advanced in age that their deafened ears did not hear him at first when he knocked upon the door. When they did appear, they were thrown into a pucker at the prospect of housing their master and two young ladies. All the furnishings were under Holland covers, and a fine layer of dust covered every surface.

There were no housemaids, after all. Just the husband and wife caretakers whose responsibility it was to keep an eye on the place. His father had arranged for his own workers to plant Adam's land and reap the harvest for him.

Adam realized he should have arranged for his caretakers' retirement years hence and replaced them with a younger, more able couple. But he had been on campaign, and the matter had slipped his mind.

It was rather too late to worry about that now.

"I will leave orders to hire a few girls from the village," he said apologetically to Marian. "I am so sorry. When I invited you to stay here, I gave no thought to such things."

"Do not worry your head about us," Marian said. "We shall manage."

She still looked ill, but she shook her head when he would have carried her up the stairs. Instead, she leaned on the arm of Isabella's maid.

"What do you mean, we shall manage?" Isabella said indignantly. Her dainty hands were knotted into fists and rested on her hips. "This house is a *disgrace,* even for a bachelor establishment. The first thing that needs to be done is a thorough beating of the carpets. And every inch of the place must be dusted."

She picked up a Holland cover and wrinkled her nose at the ancient upholstery of the sofa beneath.

"Good heavens, Adam!"

The female caretaker's lip was quivering. The poor thing blamed herself for the imperious young lady's displeasure.

"Never mind," Adam said, patting the old servant on the shoulder. "It is not your fault, but mine. It is late. You may retire."

The woman curtsied and left. Her husband came into the house burdened with baggage from the coach.

"Here, I will see to that," said Adam hastily. The old man was huffing and puffing. It would not do for the poor fellow to drop in his tracks from the exertion of transporting a spoiled young lady's wardrobe upstairs. "You may go to bed."

"Major Lyonbridge, I hope you know my wife and I have done our best."

His eyes, too, were filled with tears of chagrin at the shame of failing to do his duty by his master.

"You have done splendidly," Adam assured him. "We will discuss what is to be done for the comfort of the ladies in the morning."

"Why have you let them go?" Isabella said in disgust. "There is so much to be done."

"You are a strong, able-bodied girl who has never done a moment's real work in her whole pampered life," he said. "You can take care of yourself with the support of your maid for one night."

"Where are you going?" she cried out when he reached for the door. "There are all our things to bring upstairs."

"I am going to take care of the horses. I suggest you find whatever you and Miss Randall need for the present and carry it upstairs. The rest of this will wait until I come in from the stable."

"You are impossible!" Isabella said, stamping her foot. "Did you really expect me to live in this *hovel*?"

He quirked one eyebrow at her.

"No. But I did not invite you, did I? You insisted upon coming to take care of Miss Randall." He gestured toward the stairs. "I suggest you have at it."

"There were mice gnawing in the walls all night," Isabella told Marian with an eloquent shudder the next morning. "I barely slept a wink."

"I heard nothing," Marian said in a thread of a voice as she struggled to sit up in bed.

"You poor dear," Isabella said as she plumped Marian's pillow behind her shoulders. "It is no wonder, for you were exhausted. I was myself, as a matter of fact. Adam is a bully, insisting upon setting that punishing pace on the road. We are not his poor recruits, and so I told him, but he would not stop. I pity the men under his command."

"He needs to go back to London," Marian told her. "For the reading of his brother's will." She looked anxiously at Isabella. "I am so sorry, my dear. All of this must be dreadful for you."

"Do not worry about me," Isabella said. The thought of Philip was a dagger in her heart, but she did not have the leisure to mourn him now. She had a sick half sister to take care of—she who had never before been responsible for caring for anyone, including herself—and a baby on the way. And she had a house about to fall down around their ears that she must somehow make habitable. She would *not* bring her child into the world to the accompaniment of rodents gnawing in the walls. "You just concentrate on getting well."

"I do worry about you," Marian said. "Of all the times for me to fall ill. I am *never* ill. I shall never forgive myself if you become infected with the influenza."

"Well, I won't. I *refuse* to get it," Isabella said determinedly. She sniffed at the tray the maid brought into the room. "What is that?"

"Porridge, Miss Isabella," the maid said. "For your breakfast."

"It smells wonderful," Marian said quickly before Isabella could insist that the girl take this homely slop back to the kitchen and feed it to the pigs. She smiled at the maid when she handed her one of the bowls of porridge. "By some miracle, my appetite seems to have returned."

"It is so gray," Isabella said as she looked doubtfully at her own porridge.

"It is supposed to be that color," Marian said with a smile. "Have you never seen porridge before?"

"Not since I was in the nursery," Isabella said with a sigh. "Usually I have chocolate and sweet biscuits served to me in bed when I first wake up. Then, after I am dressed, I have breakfast with Mother. Thin toast, tea, eggs, ham—"

"A rasher of bacon and half a beefsteak?" Marian suggested with a grin.

"Oh, do not mention it!" Isabella said with a roll of her eyes. "I am *so* hungry."

"Try it," Marian said, indicating the porridge. "I see there is a pitcher of cream, probably fresh from the cow, and a bowl of dried apples. A perfectly wholesome breakfast for one in your condition, I promise you."

Isabella took a taste of the porridge.

"Not bad," she said as she poured some cream on top and fell to.

"I had better eat quickly," Marian teased her, "or you will have mine as well."

"It is not *that* good," Isabella said with a sigh. "I will have a word with the housekeeper about the food. Surely there is some proper chocolate to be found in this misbegotten corner of the world."

"As you wish," Marian said with a weary sigh. "I am as

weak as a kitten merely from the exertion of eating my breakfast. Who would have thought I could fall into such a sorry state?"

"You are ill. You will recover. And I hope you will do so as quickly as possible," Isabella said. "This house needs a lot of work."

Marian regarded her sister with dismay.

"I know *nothing* about housekeeping," Marian said. "First I was at school, and then I went on campaign with Father. Until I left the Peninsula I lived in tents or billets. I have never been responsible for a home, although I have assisted in taking care of the wounded men and keeping the hospital wards tidy. And of course I prepared my father's food and kept our quarters swept out."

"Never mind," Isabella said. "I know *everything*. All you have to do is follow my instructions and all will be well." She glanced at the walls. "This faded lavender wallpaper with the dirty white flowers is most dispiriting," she said. "Who could have chosen such an appallingly ugly pattern?"

"I believe Major Lyonbridge said the house belonged to his maternal uncle, who was a bachelor."

"A bachelor," Isabella said knowingly. "No doubt that explains it. It was probably left over from a previous century, and he could not be bothered to change it. Men are completely dead to all matters of taste."

"I am sorry to hear you say so," said Adam from the doorway, but for a change he was smiling. "How is our patient?" he asked.

"Very well," Marian said. Her cheeks flushed a becoming shade of delicate pink. Or perhaps it was a lingering touch of the fever. "I just finished eating a huge breakfast, and Isabella is about to put me to work setting mouse traps and scrubbing the floors."

He shot Isabella a look of displeasure.

"Oh, do not get all puffed up and blustery," Isabella said. "She was merely jesting."

"I have made arrangements for my housekeeper to hire two housemaids and a man of all work," he said.

"Thank you, Major Lyonbridge," Marian said, "but we should not like to put you to so much expense—"

"I should like to know why not!" Isabella snapped. "It is *his* house, after all, and he has neglected it shamefully. I am afraid we will need more help than that. This wallpaper will not do, and every floorboard in the place creaks. And *I* shall interview the prospective maids, if you please. Your housekeeper is likely to hire her relatives, and you'll have them in here eating their heads off and wasting their days in gossip and idleness."

"*You?*" Adam scoffed. "What do *you* know about hiring servants?"

"I have lived with servants all my life," she said haughtily. "And my mother taught me to keep household. There are no idle servants in my mother's house, I promise you."

Adam gave a rude snort of laughter.

"That I can well believe," he said. "Much as I hate to admit it, you are right in saying the house needs some attention. I had not noticed how shabby it had become. Indeed, my uncle did not live here above two or three months out of the year, and he never entertained while he was in the neighborhood, so it is no wonder that the house is in bad case."

"And some new linens," Isabella said. "The sheets on my bed are so worn that I put my heel through one of them when I turned in my sleep last night."

"Certainly. I will make a note for my housekeeper," he said with a resigned air.

"Never mind," Isabella said, looking purposeful. "I will talk to her. I trust the village boasts a shop or two. I will choose the linens myself. I trust you are willing to give us a sum of money for such expenses."

"Of course," he said. "But when you are choosing these

furnishings, do not forget that I am a simple soldier and not a royal prince of the blood."

"There is no danger of *that*," she said witheringly.

He gave another of those unlovely snorts.

"I must leave you this morning. Marian, I trust you will let my housekeeper know if you require anything." He gave a disparaging look at Isabella. "I am sure *you* will."

With that, he turned on his heel and left the room.

It was only there for a second, but Isabella did not miss Marian's look of longing toward his broad back.

"Never mind," she said stoutly. "We will do much better without him."

Isabella gave a speculative look around the room.

"Really, this will not be as bad as I feared if he means to let me have the place furnished as I wish," she said. "I expected to be bored witless in the country, but I always have enjoyed shopping for furnishings."

Marian gave her a look of awe.

"Isabella, you never cease to amaze me."

Isabella gave her an absent smile.

"I chose some wonderful things for the home I would have had if I had gone through with my marriage to Adam, but I suppose it would be in bad taste to have them brought here," she said.

"Yes, I think it might," Marian said with a choked laugh that turned into a prolonged fit of coughing.

"Here, sweet. Have some tea," Isabella said as she put an arm around her sister and tipped the cup of tea to her lips. "Such a pity I was compelled to return all the wedding gifts. There was a handsome mantel clock among them, and several beautiful crystal vases.

"A gracious home," she added, quoting her mother, "is made up of just such elegant little touches."

"We are only going to stay here until the baby is born," Marian reminded her.

"Yes, and then we will find a nice home for the poor

thing, and no one will ever know that the baby is mine and not yours," Isabella said with a pang.

She held her hand to her slightly rounded stomach, conscious of the tender life nestling beneath her heart. She resolutely pushed her regret to the back of her mind. Boarding the child with a worthy couple was the kindest thing she could do for it, for no one knew better than the daughter of a confirmed womanizer how a bastard child was treated in this life. Look at poor Marian, with her mother forced to marry some virtually penniless army surgeon to give her child a name and compelled to follow the drum from one rat-infested foreign hellhole to another.

If the truth of the child's paternity ever reached Philip's tyrant of a father, he might take it away from her and treat it with contempt.

No. She would not subject her child to such a fate. Better that she should find a nice, cheerful young couple with whom to leave her baby.

She found that Marian was looking at her with concern in her eyes when *she* was the one who was sick.

Isabella forced a smile to her lips.

"But meanwhile," she said brightly, "Adam has presented us with this lovely sow's ear that we must somehow turn into a silk purse, for I am not going to live in this squalor a moment longer than necessary!"

"The more servants we have about the place, the greater the danger of detection," Marian said.

"True. Servants gossip. But we will contrive," Isabella said. "We must."

If they failed, Isabella would be disgraced and there would be no way she could return to her familiar, comfortable life.

Someday it would no longer be necessary for her to hide her face—and her figure—from the world. It would even be possible for her to marry once the scandal of jilting Adam had been forgotten.

A husband.

She had flirted discreetly with several handsome and eligible young men during the past few Seasons, attentive gentlemen who had made it clear that if she were not betrothed they would gladly pay their addresses to her.

Yet when she tried to see their faces in her mind's eye, she could see only Philip's.

She loved him still. Beyond the grave.

At the same time, she *hated* him for abandoning her and dying before her.

But he was gone. She had Marian to think about now, and the health of his child.

"Are you certain this stuff is good for one in my condition?" she said, looking at the empty bowl that had held her porridge.

"Yes."

Isabella gave a long sigh.

"I suppose I shall become accustomed to it, then," she said.

Chapter 21

"You must be mad," Adam said incredulously when his father and Lady Grimsby had outlined their outrageous proposal. "Absolutely mad. I would not marry Isabella Grimsby if she came to me with Napoleon's bloody head on a plate and three regiments of crack hussars as her dowry."

"Language, Adam," Lord Revington told him when Lady Grimsby's mouth thinned to a slash of displeasure.

"Your pardon, Lady Grimsby," Adam said, "but surely you do not expect me to marry Isabella now. She jilted me at the church and ran off with my brother."

"I certainly understand that you might be vexed with her—" Lady Grimsby began.

"Vexed with her!" Adam repeated. "The woman made a laughingstock of me before all of London. With my own brother. And now he is dead."

"Well, there is no use crying over spilt milk," Lady Grimsby said. "I have told everyone who matters that Isabella was suddenly taken ill, and that is why you and Miss Randall were seen leaving the church together in Lord Revington's carriage. So your reputation and Isabella's remain quite intact."

She permitted herself the small, superior smile of one enlightening an idiot.

"Fortunately, you and the general were recalled to the Peninsula immediately afterward, so it was perfectly reasonable that the wedding had to be delayed further."

"Impossible," Adam said. "You cannot ask this of me."

"Adam," his father said sternly. "You are a decorated war hero. You and Isabella spent much of the summer creating goodwill for Lord Wellington's cause by giving the country a pretty romantic story. To give the lie to it now would embarrass not only Isabella's family and yours, but also Lord Wellington and Liverpool's Government."

"What utter nonsense," Adam scoffed. "Besides, I cannot stand the girl."

"I must confess that after her folly, she is not the wife I would choose for you," Lord Revington admitted. "Very well, you and she can break it off sometime in the future, when it will do less harm. In the meantime, Isabella is occupied in preparing your property in Derbyshire for your return, with her friend, Miss Randall, for company. All you need do is pretend you mean to go through with the marriage eventually. The Prince Regent himself commended her in my presence to a number of important men for her dedication to you and England. He called her the very flower of young English womanhood."

Adam's mouth dropped open.

"But it is nothing but an outrageous lie," he said. "You know very well that I offered Miss Randall the use of my home because Lady Grimsby threw her into the streets, where she became ill of the influenza, and Isabella insisted upon accompanying her for reasons of her own."

"Of course it is a lie," Lord Revington said, pacing before the fireplace, "but a good one. Thus you may save face, Isabella Grimsby's reputation will be restored, and, not the least of it, Philip's memory will not be besmirched by his irresponsible action in running off with your bride. Fortunately, you brought her and that other girl back in the closed carriage so no one need know she wasn't in her father's house the whole time."

"It would be better if you marry," Lady Grimsby said. "I am certain Isabella is sorry for her actions."

Adam crossed his arms and glared at them both.

"I think not," he said.

"Well, you have plenty of time to reconsider," she said with another of those superior smiles. "No one expects you to marry Isabella right now, at any rate, for your family is still in mourning for your brother's death. You can marry her at your leisure in several months. There really is no hurry. We will bring her to town at intervals, and you can be seen escorting her to one affair or another during the period of your mourning. No balls, of course. The important thing is, appearances must be preserved."

"I will *not* reconsider," Adam scoffed. "I would sooner take a viper to my bosom than that faithless little—"

Lord Revington raised one hand to cut him off.

"That will do," he said. "This distasteful business has been trying to all of us. For the next few months, you and I will retire to my primary estate so I can groom you for your inheritance. You have much to learn."

"All the while I am to pretend to be courting Isabella. Perfect," Adam said glumly. "I have a better idea."

"Now, Adam—"

"*You* retire to your primary estate and I will return to the Peninsula where I belong."

"You are my heir now! You belong in England," Lord Revington exclaimed. "You *will* do your duty, boy."

"And what about Isabella?" Lady Grimsby cried.

"My duty is with my regiment, sir," Adam told his father. Then he turned to Isabella's mother. "As for your daughter, madam, she may go to the devil, for all I care."

"You forget your company, sir," Lord Revington intervened hastily.

"I think not," Adam said, glaring at him.

"Have you no consideration for a woman's tender heart?" Lady Grimsby cried with an unconvincing sob.

Adam gave a snort of grim amusement.

"Madam, you take my breath away. A woman's tender

heart? After the way you have treated Miss Randall?" he asked.

Lady Grimsby's expression hardened.

"That incorrigible little hussy! Getting herself pregnant by some soldier and coming to England under false pretenses to embarrass my husband and me by displaying her shame to all the world. I know you feel responsible for her because she is the regimental surgeon's daughter, but it is foolish to place too much trust in persons of her class."

Adam gave a sharp look at his father, but his face displayed nothing. Obviously neither the general nor Lady Grimsby had seen fit to apprise Lord Revington of Marian's true pedigree. But then, Captain Randall's daughter was certainly a more suitable companion for their precious Isabella than Lord Grimsby's bastard.

"Miss Randall's love child can be disposed of in good time," Lord Revington said. "No one need ever know about it."

"And so everyone's history is to be revised to suit your convenience, even poor Miss Randall's," Adam said angrily. "Well, no one is going to dispose of that woman's child. How can you *consider* such a thing!"

"You take me too literally, boy," Lord Revington objected. "I meant that it would be given to a good home, of course. I am not a monster."

With that, Adam gave a strangled exclamation and strode from the room.

Lady Grimsby compressed her lips and started after him, but Lord Revington caught her arm.

"Leave him be," he told her. "He is my son. He will do the right thing."

She gave an angry laugh.

"Yes, as your *other* son did the right thing. If he had not made up to my daughter, she would not have committed this folly."

Lord Revington glared right back at her.

"Do not blame my son! If your daughter had not been perfectly willing to run away with him, he would be alive now. He said he wanted to be *worthy* of her, do you believe it? *Worthy* of the faithless little minx. Otherwise he would have stayed in London where he belonged instead of buying himself a commission and haring off to war without my leave!"

"*Your* son—" she began.

"He is dead. Let him rest in peace," Lord Revington said harshly. "I have one son remaining to me, and he will do his duty, by God!"

Marian was helping the housekeeper inventory the contents of the larder when a little flurry of excitement went up among the two new housemaids, who came running into the kitchen to tell them the news.

The master had arrived!

Marian put a self-conscious hand to her hair, which had come all undone from its chignon, and she knew that perspiration had stained her gown. Under her clothing was a soft roll of padding artfully arranged by Isabella to support the pretense of her delicate condition.

As usual, Adam looked wonderful, she thought resentfully as he strode into the kitchen in an immaculate uniform that made the most of his broad shoulders, narrow waist, and long, muscled legs.

His sun-streaked brown hair was mussed from the wind, just a little. Otherwise, he would have been *too* perfect.

She felt like an ungainly cow.

"Marian, this is no work for a woman in your condition," he said bluntly.

"By that you mean I look like I was dragged through a bush backward," she said ruefully.

"I mean nothing of the kind," he said.

"Never mind. I know very well how I must look. But I feel quite restored to health, I promise you."

"Where is Isabella? She is supposed to be taking care of you."

"I am recovered from the influenza," Marian said, "but now Isabella is feeling unwell. If you will go into the parlor, I will have one of the maids bring you some refreshment. I must go upstairs to check on Isabella."

Adam caught her hand.

"Hang Isabella. I came to take my leave of you, Marian, and I must not stay long or I will miss my transport to the Peninsula," he said. "It will be a long time before I see you again."

The significance of the uniform dawned on her.

"But you were to sell your commission," she said. "I have heard that your father insisted upon it."

"My father insisted upon a great many things, but I cannot let him have his way in this. My place is with the army. I could not go before I assured myself that you had recovered from the influenza, and you would be cared for in my absence."

"Do not worry about me," she said. She could feel the tears start in her eyes. "I wish I could go with you. Life seemed so much simpler on campaign."

"My poor Marian," he said tenderly as he reached out and caught one of her tears on the tip of his finger.

"So silly of me," she said, trying to smile. "You must think me a fool to say such a thing when you have been so generous in letting me stay in your house."

"Not at all," he said. "Ladies are entitled to a few crotchets when they are increasing, and much has happened to you in the past few months."

Isabella at that point appeared in the doorway, and her hand automatically went to her belly in a protective gesture when she saw Adam.

"What are *you* doing here?" she demanded. Marian

could see Isabella try to suck in her stomach muscles. Isabella had a prodigious appetite these days, and she had suggested that her maid casually give it out to the housekeeper that the plentiful country fare was having so deleterious effect on her mistress's figure that she was having to let out the seams of all of her gowns.

"I am going back to the Peninsula and thought I should come to see how your sister fared. Instead of finding her at rest to recruit her health, I find her working to the point of exhaustion in the kitchen with the servants while you luxuriate in bed."

Marian flinched. As a point in fact, Isabella had stayed up very late the previous evening sewing new parlor curtains by candlelight. Isabella had been working tirelessly on the house, and Marian was at wit's end with worry about her.

"Isabella has not been feeling well," Marian said. "I sent her to bed." She gave Isabella a meaningful look. "Where she should be at this very moment."

Isabella took the hint and whirled away.

"Are you certain you are quite recovered?" Adam said to Marian. His blue eyes were full of concern.

"Perfectly," Marian said stoutly.

"I have hired a midwife from the village to deliver the child," he said in a lowered voice. "She will call upon you tomorrow."

The midwife would be dismissed out of hand, of course, but Marian was touched by Adam's kindness in hiring one, just the same.

"Do not worry about me," she said again. "Adam, when you go back, you must be very careful."

He smiled.

"I have been soldiering for a good long time, my dear, and I have not yet come to grief."

"I too often have heard you described as a reckless, hellbound babe in battle to be much comforted by that," she said.

He laughed.

"You are beginning to believe all of that thrilling propaganda the War Office distributes to the newspapers about me," he said. "You should know better than that."

"You are right," she said with an answering smile. "I should."

He gave her a diffident look.

"Speaking of propaganda, you may hear talk. Rumors. That I am going to marry Isabella, after all."

"Are you?" she asked. "If so, no one has told *her* about it."

"It is a scheme of her mother's and my father's to save face. They have concocted this tale that Isabella is here, readying my house for our marriage, and I will marry her at the end of the mourning period for my brother."

"How enterprising of them," she said. "Have they an explanation for why the wedding did not take place as originally planned, then?"

"Isabella became suddenly ill, and you and I left the church to go to her side," he said bitterly.

"I see. How very neat," she said.

"I am not going to marry her, Marian," he said. "No matter how much pressure is brought to bear on me. Make sure she understands that. I will tolerate her presence in my house because her company may give you comfort during your confinement, but other than that, I want nothing to do with her."

"She was much imposed upon by your brother," Marian said, defending her sister. "It takes *two* to run away to Scotland, and he is dead now. You might spare some of your compassion for her."

"I never knew Isabella to do anything she did not want to do," Adam said. "She made her bed. She can lie in it."

He took her hands in his.

"Marian, we are never going to agree on the matter of Isabella's behavior. Let us not spend these last few moments we have together in arguing over her."

She looked up into his beautiful, compassionate eyes.

"You will be careful," she whispered as she grasped his hands.

"Always," he said as he raised one of her hands to his lips and kissed her fingers. "Take care, my dear. I will hope for a happy result to your confinement."

He grinned.

"And if it is a boy, I would very much appreciate it if you would *not* name it after me."

Marian laughed in spite of herself.

"That *would* set the cats among the pigeons, would it not?" she said. "Isabella truly wronged you."

"By jilting me?"

"By saying that you have no sense of humor."

Chapter 22

May, 1813
Derbyshire

"You have a rare talent for this," Marian said admiringly to her sister as Isabella's maid mopped her exhausted but triumphant mistress's brow with a cloth soaked in rosewater, and Marian carefully washed the small but lusty scrap of humanity that was Isabella's son. "Two hours of easy labor and out pops a healthy baby boy with no more fuss than the cook takes in removing a roasted chicken from the oven. A child could have delivered this baby."

Isabella gave an unladylike snort.

"Not precisely a rare talent I can boast about in the drawing rooms is it?" she gasped with a grimace of pain. "And if you think this was easy, you know nothing of the matter. Let me see him again."

Smiling, Marian took the now well-wrapped infant to his mother, and Isabella eagerly reached for him.

"Oh," she said with a little cry when Marian placed the child on her stomach and Isabella gasped with a sharp pain.

"You will be tender for some time," Marian said. "Is he not beautiful?"

"Beautiful," Isabella agreed dreamily. She turned to the maid. "Betty, go to my room, if you please, and bring my Milk of Roses."

The birth, of course, had taken place in Marian's room,

since she was believed by the housekeeper and other servants to be the mother. Fortuitously, Isabella's birth pains began at night, when all the day servants were gone home, and the housekeeper and her husband, because of their deafness, slept right through Isabella's ordeal.

"Ah, you are recovering more rapidly than I expected if you are already thinking of your appearance," Marian said.

Isabella gave her a look of surprise.

"The Milk of Roses is not for me, silly," she said with a peal of laughter that made her stomach ache again, but truly she did not mind.

She looked adoringly at her baby.

"It is for him. My precious baby has such reddened skin," she said. "I cannot have my son looking like a rough little farmer."

"All babies have reddened skin," Marian said.

"*My* baby will not! His name is Jamie."

Marian's mouth dropped open in surprise.

"It just came to me all of a sudden," Isabella said defensively. "I cannot help it. He is just . . . Jamie. James Edward . . . well, Randall, I suppose. Oh, look at his pretty blue eyes! Have you ever seen such a beautiful color?"

"The color of his eyes probably will change," Marian said matter-of-factly. "I believe babies are like kittens in that regard. Or maybe it is their hair that changes color. I forget. I delivered them on campaign, but I didn't often see them after that."

She paused and regarded her sister with concern.

"I suppose there is no harm in giving him a name, after all," she added neutrally.

Isabella had said she would not name her baby. That would be for his foster parents to do.

If she named him, he would be real.

Isabella had expected to feel nothing for this child except a general wish that he would do well with his foster parents. She was not overly fond of children as a rule, and she did not expect to feel any great attachment for this baby, whose conception had caused her such heartache and necessitated such subterfuge.

She had looked forward to the day when this whole unpleasant experience could be put behind her and she would fill her life once again with balls and shopping and elaborate dinners.

Now she faced the truth: She could never live that way again.

She placed a kiss on her baby's head.

She did not *want* to live that way again.

"Marian, I cannot do it," she cried out in panic. "I cannot give him to strangers. What if they are not kind to him? What if he contracts some horrible disease or meets with some accident through their neglect?"

"They are hardly strangers," Marian said soothingly. "We interviewed them most carefully. They are a respectable, relatively well-to-do, childless couple, and they will rear your child as their own. They will be discreet. The child will be known to their neighbors as an orphaned relative, and they believe he is my child, and not yours. It is the perfect situation for him."

"I don't care. They may not have him," Isabella said. She sounded hysterical to her own ears. "I am going to keep my baby."

"Calm yourself," Marian said as she took the baby from Isabella's arms. "This agitation is not good for you, or for him." The infant, apparently sensing Isabella's emotion, began lustily crying again.

"I will not give him up."

"You do not have to. We will contrive something," Marian said, looking worried. "We will simply inform the couple that I have changed my mind and I have decided to keep my baby."

"He is *my* baby," Isabella cried. "Not yours."

"I know. I know, my dear," Marian said soothingly. "I

feared this would happen. There is something about babies—this baby—that is irresistible."

"I thought I could give him away. I must have been mad," Isabella said. "What horrible person could consider such a thing once she had held her child in her arms?"

"You were desperate to preserve your reputation," Marian reminded her. "Once it was known you had given birth to a child outside of marriage, you could never return to your old life. You could never contract a respectable marriage."

"What care I about my old life?" Isabella said plaintively. "What care I about marriage? Philip is dead. And I have had enough of men." She gave the child in her sister's arms a wistful look. "Except for Jamie."

Marian smiled at her.

"It seems cruel to say so, but the ordeal of birth sometimes causes a disorder in the mother's mind. A *temporary* disorder, mind," Marian said. "You do not have to make a decision now. When you have rested, you may reconsider."

"I *have* decided," Isabella said stubbornly, but her eyes were half closed from exhaustion. "I will *not* reconsider."

"There, there," Marian said as she bent to kiss Isabella's forehead. "Sleep now. You have done splendidly."

"Where are you taking him?" Isabella cried when Marian started to leave the room with the baby.

"Just to the next room. I do not want him to wake you with his cries."

"Have the cradle brought in here," Isabella said. "I do not want him out of my sight."

"As you wish," Marian said, clearly humoring her. "He will need to be fed again soon, anyway."

Isabella managed to keep her eyes open until Marian brought the cradle to her bedside and arranged the baby in it. Then Marian closed the draperies and quietly left the room.

Despite her exhaustion, Isabella was aware of everything at that moment—the crisp cleanliness of the fresh sheets Marian and Betty had used to change her bed after the birth; the soft, deliciously cool spring breeze wafting through the window and causing the sheer white curtains Isabella had sewn to billow into the room, the scent of the flowers Marian had cut from the garden and placed in a vase by Isabella's bedside.

Jamie's soft breathing.

The sweetest sound in all the world.

Adam grinned at the chaos around him and wished Marian were here to see the faces of the officers when General Lord Grimsby informed them that from now on they would have to find other transport for their personal luggage because their extra baggage horses were being requisitioned to carry the new portable hospitals ordered by General Wellington.

He could not resist sharing the joke, and so he was writing a letter to her. He knew she would be pleased to hear about the hospitals, an improvement for which Dr. McGrigor, Lord Wellington's chief medical officer, and Captain Randall had campaigned tirelessly.

One would have thought the general had announced that food was to be discontinued until after the war, he wrote.

The requisition of his extra horse was not a problem for Adam. His modest kit contained only the requisite regimental jacket, two pairs of trousers, three waistcoats, flannel drawers, twelve pairs of stockings, six shirts, a pelisse, two pairs of boots, and one pair of shoes. All of this fit neatly into a battered satchel his batman could carry on his own horse along with his own personal effects.

Other officers, however, were far more committed to sartorial splendor than Adam.

The most vociferous of these was a conceited young lieutenant who had brought 50 boxes containing his wardrobe to the Peninsula.

He is quite the dandy, wrote Adam, *and looks quite smart in his blue velvet foraging cap with a gold tassel and border of same edged with white ermine.*

He looked into the distance, smiling.

There was no nonsense about Marian, who obviously, like Adam, preferred to travel lightly through this world.

His smile turned to a concerned frown.

She should be giving birth to her baby soon. Adam could count as well as any village gossip, and it should have been born in April at the latest.

April had come and gone. Adam wondered if something was wrong. Had Marian become ill again and lost the child? Was she being cared for properly? He did not trust that frivolous little baggage, Isabella, to put her half-sister's welfare before her own selfish impulses. The business of her running away with Philip had been hushed up, and the London Season was in full swing. He would not be surprised if Isabella had grown bored with watching the grass grow in Derbyshire and decamped to the city and the *ton*.

News should have come by now.

Please send me word of your condition, he wrote. *If you have need of anything—anything at all—send word to my solicitor. I have left instructions for him to provide you with any funds you may require.*

"Major Lyonbridge," the general barked out from the doorway at that moment. All of the men abruptly broke off their grousing and stood to attention. Lord Grimsby made an impatient gesture to indicate they should stop standing about like so many petrified posts. "A word with you in my office."

"Yes, my lord," Adam said, standing at once and following him from the room.

"I have received a letter from Isabella," the general said when they were both seated. "The child is born."

Adam felt all the breath expel from his lungs. Naturally Isabella would inform her father rather than him, so he told himself he had no reason to feel slighted.

"Is Marian all right?" he asked.

"Perfectly well, according to Isabella. She also has decided to keep her child instead of permitting that couple she had chosen to adopt it." The general's mouth was a thin line of displeasure. "This complicates matters exceedingly."

"She is a determined woman," Adam said. "It may be impossible for her to make a respectable marriage now, but—"

"That is not what I mean," the general snapped. "Hang the girl if she is determined to ruin her life. But all the *ton* thinks she and Isabella are living on your property in dignified seclusion to await your return from the war and your wedding to my daughter. I had expected Marian to be rid of the brat as soon as it was born so she could support the character of virtuous companion to Isabella. But the presence of an infant in the house is dashed difficult to explain."

He gave a weary sigh.

"The only thing to do is to send Marian and the child away."

"Send them away? Where?" Adam demanded.

"Anywhere but your house or mine," the general said. "The stupid girl! I had given her credit for better sense. If the child's father were still alive, I could force him to make an honest woman of her. My wife was right. The girl is impossible."

"Because she chose to keep her own child instead of giving him away to strangers?" Adam asked in disbelief. "It would be unnatural for her to do otherwise."

"Such sentimental drivel, Adam," the general snapped.

"Do not try to make a pretty story of this. I wash my hands of her."

Adam clenched his jaw.

"Well, I do not!" he declared. "She is living in *my* house, at *my* expense, and there she stays as long as she wishes."

"Have some sense, man! Surely you know what people will think when it becomes known there is a young woman with an infant living in your house, moreover a young woman who was on campaign at the same time as your regiment. Everyone will think the baby is yours!"

The general narrowed his eyes.

"Is *that* it? Have you trifled with Marian?"

"Certainly not," Adam said, stung. "As if I would *touch* the daughter of the regimental surgeon . . . or of my own general. Do you think I am mad?"

"*Yes,* if you are going to keep the girl in your house."

"She has nowhere else to go. You and your wife have seen to that," Adam said bitterly. "If I had not taken her from Chelsea Hospital when she was suffering from the influenza, she might be dead now, and the child with her."

"It hurts me to say this," the general said sadly, "but maybe it would have been for the best."

"You cannot mean that," Adam said slowly. "She is your daughter."

"You are right. I did not mean it." The general rubbed his eyes. "Wellington is mobilizing the army, the French are on the move, and *this* happens. Meanwhile, your father has been writing to me to insist that I release you from active service. Everyone knows a major battle is about to take place, and he is concerned for his heir's precious hide."

"I have received letters from him, too," Adam admitted. "I am not going to resign my commission, and so I have told him."

The general shuffled some papers on his desk in an attempt to make his next statement seem casual.

"We have discussed, again, the notion of your marrying Isabella upon your return," he said. "I have agreed to double her dowry if you marry her. We are wondering if you have reconsidered your previous stance."

"With due respect, my lord," Adam said stiffly, "I am *not* going to marry Isabella. I would not take that faithless little harpy to wife if it would make Napoleon Bonaparte roll over in front of Lord Wellington like a short, shaggy dog wanting to have its belly scratched. You do not have enough money to persuade me to put my head in that particular noose."

"Watch how you speak of her. Isabella is my daughter," the general said irritably.

"So is Marian. I would sooner marry *her*."

The general gave a snort of impatience.

"Then you are a fool, sir!" he declared.

Yes, Adam thought, *I am a fool. Because my mind is full of her my every waking hour.*

"You do not have to make a decision now," the general continued. "If you decide her dowry is not large enough to make you overlook her folly with your brother, we will quietly announce after a decent interval—six months to a year, perhaps—that you and Isabella have agreed you would not suit. I believe that is the way the newspapers phrase it."

"I think not," Adam said. "Six months is too long. I should like to have the pretense of a betrothal dispelled soon. The matter has been delayed long enough."

"Do not be hasty." He did not look Adam in the eye. "Your brother is gone, poor devil. Isabella no doubt repents her rash behavior. Bridal nerves were responsible, more than like. The girl is pretty, well-educated, and she knows how to hold household. You could do worse for a wife."

Adam gave a snort of grim amusement.

"Not bloody likely," he said cheerfully.

Chapter 23

"Oh, just look at him. Is he not the most precious baby boy you have ever seen?" Isabella cooed as she bathed her son.

To the household's surprise—especially since all its members believed that Marian, and not Isabella, was the child's mother—Isabella refused to entrust anyone, not even Marian, with this homely task. Adam had provided the means for them to hire a nurse, but Isabella would have none of it.

In truth, the fewer people who were exposed to the new mother and child, the better. The housekeeper and her husband—both conveniently hard of hearing, failing of eyesight, and so feeble that they rarely went up the stairs unless absolutely necessary—were the only servants who stayed in the house all night. The extra housemaids and man of all work lived with their families in the village and reported for work during the daytime hours. Isabella and Marian had little trouble staying out of their way. Any orders were conveyed to them by the housekeeper from Isabella or Marian through the intermediary of Isabella's maid.

"Hmmm?" Marian said as she tore her gaze with some reluctance from the letter that had just come in the post.

"I cannot imagine that anything Adam Lyonbridge has to say could be so fascinating," Isabella said as she admired the bright blue eyes, the slightly upturned nose, and the adorable, pursed little mouth that was Jamie. She never tired of washing him. And holding him. And nursing him. And watching him sleep. Her romantic infatuation with the baby's late father had been *nothing* compared to this.

"Major Lyonbridge has instructed his steward to give me fifty pounds as a present, presumably in celebration of my giving birth to a healthy child," Marian said.

Isabella gave her a sharp look.

"I know that expression," she said with narrowed eyes. "We are *not* going to tell him the truth. Send him a pretty note thanking him for his generosity, and put the money aside for your old age." She gave Marian a wicked smile. "Or buy some new clothes."

"It is wrong to deceive him so," Marian said with the glimmer of an answering smile to acknowledge her sister's levity.

"If his horrible father learns about the child, he could take him away from me," Isabella said. "I could not bear it."

Marian touched her sister's shoulder.

"I would never permit that to happen," she said. "Never."

Isabella picked Jamie up and held him so tightly to her bosom that he gave a protesting squeak.

"My precious," Isabella said in instant remorse as she placed a kiss on the top of his head. "I am so sorry."

"Major Lyonbridge has been everything that is kind and generous," Marian said.

"Well, Jamie is his nephew, after all, for all that we cannot tell him so."

Heedless of the fact that the whole front of her gown was wet from contact with the child, Isabella took a towel and gently dried Jamie's soft skin. This reckless disregard for her own appearance made Marian smile.

"I am not unaware of the sacrifice you have made to protect my reputation in the eyes of the world, and the sacrifice you will continue to make in continuing to pose as

Jamie's mother," Isabella said with a look of apology at Marian. "You will never make a decent marriage now."

"Do you think I care for that?" Marian said with a shrug. "Captain Randall's means were extremely modest. I never did expect to have a dowry or to make a respectable marriage. I knew perfectly well that I would have to find some employment eventually, if not in a hospital, as a companion to an elderly invalid."

"How unspeakably dreary," Isabella said. "My father would not have let that happen."

"No, instead he left me to the mercy of your mother, who sent me to Tunbridge Wells to find me a husband there. Frankly, there is not much to choose between nursing an elderly husband for food and shelter, and nursing an elderly invalid or a ward full of wounded men for money."

"When you put it that way," Isabella said wryly, "I have done you a favor."

Marian smiled at her.

"Indeed, you have," she said as she approached the bed where Isabella had laid her little one and touched his tiny hand.

"Jamie is such a miracle," Isabella said with a sigh. "Are his hands not the most beautiful things? Those tiny little fingers. Those precious little toes."

Marian laughed out loud.

"How your London friends would stare at the deterioration of your conversation," she said. Her smile faded. "Isabella, what are we going to do?" Marian asked, suddenly serious.

"Do?" Isabella said, still occupied with her son. "What do you mean?"

"When we must leave here. We cannot stay here forever. Remember, you were going to leave Jamie with a couple to care from him, and we were to go back to London, you to resume your old life, and I to find employment at one of the hospitals as a nurse."

"My father may well be angry with you for supposedly getting yourself with child, Marian," Isabella said, "but he never would let you go to work in a hospital."

"Well, he is not here, is he? He is at war. And your mother rules the household while he is gone. Believe me, I would much rather work at a hospital than live with her."

"You became ill with the influenza at that place!"

"You became pregnant on the Great North Road," Marian said tartly. "There are dangers everywhere."

"You make it sound so sordid. It was not like that at all. Running away to Scotland with Philip was so romantic, and I had been in love with him for so long. I became a bit queasy from all the bumping around in the carriage, and Philip was afraid I was going to be sick, so we stopped at an inn." She gave a reminiscent sigh. "He was so kind and understanding, even though most men would have been annoyed with me. He procured a private parlor and ordered tea and little cakes to be served. It was a pretty room with a pink brocade daybed in it. One thing led to another—it was so exciting—and soon we found ourselves—"

Marian held up one hand.

"Please! There is no need to tell me the rest."

"I was foolish to trust him," Isabella said. The hurt was still raw. "How could he have abandoned me after what we shared?"

"He was a man," Marian said with a shrug. "Who knows what was going on in his head? Remember, I was surrounded by men when I was on campaign. I have no romantic delusions about them."

"And did none of them catch your eye? Not even once?" Isabella asked slyly. "All those handsome officers, all to yourself." Her smile widened when Marian blushed. "Marian! You *did* meet someone! *Tell* me."

"I have no intention of feeding your prurient taste for gossip," Marian said loftily.

"You know *everything* about me," Isabella said wheedlingly. "The least you could do is—"

"There was no one," Marian said firmly. "No one for whom I would be suitable, that is."

Isabella's shrewd gaze went from Marian's conscious face to the letter in her hand.

"Adam," she said softly. "My poor dear."

"Do not be ridiculous," Marian said.

"It would have been impossible *before* his brother's death, even if he had not been betrothed to me," Isabella told her. "Now that he is the heir—"

"I know, I know," Marian said. "You need not belabor the point."

"And to make things worse, you are believed to have given birth to a child out of wedlock. What a dreadful tangle!"

Marian gave a careless shrug, but she could not look Isabella in the eye.

"As you said before, and rightly, it would have been impossible from the beginning," she said. "This hardly changes my situation in any way."

Isabella caught Marian's hand.

"But I appreciate your sacrifice no less," she said earnestly.

Marian squeezed Isabella's hand, and the sisters shared a poignant moment of communion.

Then Isabella had to spoil it.

"But *Adam,* Marian," she said with a roll of her eyes. "I am appalled that a sister of mine would have such abysmal taste. I am beginning to think you are Captain Randall's true daughter, after all."

"Adam Lyonbridge is a kind and generous man who has gone to a great deal of trouble and expense for us," Marian said sternly. "He owes the natural daughter of his commanding officer absolutely nothing! Nor does he owe *you* anything after the way you have treated him. I will not have you making disparaging remarks about him in his own house."

Jamie began whimpering, and Isabella rushed at once to sweep him up into her arms and comfort him.

"My poor baby," she said as she kissed him on his downy head. "Marian does not mean to frighten you."

"Indeed, I do not," she said remorsefully as she touched the baby's shoulder.

Chapter 24

Marian's breath caught when she saw the bold, now-familiar handwriting on the letter that came in the post. The ink was slightly blurred, and the edges were crumpled as if it had been through an ordeal to find its way to her.

Hands trembling, she caught it to her bosom and could have wept with nerves.

Isabella watched with haunted eyes.

Neither had slept for days.

Vitoria.

Word had been received that a great battle had been won in Spain, but the casualty lists had not yet been released.

And here was a letter in Adam's own hand addressed to Marian.

It was disquieting, receiving a letter in his dear handwriting when Marian still did not know his fate. What if he was dead? What if this was the last letter she would receive from him? What if—

"Oh, for pity's sake," Isabella snapped irritably. "Open the thing. It won't bite you."

Marian forgave her instantly. The news was that the British casualties had been terrible at Vitoria, and many officers were among the dead. Several generals. Many high-ranking officers. Wondering who lived and who had died took much of the triumph out of the victory that some said had crushed Napoleon Bonaparte's backbone.

Marian broke the wax seal and opened the letter.

She scanned it quickly and closed her eyes.

"What does it say?" Isabella asked. "It can't be anything so bad as that. It had to have been written *before* the battle."

"Yes, it was," she said. "He writes that he has drawn up a new will, and he has left Jamie and me a legacy of two hundred pounds. It was sent to his solicitor in the same post that carried this letter. He tells me that in the event that he does not survive the battle, I am to consider this house my home until—"

"Oh, for pity's sake," Isabella said again. "Just because he had the good sense to write a new will and leave you a present does not mean that he has had some premonition that he will die in battle. Adam is as big as a bear and twice as mean. He can take care of himself. I only hope my father is all right. They said some of the generals had been killed in a barrage of cannon fire. *They* know which ones. Why will they not tell us?"

Marian continued reading. She gave Isabella a sideways look.

"He mentions you."

"Kindly spare me his compliments," Isabella said dryly. "I am abundantly aware of what Adam Lyonbridge thinks of me."

"He says the general has renewed his efforts to convince him to marry you, and he depends upon me to reassure you that he has no intention of holding you to the marriage, regardless of any pressure that is being brought against him to do so. Until then, he intends to support the pretense of willingness to honor the betrothal, as he has been doing all this time, and you are to do the same until such time as it can be broken off without making your respective fathers look too foolish. He does not want any misunderstanding with regard to his intentions."

"What he means to say is he would not marry me if I were the last woman on earth. Well, you can tell your precious Major Lyonbridge that the feeling is entirely mutual," Isabella said roundly, "and that if he has any orders for me in the future he can write to me himself. I, too, will support the pretense for now, but only because it is convenient for us to stay in his house for the present."

"I am certain he will be grateful," Isabella murmured.

"And be sure to tell him that under no circumstances will I be prevailed upon to kiss his arrogant face when he returns, so he had better not expect it." She picked up Jamie and put a fond kiss on his forehead. "There are some sacrifices I will not make, even for you, my precious," she told her happily gurgling son. Her expression softened. "Oh, look, Marian," she said, utterly besotted. "See his little lips move. He is trying to talk to us. I am sure he is saying 'Mama.' Yes, my sweet Jamie. Ma. Ma."

Marian had to smile.

"I am sorry, Isabella. But it is far too soon for a one-month-old child to talk. It is merely a happy coincidence of sounds that leads you to think so, although *I* hear nothing of the kind."

"What does she know, my clever darling?" Isabella said fondly to Jamie. "She is only an old aunt."

"Very well," Marian conceded with a smile. "He *is* talking. We shall have him doing his sums next week."

"That is better," Isabella said, laughing. With a final kiss, she put Jamie down and came over to stand by Marian. She laid a compassionate hand on Marian's arm.

"We will know by tomorrow," she said. "Much as it pained me to do so, I wrote to Lord Revington as soon as we learned about the battle and begged him for news about Adam and Father. He has enormous influence in political circles and you cannot tell me that *he* has to wait until the casualty lists are printed to learn whether his son has survived. The man loathes me, no doubt. But he can hardly deny me news and still support the character of my future father-in-law."

Marian could have kissed her feet.

"Motherhood must have mellowed you," Marian said gratefully.

"Well, it has, I think," Isabella said. She turned her attention back to Jamie. "Say 'Mama,' sweetheart," she cooed. "Ma. Ma."

Then the smile was abruptly wiped from her face.

"But we will have to teach him to say it to you, and not to me," she said sadly.

Marian touched her shoulder in sympathy.

"Do not think of that now," she said.

Indeed, Marian could not have loved Jamie more if she *had* given birth to him herself.

"We are a family now," Marian said, "the three of us, and nothing will separate us. No matter what happens."

"We can neither of us marry now," Isabella said. "I do not care for myself. Jamie is enough for me, but you—"

"I am well content," Marian said. "How soon do you think you can expect to hear from Lord Revington?"

As it turned out, Lord Revington himself drove over from his country manor nearby, where he had arrived only that morning from London to deal with some matters of estate business.

Isabella hastily handed the child to Marian when he was announced. Unfortunately, he entered the room before Marian could flee up the stairs to her room.

"What is this?" Lord Revington said as he goggled at the infant. "I thought the child was to be given away."

Usually the most accommodating of infants, Jamie had commenced squalling piteously at being removed so abruptly from his mother's arms. Normally he placidly accepted Marian as a substitute, but not today.

Red-faced and juicily weeping, he was definitely not at his most appealing.

"Are you both mad?" Lord Revington said stiffly, "You

cannot keep an infant here without the whole neighborhood knowing about it sooner or later."

The two women stared at him, speechless.

"Please, my lord," Marian asked. "Have you received word of Major Lyonbridge? Has he survived the battle?"

"He has, my girl," he said as he stared at the child. "Although I should like to know what that has to do with you. Is this Adam's bastard? Why was I not told of this at once? If the child is my grandson, it is my right to decide how he is to be reared, and to make provision for his future. I would have insisted he be fostered out to—"

"He is not Adam's child," Marian said as she turned to shield Jamie's face from Lord Revington's sight.

Lord Revington had accepted the child without question as Marian's, which was good.

But if he got a good look at the child's face, he might see that Jamie's eyes were a beautiful shade of dark, cobalt blue, like his elder son's, for Marian had been mistaken in thinking they would change color. The shape of his face, as well, was very like his late father's.

Lord Revington gave a dismissive wave of his hand.

"I care not whose it is, then," he said.

Isabella bit her lip.

"My lord, we would appreciate it if—"

"Yes, yes," he said. "I will say nothing. It is no business of mine who fathered Miss Randall's child, although it does concern me that my son obviously has the charge of its upkeep. I am at a loss to account for it."

"I had nowhere else to go," Marian said. "Major Lyonbridge is a man of great compassion. It is his only reason for sheltering me along with Miss Grimsby until his return from battle."

Lord Revington gave a nod of comprehension.

"No doubt my son knew the child's father and took it upon himself to provide for it. He always was more generous than his purse would allow."

"The child is hardly in the way at all," Isabella said as Jamie continued to wail lustily. She did not dare take him back without arousing Lord Revington's suspicions, blast the man!

"My lord, you do not mention my father," she said with some apprehension.

"He, too, is well," Lord Revington said sourly.

Isabella let out her breath all at once. She found her father extremely tiresome much of the time, but she would have been sad to lose him. Moreover, she did not gladly anticipate the way her mother would receive such news. It would be like Lady Grimsby to don scarlet apparel and dance on his grave.

"Thank you, my lord," Isabella said. "It was kind of you to call on me and set my mind at ease with regard to Adam. I am very glad he has come to no harm."

"Please spare me your insincere expressions of regard for my son," he said harshly. "*You* hardly give a rap. But I suppose this little show of concern for his welfare is merely for effect."

"And I wanted to know how my father fared," she said with a cold glare at him.

"Now you know," he said, "so I will take my leave of you."

He gave a curt nod of his head in farewell and favored Marian and the still fussy child with a gaze of utter contempt as he strode for the door, straight as a ramrod.

"Well! What a dreadful old man," Isabella said as soon as she was sure he was out of earshot. "You cannot know how relieved I am to know he is not to be my father-in-law."

With that she scooped Jamie from Marian's arms and smiled smugly at her sister when he instantly quieted down, gentle as a little lamb.

"I do not know how such a sweet baby boy could have such a disagreeable old man for his grandfather," she said.

She laid her son on the bed and caressed his soft cheek. When she turned to Marian, her expression was troubled.

"Did you see his face when he asked if Jamie was Adam's son?" Isabella said with a little shudder. "You mark my words. If he ever learns that Jamie is his Philip's son, he will take him away from us and let him be reared by strangers, just for spite!"

Chapter 25

June 1814
St. James's Palace, London

The cheers of the crowd sounded hollow in Isabella's ears as she stood waiting in an impressive assembly room at St. James's Palace for the spectacle to begin.

She was wearing a new lace-trimmed, pink muslin gown with a ravishing flower-brimmed hat and flanked by both of her parents as she awaited the hero's appearance and the ceremony during which the Prince Regent would pin yet another medal upon Major Adam Lyonbridge in commemoration of his outstanding contribution to the Allied Powers' victory over the tyrant Napoleon.

She would have given anything to be back at Adam's small country property in Derbyshire instead, watching her sturdy little son chase butterflies in the grassy meadow near the house. From long habit, her eyes kept straying from the rather formal grouping of Adam's relatives and her own toward the floor by her skirts to determine her child's whereabouts.

For a moment she would feel a thrill of panic at not finding him, but then she would remember that the boy was safe with Marian in the gallery with all the townspeople and other common folk. Isabella had insisted that they be accompanied by a burly man from her father's household for their protection, but she worried that the burliest man in Creation could not protect her vulnerable son from contracting one of the common illnesses that were cheerfully borne by the lower classes.

For the past two nights, Marian and Jamie had slept in lodgings in town, while Isabella stayed in her family home in Mayfair with her mother. Isabella had never before been separated from Jamie at night. Did he cry for her in his sleep? Was he refusing to eat?

Or was he so content with Marian that he would learn to love her more than he loved his own mother?

Jamie no longer called her mama. That now, to Isabella's regret, was Marian's title. He called *her* Aunt Isabella, not to acknowledge a relationship that must never be acknowledged, but as any child would call a close friend of his mother's. It had taken weeks to break Jamie of calling both of them mama. Once in a while he forgot, and it was exceedingly sweet to Isabella's ears. She tried in vain to convince herself that it was better this way. Marian *was* his mother in the eyes of the world, and the sooner Isabella became accustomed to the idea, the better for the three of them.

Isabella absolutely hated the fact that her mother regarded her sweet little son in the light of an embarrassment that must be hidden from the world. When the three of them had arrived from the country, her mother had been quick to parcel off Marian and Jamie to lodgings before anyone significant might see them. Lady Grimsby had looked at Isabella's precious son as if he were a bug, and not a very interesting one at that.

Of course Isabella understood the necessity of not acknowledging her son as hers. It was the price she had to pay for the safety of seclusion during Jamie's birth at Adam's house, and for not having him taken away from her and Marian by that dreadful Lord Revington.

Just as the travesty of her appearance today was a price she had to pay for the preservation of her precious reputation.

The brave, loyal, beautifully dressed and coiffed fiancée must be produced at the important ceremony that was to honor the gallant war hero whose house, supposedly, she had been readying for their life together. Thanks to the pretty stories that her father and mother had been tireless in circulating about the war office and polite society, everyone was expecting to see a tender reunion of the faithful lovers separated for so long in the service of Mother England.

Once the Peace Celebrations were over at the end of the summer and the *ton* retreated from London to various fashionable watering holes, Isabella, Marian, and Jamie would retire to a small rented house of their own in the country for the summer.

That was *her* price for participating in this farce.

When Adam entered the assembly room, a cheer went up in the gallery full of townspeople. Everyone stood just a little straighter because Adam, even Isabella had to admit, had that effect on people.

He was freshly barbered and dressed in a spotless uniform lavishly decorated with gold braid. His boots were so shiny Isabella was certain one could see one's reflection in them. His blue eyes were the color of a summer sky, and when he smiled to acknowledge the cheers, his strong, white teeth formed a pleasing contrast to his tanned face. Nature had given Adam Lyonbridge rather nondescript brownish hair, but the streaks put in it by the sun made it appear to be gilded with gold. Isabella could hear a chorus of feminine sighs from the gallery.

Intellectually, she knew that he was magnificent, and every woman in the assembly room would give her right arm to exchange places with Isabella right now.

But impressive as Adam might appear to these people in his shiny new uniform, Isabella was not fooled. Underneath all of this fine trimming was the same old Adam, a barbarian who was happier on campaign, stomping about in his heavy boots and cheerfully dining on the burnt carcasses of small birds he tore apart with his dirty hands. Isabella suspected he preferred the company of his horse to that of any female.

She knew perfectly well that he would have made her a dreadful husband if she had been spiritless enough to marry him.

Isabella could summon up nothing more than a vague feeling of gratitude to him for sheltering her and her son all these months. It argued for a compassionate heart, she had to admit. But he did so out of pity and a sense of duty to Marian, his commanding general's natural daughter, after all, and not because he had any regard for Isabella herself.

As expected, he walked straight to their party and exchanged bows with his father and the general. He kissed Isabella's mother's hand, and then he turned to Isabella.

Isabella could hear the sighs of expectation waft over the gallery in the sheer romance of the moment.

Only the conviction that Adam disliked her as thoroughly as she disliked him enabled her to initiate this shameless deception with a clear conscience.

Isabella sank into a deep curtsy, and the gallery erupted into applause. Adam gazed solemnly into her eyes and raised her. Then he took her gloved hand in his and turned it slightly to place a lingering kiss at the pulse point of her wrist exposed by the edge of her short white lace glove.

One of the female members of the gallery audience caused a small flurry of commotion by fainting dead away. Isabella felt her cheeks grow warm with embarrassment, so she supposed it was fortunate that she would appear to be blushing like a good little maiden.

Imagine *Adam* bestowing such a sensual greeting on her, and in *public,* the wretch. He did it to spite her, no doubt. His eyes were hard as flint during the whole disgraceful process.

She could see him ensconced with her father and a half dozen officials at Whitehall to orchestrate his kissing of her wrist. She could not believe the barbarian Adam was capable of such a romantic gesture on his own.

"Welcome home, Major Lyonbridge," she said, gritting her teeth in a smile for the benefit of their audience.

"Thank you, Miss Grimsby," he said. In a lower tone he added, "Where are they?"

"Who?" she whispered.

"Marian and the child, of course," he said. "Did you leave them in the country?"

Isabella gave a shift of her eyes toward the front of the gallery, where she could see a portion of Marian's face peeking around the enormous hat of a stout, middle-class matron. Adam must have understood her message, for he gave a brief nod of acknowledgment before he turned to reply to some remark made by his father.

At that moment, the Prince Regent entered the room at the head of an impressive procession of his courtiers and various titled noblemen. Princess Charlotte accompanied him, which caused a slight stir among the masses. Once Adam and the family bowed deeply to the king, the plump, pretty princess came forward, all smiles, to have the gallant hero presented to her.

The princess was presently in disgrace for refusing to marry the prince her father chose for her, so it was a compliment to Adam of no mean order that the Prince Regent permitted her to attend the ceremony.

"On behalf of the women of England," the young princess said in a strong, beautifully modulated voice, "I salute you."

"Your highness does me too much honor," Adam murmured as he went down on one knee with athletic grace and kissed the hem of the princess's gown. He rose to thunderous applause and cheers.

More feminine sighing and swooning from the gallery.

Isabella rolled her eyes in disgust.

Then all was silent as the Prince Regent stepped forward to pin a medal on the breast of Adam's uniform and deliver, on behalf of a grateful nation, his congratulations and warmest thanks to Adam for his bravery in the battle against England's enemies.

Isabella heard none of it. A child gave a cry from the gallery.

Was it Jamie?

Was he hungry? Bored? Thirsty? Her blood ran cold with an even more dreadful thought. Had some dirty brute snatched at him and tried to abduct him? Isabella normally did not pay much attention to what happened among the lower orders, but now she recalled some talk of a lively business among thieves in snatching well-nourished young children to sell to the highest bidders.

Would this interminable ceremony *ever* conclude?

"Well done, my boy," General Lord Grimsby said in congratulatory tones to Adam when the tedious affair was over and the Prince Regent and Princess Charlotte had withdrawn with their entourage. Various high-ranking officers and public officials stood about, pounding Adam on the back and giving him bluff, hearty congratulations.

Adam smiled and bowed and expressed his thanks. Because everyone expected it, he took Isabella's dainty hand and tucked it into his arm as he strolled across the room in a positive sea of well-wishers and searched the departing members of the gallery for Marian.

It was *her* face that had been before him every moment from the time he learned that the enemy had been beaten and he was to go home. And suddenly he saw her.

She gave him a shy, self-conscious smile and would have hurried on if he had not abandoned Isabella and come to plant himself before her. The wide-eyed child looked up at him with consternation, and his lower lip trembled.

"Do not be afraid, lad," Adam said kindly to him. The child inched closer to Marian and put his finger in his mouth. "I do not bite."

Adam's hungry eyes devoured Marian. She was dressed in a fine green gown with a matching pelisse and a blond straw hat trimmed with green ribbons and yellow artificial flowers. She looked fresh and new in the midst of all this tedious ceremony.

"Everyone is staring at us," she whispered. Her cheekbones grew pink with embarrassment. "You must permit me to take my departure."

"Adam, surely you were told that my parents are having a celebratory breakfast in your honor," Isabella said from beside him as she took his arm. "I am certain some of the guests have already begun to arrive and are waiting for us to appear."

"Let them wait," he said through his teeth. "Why was Miss Randall in the gallery? Why was she not among your parents and the honored guests?"

"Please, Major Lyonbridge," Marian protested. "It does not matter."

"It bloody well *does* matter," he said, earning a frown from Isabella at the vulgarity of his language. "And is Miss Randall invited to this celebratory breakfast?"

Isabella hesitated.

"I really must go," Marian said, clutching the child to her. "Come along, Jamie."

"Miss Randall is going with us," Adam told Isabella. When Lord and Lady Grimsby came up to them, he added, "And her son, too."

Conscious of the curious faces surrounding her, Lady Grimsby gave a false, sweet smile.

"Of course, Miss Randall is always welcome in our home," she said with a creditable pretense of graciousness.

Her lip curled slightly as she looked down at Jamie. "And that little boy, too, of course."

The party would have moved on, but General Lord Grimsby blocked their way as he stared so avidly at Jamie that the child began to whimper in fright.

Marian picked him up to console him and the general fell into step at Adam's side as he herded Isabella and Marian forward.

Tears glistened in the old man's eyes.

"Are you all right, my lord?" Adam asked him.

"Wrong side of the blanket be damned," he whispered huskily, "the boy is my first grandchild. Handsome lad, is he not?"

"He is that," Adam agreed, but his mind was full of Marian.

When they arrived at Lord Grimsby's town carriage, Adam and Isabella managed to squeeze Marian and the boy with them into the forward seat designed for two. Fortunately, Jamie was small enough to sit on Marian's lap and Marian herself was not much bigger. The big man who had accompanied Marian and Jamie to the ceremony was told to walk back to the general's house.

Lord and Lady Grimsby sat across from them, which made it impossible for Adam to exchange another word with Marian. The general's wife glared at Marian and her child throughout the trip to the town house in disapproving silence. Marian stared back with her chin raised in defiance.

"What is your name, lad?" the general asked the child in bluff good humor. His wife gave him a look of utter disbelief.

"Jamie," the boy replied as he leaned shyly against Marian's shoulder. He looked across her to Isabella. "Mama," he said happily and crawled over Marian to sit on Isabella's lap.

Lady Grimsby looked as if she might have an apoplexy.

Good, thought Adam.

Isabella hugged Jamie, and he gave her a smacking kiss on the cheek. Adam watched in surprise as Isabella's expression visibly melted. She hugged the little boy close.

"Jamie is a bit confused," Isabella said to her parents, "because the three of us lived together for so long after he was born. It was a habit he fell into, calling both of us mama when he first learned to talk."

Lady Grimsby curled her lip at Marian. It was clear whom she blamed for this awkwardness.

"I missed you, Mama," Jamie told Isabella.

"He really is a very bright child," Isabella said proudly. "He learned to talk quite young."

At that moment, the carriage drew up before Lord Grimsby's town house, and Adam could see a small crowd gathering in front to welcome the hero.

Adam got out of the carriage to a smattering of applause and cheers. He acknowledged them with a bow, then reached back into the carriage for Isabella's hand.

"Smile, my dear Isabella," he said to his erstwhile fiancée. "Remember that you have waited with glad anticipation all these months for my return."

"Oh, *do* be still!" she snapped as she opened her jaws wide in a realistic imitation of a beatific smile.

Jamie stood in the doorway of the coach and looked about him in wide-eyed interest.

"For pity's sake, give that little urchin to its mother before someone sees it," Lady Grimsby snapped, breaking her silence.

Isabella looked as if she might object, but Lord Grimsby broke in.

"It would be best, Miss Randall, if you and the child stayed in the carriage and alighted from the stables. You can then slip unobtrusively into the house."

"See here, sir," Adam said in consternation. "Surely that is not necessary."

"Please, Major Lyonbridge," Marian said, looking discomfited. "It would be best."

"Are all those people here to see us?" Jamie asked. His blue eyes were sparkling.

"Yes," Adam said as he reached into the carriage for the boy and hoisted him to perch on his shoulder. He held onto him with one hand and held his free hand out to Isabella. She *smiled* at him—a real smile, this time, and not one of those stiff social masks for effect. Jamie laughed in sheer exhilaration.

"Stubborn, stubborn man," Marian muttered behind him as she fell into step behind Lord and Lady Grimsby.

Marian wondered what pretty story Lord Grimsby and his wife would concoct now to account for the inconvenient existence of one small, fatherless boy who grinned at all of Adam's and Isabella's well-wishers with puckish delight.

Chapter 26

"Disgraceful. Utterly disgraceful," said Lord Revington under his breath to his son as he watched a smiling Miss Randall wipe the telltale crumbs off her child's face after he had made a pig of himself with several dainty cream cakes from an ornate platter. "Flaunting her love child before the *ton*."

Adam felt a pang of guilt. He had acted impulsively throughout the morning, and thus held Marian up to public scrutiny and criticism, when his objective had been to lend her his support.

He had been outraged to see her relegated to the gallery where she would be jostled by the raff and scaff of humanity at the decoration ceremony.

He had been appalled by the general's suggestion that she hide in the carriage with the child and alight in the stable so she could make an inconspicuous entrance to her father's house, as if her mere existence was an embarrassment to him.

She deserved better from her own father, even if the connection could not be acknowledged. Adam was convinced that if the general had taken a proper interest in Marian's welfare sooner, she would not have come to England pregnant by some dead, nameless soldier.

Marian was a modest young woman with a good head on her shoulders. He had never seen the least sign of wantonness in her. It occurred to Adam, not for the first time, that this man, whoever he was, might have forced himself upon her. No matter how lonely she might have been, Adam could not imagine her surrendering her virtue lightly.

The thought of Marian enduring such insult made him want to seek out the fellow and . . . it was fortunate for the man that he was already dead. Adam consigned his soul to the hottest part of hell.

Even worse was the thought that Marian might genuinely have loved the fellow and still could be mourning him.

"Take that murderous look off your face," Lord Revington said under his breath. "You are quite frightening the ladies."

Adam blinked and muttered an apology.

His father put a hand on his arm.

"You know these fighting men," he said genially to the nearest guests. "You can take them off the battlefield, but they find themselves still fighting the war during introspective moments."

"It must have been so exciting," said one pretty, well-dressed miss as she insinuated herself closer to Adam. Several others stepped forward as well, doing their best to squeeze their friends out for a place near the conquering hero.

Adam barely restrained himself from rolling his eyes.

"Do tell us about your adventures," another girl said.

"They are not pretty stories for the delectation of nosy ladies," Adam said. "If you will excuse me—"

He gave a short, abrupt bow and walked away.

Lord Revington scowled at his son's broad back, but Adam's rudeness did not have the effect of discouraging his fair auditors from admiring him.

"So masterful," sighed one of the ladies, whom Lord Revington recognized as the daughter of one of the richest and most powerful peers in the empire.

"One just knows his gruff manner conceals a sensitive soul," said another, who promised to be equally well-dowered, as she followed the major's progress through the room with avid eyes. She licked her soft pink lips. "Lucky, lucky Miss Grimsby."

The girls exchanged a romantic sigh.

This little scene had the effect of cheering Lord Revington immensely.

He would have no trouble finding a bride for his son when news of his broken betrothal became public.

Lord Revington watched his former friend, General Lord Grimsby, with cold eyes as he regaled some of his cronies with what were sure to be overembellished tales of his own gallantry during the war. Nearby, his harpy of a wife tittered and gushed at an elderly and powerful marquess, trilling at his every pronouncement as if he were the most amusing wit in the kingdom, no doubt to help promote her husband's career.

There was no love lost between the general and his wife, but they were united in their ambition.

Isabella, Adam's betrothed, had ignored him and the guests completely during the breakfast being held in his honor. She had a sulky look on her face as she watched that brazen hussy, Miss Randall, fuss over her child. Adam would not hear a word against Miss Randall, no doubt from loyalty to her father, the late surgeon of his regiment. The soft-hearted Adam had offered her the shelter of his home when Lady Grimsby had thrown her out of her house—and so the little tart deserved!—and the sly girl repaid him by flaunting herself and her love child in public.

It would not take long for gossips to latch onto the notion that the boy was Adam's, especially if it became generally known that he was born at Adam's house.

For all of the girl's protestations, Lord Revington himself would have persisted in suspecting the child was

Adam's if his son had not looked him straight in the eye and denied it.

Adam had many skills, but lying convincingly was not among them.

Lord Revington frowned when Adam gave the boy a casual caress on the head when he passed him and his mother. The boy looked up at him with hero worship in his eyes.

Adam was completely without guile. And his gallantry toward the unfortunate Miss Randall was bound to bring him to grief unless his father took a hand in the matter.

It was time to find Adam a new fiancée—a good one this time—to distract him from the surgeon's daughter.

"The masses have been given their pretty story," Lord Revington said when Lord Grimsby and Adam joined him in his library the next day. "I think we may now consider the betrothal at an end."

"I had assumed we would continue the present arrangement until the end of the summer," the general said with lowered brows. "When the Congress convenes in the autumn to deal with the mess Napoleon has made of the map of Europe, all eyes will be on Vienna. Why not wait until then, when Adam and Isabella's decision to part ways will attract less attention?"

"Because my son must get on with his life," Lord Revington said coolly. "This dancing attendance on your daughter is a waste of his time. He should be looking about him for a proper wife."

Adam gave a short laugh.

"There is plenty of time for that, Father," he said. "Although I would be relieved to put my betrothal to Isabella behind me, I am in no hurry to acquire another fiancée. I have spent time enough away from my regiment. Indeed, my leave is almost expired."

"What foolishness is this?" Lord Revington demanded. "We agreed, sir, that you were to resign your commission when the war was concluded. Napoleon is beaten. Now you must take up your responsibilities as my heir. And set up your nursery."

"Being your heir has responsibilities?" Adam scoffed. "I do not recall that Philip found his responsibilities as your heir too onerous. It seemed to me that he spent all of his time in idleness here in London, and gambled and drank and wenched to relieve his boredom."

Lord Revington clenched his teeth.

"I made many mistakes with your brother. I should have kept him closer at hand. As I mean to do with you, sir."

"What? You would keep me on leading strings?" Adam said with a glimmer of dark amusement. "You'll catch cold at that, I'm afraid."

"If he repudiates his engagement to Isabella now, he'll make a laughingstock of me, Lord Wellington, and the Prince Regent to boot," Lord Grimsby protested.

"He will do no such thing," Lord Revington said. "A small, dignified announcement will appear in the press to signify that the couple has agreed they will not suit, and so forth. Then Adam will be free to look about him at the rest of the debutantes. Fortunately, due to the Peace Celebrations, all the eligible girls will spend most of the summer in London instead of retreating to various watering holes. Vastly convenient to have 'em all in one place so Adam can take his pick."

"Do you never *listen?*" Adam asked, goaded. "I have told you, I am not resigning my commission. And I have no intention of looking over the field of debutantes and offering for some silly chit who will be just as bad as Isabella."

"You can trust me to guide you in this matter, my son," Lord Revington said.

"Not on your life," Adam said dryly. "*You* are the one

who chose Isabella for me, and we know how felicitously that turned out. Next time I become betrothed, *I* will choose the lady."

"But Isabella—" the general protested.

"Is a free woman," Adam said dryly. "Let us repair to your house at once to give her the good news."

The general gave a sigh of capitulation.

"I suppose it is for the best," he said. "It occurs to me that Isabella, too, is in want of a spouse, and, in truth, she is not getting any younger."

The three men stood, preparatory to leaving Lord Revington's house for General Lord Grimsby's. Lord Revington put his hand on Adam's shoulder.

"Now, about the matter of your resigning your commission—" he began.

"Not until you have your spoon planted firmly in the wall," Adam said cheerfully. "Which, happily, will not be for many years."

"And so my betrothal is at an end," Isabella said dramatically to Marian as she bounced a laughing Jamie on her knee. "The announcement will appear in the newspaper next week."

Marian forced down the thrill of sheer happiness that coursed through her heart at such news.

Idiot!

Just because Isabella's betrothal was to be brought to an official end did not mean the magnificent Major Lyonbridge was any less lost to Marian now than he had been in the beginning.

On the contrary. At the beginning of their acquaintance, he had been the second son of a wealthy and powerful viscount, and she the daughter of a virtually penniless regimental surgeon.

It would have been a vastly unsuitable match then.

Now Major Lyonbridge was his father's heir, and when one considered his celebrity status as one of Lord Wellington's most decorated officers, he could look as high as he chose for his bride.

It was exceedingly unlikely that his choice would be the illegitimate daughter of his commanding officer, who he and the world believed had given birth to an illegitimate child. Indeed, few gentlemen would be willing to espouse her after her fall from grace.

"I hate being separated from him," Isabella said, and Marian blinked.

"Not Major Lyonbridge, surely?" she said.

Isabella rolled her eyes.

"Jamie, silly! Mother refuses to have you stay at our house, and I hate the thought of your being forced to stay in lodgings with Jamie. A child needs room to run and play."

Her voice broke.

"A child needs his mother."

"I know, sweet, I know," Marian said soothingly as she patted Isabella on the shoulder.

Isabella looked at her sister with tears in her eyes.

"I am the most selfish beast in nature, to be complaining to you." She took Marian's hand and squeezed it. "I don't know what would have happened to me or Jamie if it had not been for your sacrifice."

Marian smiled at her sister and put her free arm around Jamie so they were joined in an affectionate hug.

"Your friendship and Jamie's love have brought me so much joy," she said. "I did not know how lonely I was until I met you. As for these rooms, I assure you I am in high cotton. These are the most luxurious lodgings I have ever occupied. It was good of your father to arrange to have us moved into them from those poky little rooms we had when we first came from Derbyshire. I feel much safer here."

A knock sounded at the door.

Marian and Isabella exchanged a concerned look.

"Who can that be?" Isabella whispered.

Marian gave her a mocking look of terror.

"Do you think we should . . . open the door and find out?" she asked.

Isabella sat forward on the sofa and shielded Jamie with her body as Marian opened the door. She persisted in her fear that some unknown villain might snatch her tender son if she and Marian did not remain vigilant at all times.

"Major Lyonbridge!" Marian exclaimed.

"Good afternoon, Miss Randall. I hope my visit is not inconvenient—" Adam began as he stepped inside the room. His words stopped abruptly when he saw Isabella. "Oh, I say. This is awkward."

"Not at all," Isabella said wryly. "Perhaps Jamie and I can go for a little walk." She nodded her head to indicate her maid, who had been sitting quietly in a straight chair by the unlit fireplace. "Betty will stay to play propriety."

"What I have to say to Miss Randall is for her ears only," Adam said.

Isabella opened her mouth to protest.

"It is all right, Isabella," Marian said, not taking her eyes off Adam's earnest face. "In truth, I have not much reputation left to protect, have I?"

Pursing her lips, Isabella looked from one to the other for a moment.

"Very well, then. Come along Jamie. You, too, Betty."

The maid stood and would have taken Jamie's hand, but the child darted around her to tug on Adam's pants leg.

Smiling, Adam picked him up.

"Please, sir. Will you give me a ride on your shoulders?" the boy asked with a sunny smile.

"Later," Adam said, his eyes still on Marian. "After I have talked with your mother."

"Come along, Jamie," Isabella said again.

With a concerned look at the two of them, she took the child and the maid away with her.

And then they were alone.

Marian's throat was so dry all of a sudden that she could hardly speak, but she managed to choke out the words.

"Please be seated, Major Lyonbridge," she said in a voice that sounded too high to her own ears. "May I offer you some tea?"

He stepped forward quickly and took her shoulders in his big hands. When he spoke, his lips were inches from hers.

"I did not come for tea," he said huskily.

Chapter 27

Now he had frightened her.

Marian's eyes were huge in her face and Adam could see her throat work convulsively above the prim, pleated collar of her blue cambric gown.

Bloody hell.

He forced his hands to release her, one finger at a time. He stepped back and took a deep breath.

"This is not the way I meant to begin," he said ruefully.

Her magnificent green eyes narrowed.

"Adam Lyonbridge, if you have come in all this ceremony to offer me a slip on the shoulder, you can turn yourself around and go back out again!" she said, hands on hips and ready to tear a strip off his hide.

He laughed in pure exultation. How he adored her!

Before even he knew what he was about, he had seized her about the waist and given her a whirl that threatened to sweep the teapot off the table.

"Major Lyonbridge!" she snapped as she gave him a smart cuff on the shoulder. "Put me down at *once!*"

"*This* is why I cannot live without you," he said as he put her on her feet.

"Well, that is vastly unfortunate under the circumstances," she said, all in a huff, as she straightened her clothing.

"Marian, I want to marry you."

"Do not be absurd," she scoffed. "Your father would

never permit it. He wants you to marry an heiress, and he has every right to expect this of you."

"I can deal with my father. The question is not what he wants, but what you want. Will you marry me, Marian?"

Marian's lips worked, but nothing came out.

"I have made a proper botch of this, have I not?" he asked with a sigh as he ran one hand through his hair. "I meant to lead up to this with careful arguments. With all the delicacy in the world, I would have pointed out that a husband would be very convenient for you now that you have a child to rear. I would have professed my admiration for your courage in bearing your hardship. I would have promised to care for your son as my own, and love him as well as any natural father might do, for, indeed, I have a strong affection for him already."

"How is that possible? You have known him only a short while," she said.

"I was acquainted with you an hour when I knew you were the right woman for me."

"What? While I was up to my wrists in blood at the regimental hospital?"

"Even then." He smiled. "I would snatch me up, if I were you. You are not likely to receive a better offer."

Marian pursed her lips, but he could see the glimmer of a smile at the corners of her mouth.

"Major Lyonbridge, your flights of romantic fancy quite overwhelm me," she said dryly.

"I am a soldier, not a poet," he said. "I could not speak before because I was betrothed to your sister. But now that I am free of her, I can marry to please myself."

"Your father will never agree, and I will *not* embark upon a flight to the border with you. I have a child to think of."

He gave a cry that was almost savage and pulled her into his arms again.

"Adam!" she exclaimed as her body fit perfectly to his.

He gave a growl of satisfaction. He framed her face with his hands and lowered his lips to kiss her.

She gave him a thump on the chest with the heel of one hand.

"What do you think you are doing?" she snapped.

"That," he told her, "was a yes. Even *I* know that when a woman starts setting conditions, she has already accepted a man's offer in her mind."

He captured her wrists and held them behind her back so that they were breast to breast. He could feel her heart beating. She did not insult his intelligence by struggling, and he respected her for that.

Instead she gave a little whimper of anticipation as he took her lips with all the long-stifled desire in his heart.

They were both breathless when he ended the kiss.

Somehow during this long, satisfying exercise he found that he had released her hands and they were now clasped tightly around his neck. Some of her thick auburn hair had worked loose from its pins.

He adored the half-lidded look she gave him.

"Yes?" he prompted.

"Your father will never agree," she said, but her eyes were full of hope.

"He will agree," Adam said solemnly, "because in exchange for the privilege of marrying you, my dear, I am willing to pay his price."

"His . . . price?"

"I will resign my commission," he said glumly, "and let the old man groom me to be his heir. By this time next year, I will know all there is to know about corn and livestock, heaven help me."

"No," Marian said as she turned away from him. He could hear the tears in her voice. "I cannot allow you to make such a sacrifice. You would regret your choice someday and blame me. You would blame Jamie. You would not mean to, but you could not help it. "

"Never," he said as he turned her around to face him. "I can do it. I can do *anything* if I have you at my side."

"You love me that much?" she asked wonderingly. There was no coyness at all in the question.

"That much," he said, smiling. "Kiss me again before they come back."

Her response this time, though warm, was a trifle absent.

When he released her, she bit her lip.

"Out with it, girl," he said with a sigh. "What is going on in that clever little brain of yours?"

"The marriage will cause a dreadful scandal," she said. "Perhaps it had better be Gretna Green after all."

"Not on your life," he said vehemently. "I will not marry you in secret, as if I were ashamed of you. We are going to be married in a church. Those members of our respective families who wish to be present will be welcome. Those who do not can go to the devil."

With that, he grasped her shoulders and kissed her again.

This time, she returned his ardor so convincingly that he had to take several calming breaths to keep himself from taking liberties that would rightfully earn him a smart slap on the jaw and a scold from his beloved that would leave his ears ringing.

She was a *mother,* for heaven's sake. And her child would be returning to her lodgings at any moment.

With Isabella.

Thinking of his erstwhile fiancée had the effect of dampening his ardor like magic, so when Isabella, Jamie, and the maid entered the room in response to a knock on the door a moment later, he and Marian were having a practical conversation about how best to approach his father and hers on the subject of their wedding.

First, though, Adam had to apply to Marian's closest male relative for her hand in marriage.

"Jamie, I should like to marry your mother," he said

solemnly as he knelt so he could look eye to eye with the child. "Is that all right with you?"

"Will you give me a ride on your shoulders?" Jamie asked coyly.

"Yes," he said, smiling. If only it could be that easy.

"Will we come to live with you? And your horse?"

With a great effort, Adam kept from laughing.

"Yes," he said.

"Can my other mama come live with us?" the boy asked as he looked at Isabella.

"No," three adult voices said at once.

"I cannot like this scheme of yours," Isabella said to Marian when Adam had left. "I suppose it will do no good to ask you to think it over carefully."

"I am to call him Papa," Jamie interjected brightly. "He said I am to have my own pony."

Isabella gave a snort of annoyance. Men were always great with promises when they wanted something. Witness Philip Lyonbridge, who promised undying love, and see how quickly he went off without a word to get himself killed in the war once he got what he wanted from her.

Adam's bribes were more tangible, at least. Jamie would have a pony. And Marian would have a ring on her finger if she did not make Isabella's own foolish mistake.

"Marian, do not give in to . . ." she stole a look at Jamie to see how close he was attending. Naturally his whole attention was focused on her. She gave a huff of annoyance and stared meaningfully into her sister's eyes. "Not until his ring is on your finger."

"Certainly not," Marian said. Then her mouth dropped open. "Oh, dear. Eventually he is going to know . . ." She glanced at Jamie. "And then I will have some explaining to do."

Isabella closed her eyes. That was the problem with telling falsehoods. There never seemed to be an end to it.

"You cannot marry him," she said. "Please, you *cannot*! For if you do, you will have to take him into your confidence, and his horrible father will learn . . . and you know what he might do."

Marian's eyes grew hard.

"And you might be prevented from making a suitable marriage if it becomes known that . . ." She glanced again at Jamie.

"Betty, please take Jamie to the other room and put him down for his afternoon sleep," Isabella said in frustration.

The maid, who had kept an impassive face during the interchange between the sisters, gave a little nod of assent and took a protesting Jamie away.

"I am not sleepy," he said tearfully.

"Come along now, Master Jamie, do," the maid said in hushed tones as she towed the boy out of the room.

"Is that what you think?" Isabella demanded of Marian when the maid and Jamie were gone. "That I would sacrifice your happiness because I want to make a good *marriage?*" She gave a snort of derision. "Marriage, my dear, is vastly overrated."

Marian raised one eyebrow.

"How would *you* know?" she snapped.

"Touché," Isabella said dryly.

Marian put her hands to her reddened cheeks in consternation.

"Oh, Isabella, forgive me. I do not know what possessed me to say such an unkind thing to you!"

Isabella rolled her eyes.

"You really want this man, do you not?" she said with a sigh. "Really, I am still at a loss to account for it. What is going to happen to Jamie, may I ask, while you are fleeing to Gretna Green with your gallant major?"

"We are not going to elope," Marian said. Tears of emotion shone in her eyes. "He insisted that he would not marry me in secret, as if he were ashamed of me."

"So much for the three of us being a family," Isabella said wistfully.

"Families are still families, even if their members are not all together. You, Jamie, and I will be no exception," Marian said earnestly. "Please, I want him, Isabella. So much. It will be difficult for you, I know."

Difficult.

What an understatement!

Isabella's stomach quivered at the thought of the questions, the pitying looks, the *humiliation* of trying to hold on to the shreds of her dignity when her former fiancé married her half sister in such indecent haste and the gossips made a nine-day wonder of it all.

This anticipated ordeal paled to insignificance, though, when Isabella considered that her son would be living with Marian in Adam's house, and Isabella would be relegated to the status of mere visitor.

How could she bear it?

But how could she *not* bear it?

Her son would be reared by loving parents in Marian and Adam. It would be the best thing for him. Only a selfish person would stand in the way of his happiness and that of her loyal half sister. Isabella, herself, reputation intact—more or less—would resume the life she had known before Jamie's birth, that of brainless miss and ornament to Society.

If Isabella wanted to see her son in the future, she would have to be very, very conciliating to Adam.

She could do it, she thought as she mentally gritted her teeth.

For Jamie she could crawl on her hands and knees to the man, if she had to.

Chapter 28

Adam regarded the delicate miss, clothed all in white with a wreath of pink roses and trailing white ribbons in her blond curls, with attentive courtesy during their introduction, even though he had not the slightest interest in becoming acquainted with her.

It was not *her* fault that his father was thrusting every debutante of long pedigree and passing looks at him tonight. The man did not have a subtle bone in his body.

Adam was at Almack's, that Holy of Holies of marriage-making, and the hunt was on. Every patriotic peer, it seemed, was eager to secure the celebrated war hero—and incidentally heir to his father's title and fortune—for his darling little girl.

This particular darling little girl batted her long eyelashes at him. Her big, blue eyes shone with hero worship. He had no choice but to dance with her or embarrass her and her parents before the eyes of the *ton*.

Adam offered her his arm and escorted her to the dance floor as his father watched with a smug look of satisfaction.

He and Marian had agreed that he would break the news to his father that day, but Lord Revington had been absent from his home when Adam called on him, and there had been no opportunity to talk to him at the ball, not that Almack's was the appropriate place to inform his father that he had proposed marriage to a young woman the world believed to be the daughter of his regimental surgeon and the unwed mother of a child besides.

That little ordeal would be an appropriate end to a frustrating night. Mercifully, whether his father accepted his marriage to Marian or washed his hands of him, this tedious audition of nubile young debutantes would cease.

"Well, what did you think of her?" Lord Revington asked after Adam had danced with the girl, left her in the care of her mother, and returned to his father.

"She wanted to know all about the war. Details of certain battles." Adam gave a frown of distaste. "Specifically, the number of my kill and the manner of my killing them. The more gruesome the details, the better."

"You did not tell her, I hope," Lord Revington said. "The poor little thing would be having nightmares for weeks."

Adam gave a snort of derision.

"Not she. You should have seen the poor little thing's eyes sparkle with avid delight when she asked," he said dryly. "I have seen the phenomenon before. These Society misses may look like sugared meringues, but they have a peculiar taste for horrors."

"Well, then, what think you of Miss—"

"Father, I will give you a full report at the end of the evening on each one of them, I promise you, if you are still interested then."

It had been like this ever since the announcement releasing him from his betrothal appeared in the newspapers. Officially, Isabella had broken off their engagement, and Isabella also was at Almack's tonight so they could present the appearance of a civilized severing of their relationship before the world.

Perhaps it would have been in better taste for one of them to remain at home, but both fathers were adamant that they appear at Almack's tonight.

The fathers were eager to find their troublesome offspring new prospective spouses. It was a testament to the standing both the general and Lord Revington enjoyed in Society that the patronesses granted vouchers to Isabella, who had jilted the war hero, and the war hero himself, for, as a rule, there were not many military gentlemen to be found in the exclusive company at Almack's.

Major Lyonbridge, however, was heir to his father's title and lands, and therefore a very handsome *parti,* so an exception was graciously made.

"When will this farce be at an end?" Isabella asked Adam when they shared a dance at one point. She looked as bored as he felt.

"Not soon enough for me," he said. "You have changed. There was a time when you lived for balls."

She made no reply, because at that moment the pattern of the dance obliged her to circle with the other ladies in the center while the gentlemen circled them in the opposite direction.

It was a country dance, for to perform a waltz together would suggest to Isabelle and Adam's well-wishers that there was some hope of their reconciliation. The purpose of the dance was, on the contrary, to show the world not only that neither bore the other ill will, but that they could dance together in perfect civility without looking the least conscious.

"I will be glad when I am married to Marian," he said wryly when a movement of the dance brought them back together. "I feel like a perfect fool, being obligated to support the character of a man hanging out for a wife. These little debutantes are even sillier than you were when you were their age."

"As I live and breathe, a compliment!" Isabella exclaimed. "A backhanded one, to be sure, but a compliment, just the same. Perhaps you took too many blows to the head in the Peninsula."

He laughed, then clamped his mouth shut. It would not do to appear to be enjoying himself *too* much in Isabella's company, or her father would start campaigning for their marriage all over again.

"I thought you a complete blockhead, you know," she said with a sigh.

He raised one eyebrow.

"An opinion that has not altered, I trust."

"Not at all," she said with an airy smile as the dance ended.

He bowed, Isabella curtsied, and he returned her to her mother. He bowed to both ladies, noting the identical, fierce smiles of dismissal on their too-similar faces.

Adam smiled back and rejoiced mentally, once again, at his deliverance from marrying Isabella. Some other fellow would be left with her on his hands when she aged into a perfect copy of her difficult mother.

He would tell his father tonight that he intended to make Marian his bride. Then, as a courtesy, he would notify the general. He would not ask permission for Marian's hand, for that would be ridiculous.

Once that hurdle was accomplished, it would remain only for Marian to choose the church in which she wished to be married.

That, and the necessity of resigning his commission so his father could turn him into a gentleman farmer and a politician as well, if the old man had his way.

Adam would hate it, of course. He would make an abysmal gentleman farmer. All his skills were confined to those required for soldiering.

As for being an ornament to Society and a budding politician, there was nothing he cared for less. He consoled himself in the sure knowledge that once the polite world learned he was about to espouse the daughter of his regimental surgeon, he need never worry about the obligation to attend a ball at Almack's again.

Lord Revington, Adam devoutly hoped, might, in time,

forgive him for his misalliance; the Patronesses of Almack's, he knew, would not.

Adam smiled as he thought of Marian.

He was a lucky man. There was no nonsense about Marian, only loyalty, courage, and all that womanly beauty. She didn't give a hang for Almack's.

What a wife she would make for a career soldier! It was an everlasting pity that he was not destined to remain one.

Lord Revington's reception of Adam's news was not pleasant, nor had Adam expected it to be.

"Blast it, boy. You have gotten the little chit with child," the old man said with forbidding scowl. "How could you have been so stupid?"

"Of course I have not," Adam said, taken aback.

His father seemed a bit mollified at that.

"You relieve my mind," he said. "But even if the girl were breeding, there is no reason to marry her."

"There is *every* reason to marry her. I love Marian," Adam said.

"Love," Lord Revington scoffed. "I cannot think of a worse basis for marriage. You must trust your elders, boy, to choose correctly for you."

"You chose Isabella," Adam said dryly, "and we have seen how well *that* answered. We had her running off to the border with my brother on my wedding day. Marian, at least, is made of sterner stuff."

"She has borne a child without benefit of marriage, sir!" Lord Revington exclaimed. "Do you want to be made a laughingstock before all of Society?"

"Do you mean, *more* of a laughingstock than I was made the day the bride *you* chose for me ran off with my brother?"

Lord Revington gave a dismissive wave of his hand.

"No one knows about that," he said. "No one who matters, at any rate."

"So it didn't happen," Adam said sardonically.

"Precisely," said Lord Revington, taking the comment at face value. "This would be so much worse. My son to marry the daughter of an army sawbones? Every feeling revolts."

"It gets worse. The truth is, Marian is not the daughter of Captain Randall at all, although she did not know this until recently. She is actually the natural daughter of Lord Grimsby and a young woman who married Captain Randall before Marian was born. Lord Grimsby was married, of course, and could not do right by her. Marian and I agreed that you have a right to know the truth if she is going to marry into your family."

Lord Revington closed his eyes for a moment to get a grip on his temper.

"And you would *marry* this woman? Grimsby's *love child* is to be the mother of my grandchildren? I think not."

"If you accept Marian as my wife," Adam said, "I will resign my commission and put myself in your hands to be groomed as your heir."

Lord Revington looked up at that. He would have said something, but Adam held up one hand to stop him and continued.

"But if you do not accept Marian with every honor as my wife," Adam said, "I shall not resign my commission. Marian and I will leave with my regiment, and you will never see me—or your only grandchildren—ever. I will not expose my children to your disdain."

"The insolence! You *dare* threaten *me*?" Lord Revington shouted.

"Yes! For Marian I would dare *anything*."

"You mean it, by God," his father said bitterly. "You really will turn your back on your responsibilities as my heir for that girl if I do not dance to the tune of your piping. I thought you had no guile in you. Instead, I find you are a manipulative, conniving—"

"I am," Adam said with a wolfish smile. "And I learned

it by following my father's excellent example. Do you give your consent?"

Lord Revington gave his son a fulminating glare.

"I have no choice," he said in resignation. "I wish you joy of the little hussy."

"Thank you, Father," Adam said.

"I expect you to keep your part of the bargain. At the end of the summer, after the Peace Celebrations, I expect you to resign your commission."

Adam bowed.

"Agreed," he said. "Good evening, Father. I must leave you now, for I have another call to make."

Lord Revington gave him a look of disapproval.

"You are going to fly into the arms of your inamorata, I suppose," he said in disgust.

"Sadly, no," Adam said with a sigh. "I am going to call on Lord Grimsby to inform him that I am going to marry his daughter. The sooner this business is settled, the better."

"You wish to marry Marian," General Lord Grimsby repeated blankly. Then his eyes brightened, he shot to his feet, and he raced across the short distance to where Adam was standing and pumped his hand enthusiastically. "Excellent, excellent. Marian is a fine girl. You will not be sorry."

"I know I will not," Adam said.

"Let us drink to the match, then," the general said. He left off wringing Adam's hand to busy himself at the decanters. "By Jove, I never thought to see the girl settled so well, not after that business with the child."

He handed Adam a glass of port.

"I must insist, though, that you leave Marian and the child in England when your regiment goes on its next assignment. Following the drum, even in peacetime, is no life for a woman. I believe the regiment is to be stationed in Scotland next, and—"

"I will not be going to Scotland," Adam said.

Lord Grimsby looked surprised for an instant, then he gave a knowing laugh.

"Of course," he said. "Forgive me, boy. You will be wanting further leave for your honeymoon. Well, do not make it a long one. You will be needed back with the regiment, and—"

"I am resigning my commission at the end of the summer," Adam interrupted. "It is my father's price for accepting Marian as my wife. I am to be groomed for my position as his heir. He also has political aspirations for me. He has no doubt he can persuade Lord Liverpool to appoint me to some prestigious office in the Government."

"What? I am to lose my best officer at his whim?" He gave Adam a long look. "And you agreed to this?"

"I have given my word," Adam said.

General Grimsby's eyes narrowed.

"You know," he said carefully, "if you have got the girl with child, other arrangements may be made—"

Adam clenched his jaw to keep from planting his future father-in-law a facer.

"I have *not* got Marian with child. You should be ashamed of yourself for suggesting such a thing."

"And you want to marry her, anyway."

"I love her."

"Well, my boy," the general said genially. "I could not be more delighted to have you as a son-in-law, even though the relationship cannot be officially acknowledged. You understand, of course."

"Completely," Adam said tersely, resentful, on Marian's behalf, that the world perceived theirs as an unequal match. She was worth a hundred of any of the spoiled little debutantes his father had tried to foist upon him at Almack's. "The marriage will take place in three weeks at the parish church near my property in Derbyshire."

"Three weeks! Could you not wait until the summer is over? You said she was not with child!"

"And so she is not. We *could* wait, but we will not," Adam said. "I hope you will grace the wedding with your presence."

"I would not miss it," he said heartily. Then he looked sheepish. "I am afraid my wife—"

"Lady Grimsby may attend or not, as she wishes. And Marian would like for Isabella to attend. As her bridesmaid."

"I say," Lord Grimsby said, frowning. "Will that not give rise to talk?"

"*More* talk, do you mean?" Adam suggested sardonically.

Lord Grimsby gave a snort of agreement.

"It matters not, I suppose," the general said. "Isabella is at Marian's lodgings more often than she is here. The girls are thick as inkle weavers, much to her mother's displeasure."

He gave an eloquent shudder, and by that Adam knew that he had been suffering for his wife's disapproval of the friendship between Isabella and Marian.

Adam refused to feel sorry for General Grimsby and the abuse his difficult wife would no doubt heap on his head when she learned the news of the impending marriage, although Adam could not quite condemn the general for the amorous indiscretion that had given him his gallant Marian.

"Very well, then," Adam said, bowing as he prepared to take his leave.

When he opened the door, he found a breathless Isabella approaching the room.

"My maid told me you had come to the house," she said anxiously. "Is all settled?"

"Did *you* know of this, miss, and not a word to me?" her father demanded.

"Of course, Father," Isabella said. "I have come to tell

you that Marian will require a hundred pounds for the wedding, and I expect you to make her a decent dowry. Another five hundred pounds should do it, do you not think, Adam?"

"Six hundred pounds!" Lord Grimsby exclaimed.

"Timing, Isabella," Adam murmured. "The money does not matter. I can afford to give Marian a decent wedding, and to support her and the boy. I have my savings, and I received a legacy from my—"

"The money *does* matter, and you know it," Isabella insisted. "Knowing your beastly father, he will make you some miserly allowance during his lifetime to punish you for marrying against his wishes, and he is such a mean old buzzard that he is likely to live forever. Besides, my sister's honor requires that she bring a dowry to your marriage. Would you see her shamed by coming to you with just the clothes on her back?"

"And her bastard child," the general said sardonically. "Do not forget *that* little inducement."

Two pairs of wrathful eyes turned on him.

"Who are *you* to cast those particular stones, Father?" Isabella demanded.

"I will not have Marian disparaged over something that obviously happened to her after Captain Randall's death when she thought herself all alone in the world," Adam said angrily. "The boy will be my son. He will take my name and live in my house, and he will be brought up with any children Marian and I may have together."

"Six hundred pounds," General Grimsby said in a small voice. "And what your mother will have to say, Isabella, I cannot bear to think."

Chapter 29

Marian's wedding day dawned clear and sunny, without a cloud in the blue summer sky. A recent rain had washed the world new again and caused the flowers she and Isabella had planted near the house in the spring of the previous year to burst forth in glorious bloom.

As Marian stood at the window of her room in Adam's house in her white nightrail, Isabella came to stand beside her.

Adam, of course, was staying at his father's manor house until after the wedding.

"You shall have a beautiful day," Isabella said.

"I know," Marian said, turning with a smile to give her sister a hug.

She thrust to the back of her mind the fact that soon Adam would have to resign his commission. Part of her was glad, because dreadful things could happen to a soldier—even an officer—in peacetime as easily as in war. But part of her was apprehensive, for she knew he would hate being a gentleman farmer dogged by his father all his days.

For her part, Marian knew she was no housewife. She had known little in her adult life except campaigning and nursing the sick, and such skills, most unfortunately, had not translated into those required for running a household efficiently. Isabella, not Marian, had taken over these responsibilities when the two young women came to live here before Jamie was born.

Marian was useless when it came to supervising the maids. She found it easier to do the work herself than to delegate the household tasks to others.

But if Adam could learn to be a viscount, Marian would learn to be a viscount's wife. Somehow.

Adam had chosen *her* over his career. He had chosen *her* over the most beautiful and well-dowered young women in the kingdom.

It was up to *her* to make sure he did not regret it.

"It is time to dress," Isabella said with a grin. "Now the fun begins."

The maid would dress Isabella first, Isabella explained, so that Marian would be as fresh and uncrushed as possible when she went to the church.

Isabella's figure was not quite so slim as it had been before Jamie's birth, but she looked extraordinarily beautiful in the sunny yellow gauze gown she had chosen for her sister's wedding.

Marian answered Isabella's cheerful remarks with an absent smile as Betty put the finishing touches on Isabella's coiffure. She kept walking to the wardrobe door, which was open to expose the dainty, lace-trimmed white gown and veil that Marian was to wear for the ceremony, to feast her eyes on the pretty costume.

She had argued in vain that a white gown and virginal wedding veil were highly inappropriate for an unmarried woman who had given birth to a child. Isabella, who knew Marian was no such thing, was adamant.

There was going to be gossip about the wedding, anyway, she reasoned. Marian might as well wear what she wished.

At nine o'clock, one of Lord Revington's open carriages swept into the yard, and Marian and Isabella, accompanied by Betty and an ebullient Jamie, were assisted inside by one of the viscount's liveried footmen.

Jamie kept bouncing on the seat in his excitement.

"Adam is going to be my papa!" he said.

The look on Isabella's face caused Marian to reach out and touch her sister's shoulder. It would not be easy for Isabella to endure the prospect of being separated from Jamie. She would always be a welcome visitor in Marian and Adam's home, but from now on she would live apart from her precious son.

If that dreadful Lord Revington dared slight Jamie in any way, he was going to be sorry!

Marian found upon arrival at the church that all the neighbors and village residents had turned out to greet the bride. When the footman handed her down, her well-wishers applauded for her. She gave them a brilliant smile.

At that moment, all her doubts were banished.

This was her wedding day, and, today, it seemed, everyone loved a bride. She was determined to enjoy every minute of it. How could she not be happy? Soon she would be Adam's wife!

Little girls ran up to her with flowers in their small, plump fingers, and Marian gathered all the pretty summer blossoms in her arms. She would have carried them into the church, but Isabella took them from her and handed them to a footman to place in the carriage.

At that moment, Lord Grimsby walked out of the church and took Marian's arm. His eyes were moist with tears of emotion. He cleared his throat.

"Today, I stand in the place of your father," he said huskily, "and I beg you to grant me the honor of escorting the bride."

"With all my heart," Marian said, and meant it.

Marian wished she could have been escorted to her wedding by Captain Randall, the only father she had ever known, but General Lord Grimsby would do as a substitute today.

He would do very well.

"I have something for you," the general said. He handed her a small velvet pouch.

Marian felt a lump in her throat as her fingers drew the familiar smooth, cool, white necklace from it.

Her mother's pearls.

She had never expected to see them again after the day she had cast them on the general's desk with anger in her heart, let alone wear them on her wedding day.

"Thank you," she whispered as the general clasped them around her neck for her. She kissed his cheek.

Lord Grimsby gave her a sentimental smile.

"You are so much like her. Especially today," he said. He patted Jamie on the head. "Go with—" he indicated the maid and gave Isabella a questioning look.

"Betty," Isabella said.

"Betty," Lord Grimsby repeated. "Go with Betty into the church now, lad. There is a place for you right up front near the bride's family, where you may see everything. Betty, it is the pew behind my wife's."

The maid dipped a curtsy, took Jamie's hand, and shushed him, for his excited chatter was loud as he hastened inside to see his first wedding.

"Thank you, Papa," said Isabella with a radiant smile.

"Yes, thank you . . . my lord," said Marian.

Mrs. Peevey, the housekeeper at Lord Revington's manor house, approached Isabella with a prettily arranged cluster of violets and pink roses in her hands. The flowers were tied together with long curling silver ribbons. She whispered something to Isabella and, beaming, went back into the church.

"Look, Marian," Isabella said. "Your wedding bouquet, from Adam."

"How beautiful!" Marian exclaimed. Her vision blurred slightly.

"None of that, my girl," Isabella said, smiling. "It will not do for you to go to Adam with a red, running nose." She placed the bouquet in Marian's white-gloved hands. "These are very pretty. Not too ostentatious, not too simple. Charming and elegant. I would not have credited Adam with such good taste."

She gave Marian a mischievous look.

"Someone else must have chosen them for him."

So it was with laughter on her lips that Marian walked to her bridegroom on her father's arm.

Adam stood straighter when he saw his bride and the general come into the church. She was so lovely, she took his breath away.

Was there ever so perfect a bride?

Her brilliant red hair was caught up in a sparkling crystal comb, and a fine lace veil cascaded down her back. The bodice of her dress was low and sleeveless to display a ladylike portion of her generous bosom and beautifully molded arms.

She looked . . . happy. Radiantly happy.

He knew he was grinning like a fool. He could not help it.

All of the officers of his regiment who could be gathered were present to do honor to the major's future wife.

His father's face was impassive, which was about the best that could be hoped for. Unlike the other guests, Lady Grimsby had not stood to face the bridal procession when Marian entered the church. How like her to choose this slight as a means of registering her disapproval.

Adam felt his grin grow wider.

His future son, Marian's Jamie, was standing up in the pew behind Lady Grimsby. The maid who was supposed to be minding him was facing the back of the church, no doubt sighing sentimentally at the pretty picture presented by the distinguished General Lord Grimsby and his radiant daughters.

So no one but Adam noticed that Jamie was leaning over the back of Lady Grimsby's pew, methodically picking apart the expensive peacock feathers on her fashionable hat.

* * *

Marian knew that a proper bride should be shy and hesitant, so she was grateful for Lord Grimsby's measured tread to the altar and the firm hand he kept on her arm.

If not for that, she might have floated up the length of the church—or raced to the front like a hoyden.

She had seen Adam in his regimental dress uniform often enough before today, and as usual he was devastatingly handsome in it. His sun-streaked hair was freshly trimmed. But it was the big, beautiful smile on his face that threatened to make her eyes fill with sentimental tears.

That was when she truly believed what he had been telling her these past few weeks leading up to the wedding—that it made no difference at all to him what he had to sacrifice in order to marry her.

He loved her. He truly loved her.

"You are beautiful," he whispered when Lord Grimsby solemnly placed her hand in his and stepped back.

"So are you," she said breathlessly as she looked up into his blue, blue eyes so full of love and promise.

They made their vows in clear, confident voices. The pastor pronounced them man and wife. And when it was time for him to kiss the bride, Adam did so with a mere decorous brushing of the lips.

"Later," he told her with a promise in his solemn eyes when she gave him a quizzical look. He looked as if he might eat her up, and she quivered with anticipation.

Then they turned to face the congregation, which broke into simultaneous applause. The members of Adam's regiment preceded them down the aisle, and once the party had walked out of the church and into the sunshine, they held their crossed swords aloft in a canopy of Toledo steel so the newly married couple could walk under the blades.

A small, elegant wedding breakfast was held immediately after the ceremony at Adam's house for members of the couple's family, friends, and the leading members of the gentry in the neighborhood. When the last crumb of fruitcake had been consumed, the guests drifted away with good wishes on their lips.

The last to go were Isabella and Betty, who had a difficult time persuading Jamie that he was to go to Lord Revington's estate with them to spend the afternoon and the night. He could come back tomorrow.

Jamie's lower lip was out. He wanted to stay with Mama and his new papa now. Had they not said they would all live together, the three of them?

Happily, all the cake was not gone after all! Aunt Isabella had saved a piece for him. See? She knelt down to show him that she had wrapped the cake in a serviette and placed it in her reticule. It was their secret, mind. If he was very, very good, he would have some with hot chocolate after dinner.

There was nothing Jamie liked better than cake and hot chocolate.

"I love you, Aunt Isabella," he said, putting his little arms around her neck.

"I love you, too, darling," she whispered. With that, she picked him up and jiggled him to make him laugh. Then she settled him on one hip, nodded for the maid to follow, and went out to the carriage Lord Revington had placed at her disposal.

Chapter 30

Marian went up to undress for bed an indecently short time after it was dark. Adam's elderly housekeeper—*her* housekeeper, too, now—helped Marian out of the pink muslin gown she had donned after the wedding guests had left and into the white lace nightrail that had been a gift from Isabella.

She blushed when she saw her reflection in the glass.

"Mr. Adam will be pleased, ma'am," the housekeeper said with a sentimental sigh. She cast a complacent eye over the bouquets of pink roses in crystal vases, the bowl of strawberries with cream, the bottle of chilled champagne resting in a silver bucket placed next to the bed.

White curtains fluttered at the open windows and the sweet fragrance of flowers from the garden wafted into the room. The housekeeper lit more of the white candles placed in silver holders on the table and mantel.

At a soft knock on the door, Marian self-consciously drew her hands up to cover her bosom, which was barely concealed by the delicate lace of the nightrail. Then she laughed at herself.

"Come in," she called out.

Adam walked into the room and stared at her.

She stared back.

Marian had seen many men in varying degrees of nakedness due to her father's occupation, but never had she seen such a glorious sight as Adam in undress.

His long legs were encased in skin-tight pantaloons, and his white shirt was open at the throat to reveal the long column of his throat. His hair obviously was just washed. It was still a bit damp at the ends. His face was freshly shaven out of consideration for his bride's delicate complexion, and his eyes were so ardent that Marian felt her knees grow weak.

"You may go," he said to the housekeeper, but his eyes were still on Marian.

The housekeeper fanned her flushed cheeks and dipped a curtsy.

"I wish you joy," she said before she turned and left the room.

Adam approached Marian and kissed her hand. Then he turned it in his long fingers and kissed her wrist.

"I have seen that trick before," she said with narrowed eyes.

He gave her a sheepish grin.

They were both remembering that moment at the decoration ceremony, when he caused women to swoon in the gallery by saluting Isabella in just this way.

"I know," he said softly. "Amazingly effective, is it not?"

She closed her eyes.

"Amazingly," she whispered.

Adam took this opportunity to place hot, sweet kisses on her closed eyelids, and then her lips.

His arms came around her waist, and she trailed her fingers through his wonderful smooth hair as she returned his increasingly passionate kisses with equal passion. He drew the short lace sleeves of her gown down so that he could place small, perfect kisses on her shoulders. His hand molded her breasts, and soon she found the bodice of her nightgown pulled down around her waist. Breathing hard, she pulled his shirt from the waistband of his pantaloons and ran her hands underneath the shirt to caress the warm skin of his muscular, lightly furred chest.

Adam then put her away from him and stood back, but only so that he could remove her gown completely from her exquisite body. He could only stare for a moment. She was as perfect, as pure as any classical statue. Her green eyes were alight with passion.

"You are so beautiful, my bride," he whispered.

In one smooth motion, he drew his shirt off and threw it on the floor. His pantaloons followed. Then he picked Marian up in his arms and gently placed her on the bed.

He cupped her face in his hands and kissed her with all the hunger in his soul. She was whimpering with need by the time he released her lips.

His bride.

He caught her in his arms so that every beautiful inch of her skin was pressed intimately to his. He felt, rather than heard, her breath catch. She was bracing herself.

He smiled in the candlelit half-light.

"Not yet, my darling," he said as he placed tender kisses on her upturned face. His hand spanned her flat belly completely. "I am not at all in a hurry to see this end."

Adam could hear the maids giggling through the open windows of the house as he sat on the veranda overlooking the gardens, sipping his morning coffee and awaiting the appearance of his bride.

The cook and maids had arrived sometime in the dawn from the village, and shortly thereafter the fragrance of fresh-baked pastries filled the house.

Flaky pastries filled with strawberry jelly rested on a pretty china plate on the table next to a bowl of strawberries and cream.

Apparently his staff was under the impression that newlyweds could subsist entirely on such dainty morsels. He certainly hoped there would be something a bit more substantial for dinner.

Then Marian appeared in the doorway, and he forgot all about the demands of his stomach.

She was dressed in a sea-green gown, and her hair flowed down her back, tied with a yellow ribbon. Her face was delicately flushed and her gorgeous green eyes were languid.

"Good morning, my sweet," he said. "Will you have a cup of coffee?"

"I am sorry to be so late. I should have been up well before now, pouring coffee for *you,*" she said. He noticed that she moved without her usual grace.

His bride was sore.

His virgin bride.

How very unexpected.

"At the risk of spoiling the mood, my love, I have questions," he said.

Marian bit her lip and sat down with a sigh.

"I thought you might," she said ruefully.

He looked toward the house to make sure there were no maids lingering close by. He lowered his voice, even though he could see no one.

"Delightful as I find the prospect of being Jamie's father," he said, "I am rather wondering where he came from."

"He is Isabella's son," she said, also whispering.

Adam nodded.

"I thought he might be. Isabella has permitted your reputation to be lost to preserve her own."

"It was not like that. It was *never* like that," Marian said.

"What *was* it like, then?"

"She was afraid your father would take him away from her if he knew."

Adam nodded again. Sadly.

"He is Philip's son."

Of course. Why had he not known it at once? The boy had the same dark hair. The same mischievous, dark blue eyes. He was Philip to the life.

"Yes. She could not bear the thought of having him reared by your father, who was sure to place him with strangers who might not be kind to him. Isabella is all too aware of how a bastard is treated in a great man's household, since her father produced so many of them."

Adam knew Lord Revington would have done it, by God. He would have torn Jamie away from his mother, no doubt with Lord and Lady Grimsby's blessing.

"I am nobody," Marian continued. "I might be allowed to keep my child. And I was eager to avoid a marriage Lady Grimsby was determined to arrange for me. We informed Lady Grimsby that I was pregnant. We assumed we would be permitted to stay in Lord Grimsby's country house in seclusion for fear of scandal, and no one would be the wiser. We did not expect her to cast me from the house. Your timely rescue and the use of this house was a godsend."

Adam shook his head.

"No wonder Isabella hovers over Jamie like a hen with one chick."

"She *is* a hen with one chick," Marian said ruefully. She gave him an anxious look. "You said you would rear him as your own son and love him as your own son," she said. "He is innocent, Adam. You are too good a man not to honor your promise."

"He is Philip's own child," Adam said wonderingly. "Did you think I would not love him all the more if I had known? Having him in the house will be like having something of my brother restored to me."

With a little cry of happiness, Marian rose from her chair and ran to Adam to throw her arms around his neck.

"Thank you, my darling," she whispered. "I knew you would understand."

Chapter 31

Marian hated being the mistress of a household. The maids who came up from the village for work each day, she was quite sure, despised her for being so ignorant about household matters.

Her elderly housekeeper tried to teach her, but Marian was hopeless. Absolutely hopeless.

She had no eye for a table left undusted by a lazy maid, and when the housekeeper gently informed her that it was time to turn out the linens for washing, she had no idea what an ordeal it was simply to ensure that she and her husband would be sleeping on clean sheets at night.

Isabella had taken care of all these things when she was living here, and Marian sorely missed her. Her half sister had enjoyed ordering all the servants about, and woe to the maid who halfheartedly pursued her duties. Each meal was perfect when Isabella was here.

And Jamie was never this mischievous when Isabella was in the house.

Marian had spent months on campaign and long days caring for the wounded soldiers in the regimental hospital. She assisted Captain Randall in his surgery and occasionally even set a broken arm or leg herself if the surgeon was not available.

She had thought she was exhausted at the end of those days, but she had no idea, then, of how difficult it was to stay one step ahead of one small, usually grubby little boy whose talent for inventing new ways to do injury to the carpeting, painted walls, and his own small precious person was enough to turn Marian's hair white.

Late that afternoon, Adam came into the house ready to drop from fatigue after being harangued by his father all day, and he stopped dead on the threshold at the spectacle of his wife and the nursery maid chasing Jamie through the room. The little devil had a whole pot of jam in his hands and obviously had partaken liberally of its contents, from the look of his berry-stained face, before his theft was discovered.

He managed the glimmer of a smile when Marian skidded to a stop before him.

Her hair was coming loose from its pins, her gown was rumpled, and she looked as if she might cry at any moment.

Adam held out his arms.

Marian walked into her husband's embrace and pillowed her head on his chest with a long sigh of relief. She had wanted to comb her hair and tidy herself so she would look presentable when her husband came home to her after a day of being put through his paces by his imperious father. But before she knew it, the day had gotten away from her.

It seemed odd to see Adam out of uniform, but it made no sense for him to wear his scarlet coat when his father was taking him all over his nearby estate. The brown coat and scuffed boots made him look diminished, somehow. Not quite so handsome and impressive, although just as dear.

He will look like this from now on, she realized.

"My poor darling," she said. "You did not look this exhausted after Salamanca."

"Neither did you," he said as he kissed the top of her head. "Lord, you smell good. I have been in the cattle barn for most of the day learning more than I ever wanted to know about breeding and feeding and milking and branding and birthing cows. I will never feel the same about a beefsteak again."

"Papa! Papa! Papa!" cried Jamie as he raced from the other room and ran straight at Adam, who gave a grunt of pain when he plowed right into his knees.

Adam picked the child up and gave him a kiss on the nose. Jamie buried his jam-stained face in Adam's shoulder and left a sticky mulberry smear on it.

"And have you been good for your mother today, Jamie?" Adam asked. Marian had to smile. He sounded every bit the patriarch.

"Yes," Jamie said without a trace of guilt on his face.

Marian was tempted to tell Adam that the housekeeper's cat would not agree with this sunny assessment of Jamie's behavior after he escaped from the nursery maid and chased the poor cat around the kitchen, which caused the cook to drop a fresh-baked pie on the floor and threaten to give her notice. Marian and the housekeeper practically had to get on their knees to avert this calamity.

That was *before* the little devil stole the jam jar and left sticky handprints all over the wainscoting in the dining room. The nursery maid was in tears, and Marian supposed they would have to hire another one in addition to her, for it was plain that Jamie was too much of a handful for Marian and one skinny girl to control.

Adam gave Marian a rueful smile, as if he could read her mind. He gathered her close with his free arm so the three of them were huddled in a cocoon of comfort.

"We will weather these rough seas somehow, my love," he said softly as he kissed the top of her head again, and then Jamie's. "We have much to learn about being a family, but we will do so in time."

"Thank you, Adam," Marian said with a sigh. "It is a good thing you did not expect to come home to a smoothly running household. Dinner will be late because the cook was too upset to begin it on time."

"The cook was upset? About the jam jar?"
"About the cat."
"The cat?" Adam said, mystified.
"Never mind, love," Marian said with a sigh. "I will tell you later."
"After Jamie is in bed," Adam whispered with his secret smile.
"Yes, then," she said longingly.

At eleven o'clock, Jamie was wide awake and insisting that Marian read him another story.
"Can you not give him some warm milk?" Adam said in desperation from the doorway. The child's eyes were heavy with exhaustion, and his voice was high and cranky, but still he would not rest.
"I want Aunt Isabella," Jamie said tearfully.
"I know, darling," Marian said with a sigh. "I know."
Adam came over to the bed and sat down on the other side of Jamie. He put his arm around him.
"Perhaps you would like me to read for a while," he said to Marian.
"Oh, yes, Adam," she said gratefully. "Thank you."
A half hour later, Adam allowed his voice to trail off when he saw Jamie had at last fallen asleep. Unfortunately, so had Marian.
Adam stepped around the bed, where Marian was lying next to the child, and gently shook her shoulder.
"Come along, love. He is asleep at last," he whispered into her ear.
She smiled in her sleep but did not wake.
"Marian," he whispered again.
She gave a small frown and burrowed back into the pillow when he took her arm and tried to coax her out of bed.
"Go 'way," she murmured.

Adam's bride was sound asleep. At least she didn't snore.

He thought longingly of his wedding night. The flowers, the candles, the champagne, his lovely bride, eagerly returning his caresses, and Jamie, being entertained elsewhere.

Adam should be disappointed tonight, but in truth he had to admit he was so tired that he feared he could not have risen to the occasion, so to speak, even if he had found an eager bride waiting for him in their bed.

He was not willing to sleep apart from her, however.

He lifted his bride carefully into his arms, not so much to avoid disturbing her slumber as to avoid disturbing the child's. Heaven forbid he should wake and demand another story.

Marian roused a bit as he carried her down the hall to her bedroom.

"Adam," she said softly.

"Yes, sweet," he replied.

"I am afraid I am a very bad wife."

He smiled.

"Why is that?" he asked.

"All I can think of is sleep tonight."

"Me, too, love. Pray, do not give it another thought."

"That's all right then," she said, and drifted back to sleep in his arms.

"No, no, *no!*" shouted Lord Revington, goaded beyond endurance by his heir's blockish stupidity. They were going over the estate accounts, and the perverse boy had not been listening to a word he said, obviously, or he might by now have retained *something* of his father's instruction.

"I am sorry, Father," Adam said, running a hand through his hair. "This is all so new to me."

"I know. I am trying to be patient," Lord Revington said wearily. "I will not live forever. You must be ready to step into my shoes when I am gone. And that wife of yours had better give you a son, or the title will revert to the crown when you are dead."

"I know, I know," Adam said, strangely reluctant to dwell upon the possibility of his father's demise. If Lord Revington only knew how unlikely it was that he and Marian would produce a son at this rate, he would have an apoplexy. In the two weeks of their marriage, they had fallen asleep together right after Jamie did two nights out of three.

But when they did not . . .

"You have the silliest look on your face," Lord Revington complained. "Do try to pay attention."

"Yes, Father," Adam said with a sigh.

Chapter 32

Lisbon, Portugal

The guard stationed in front of the colonel's tent scowled at the filthy, barefooted man before him. He wrinkled his nose. The fellow smelled like he had been dwelling among pigs and wallowing with them in their pigsty.

He had dark hair matted down with perspiration and a heavy beard. His arms and legs were matchstick thin.

"The colonel," the man muttered in a heavy Spanish accent. "I must see him at once."

"Begone," the guard said. "The colonel does not see every beggar who comes here demanding his attention."

"He will see me," the man insisted.

At that moment, the colonel himself came to the flap of the tent. He wrinkled his nose at the filthy man, as the guard had done. The colonel was a fighting man, and he was not happy to have been ordered to stay behind to keep the peace as the last troops prepared to be shipped home to England. He had little patience for the uncouth natives and their endless complaints.

"What is this?" the colonel demanded of the guard.

"This filthy peasant says he must see you, sir. Shall I put a hole through his leg?" He gestured to his firearm and waited in expectation, apparently, for the peasant to shriek with alarm and go scurrying back into the trees from whence he came. Instead, the fellow merely looked at him.

The colonel frowned at the guard. He was not one to tolerate levity of this sort on duty.

"Be off with you," the colonel said to the Spaniard.

At that the man stood straight, and the colonel perceived that he was much taller than he at first supposed.

"Who are you?" the colonel asked.

"I am merely José Garcia, my colonel," the man said with a grin, in his execrable English. "As of late in service to a certain French general."

The colonel gave a hearty laugh and clapped the peasant on the back as the guard's mouth fell open in astonishment.

"Close your mouth, man, you look like an idiot," the colonel said good-naturedly. "Do you not recognize him?"

The guard merely looked blank.

"It is a good disguise," the colonel said, clapping the peasant on the back again.

The guard peered at the peasant and noted that his grin revealed a mouthful of perfect white teeth.

"Tell him who you are," the colonel said to the man.

The peasant drew himself up to his full height and stood at attention.

"Captain Philip Lyonbridge," he said crisply in perfect, aristocratic English. "At your service."

He smiled at the colonel.

"I hope you enjoyed the copies of the French orders at Vitoria and the other papers I found lying about where any sneaking Spanish scoundrel could make off with them."

"That I did, my boy. That I did," the colonel said. "Good work, Lyonbridge. Glad to see you alive. That was damned dangerous work you were doing, damned dangerous. Let us have a drink before we notify the British Government that instead of being killed last year, you have been working as a spy behind enemy lines."

* * *

"He's asleep," Marian whispered as she crept into the parlor, where Adam was reading a newspaper.

"At last," he said, holding his arms out for her. He kissed her on the top of her head. "To bed, wife. Shall I carry you, most romantically, up the stairway?"

She looked sorely tempted, but practicality asserted itself.

"Let us just get up the stairs as quickly—and as quietly—as we can," she said, taking his hand and running toward the stairway.

Stifling their laughter, they almost made it to the top of the stair before they heard a peevish little voice cry out tearfully, "Mama! Where are you, Mama? I want another story!"

"Do not look so glum, my dear," Marian said to Adam as she poured his morning coffee for him. "I am sorry about last night," she said in a lowered voice.

"There will be other nights," he said, smiling bravely.

The sound of the front door knocker reached them, and Adam's brows rose in surprise.

"Now, who would be calling on us at this hour?" he asked.

"Lord Revington to see you, sir," the housekeeper said with a little dip of a curtsy in Adam's direction. "Ma'am," she added to Marian.

"Lord Revington. At this hour," Marian said wonderingly.

Adam started from the room, but he caught Marian's hand and took her along with him.

"Father?" Adam asked, alarmed, when he reached the parlor and found his father furtively dashing tears from his eyes. "What is wrong?"

"Nothing is wrong," he said. When he raised his head, Adam could see the smile on his face. "Your brother is alive."

He handed Adam the letter in his hand.

"A spy?" Adam said in astonishment as he looked up from the letter. "Philip has been spying on the French all this time?"

"Yes," Lord Revington said. "He is on his way to London from Lisbon."

"This is wonderful news—the best news!" Adam said. "By God, wife, we're off to Scotland!"

He took Marian's hands and did a little dance with her around the room that left her breathless.

"See here, boy, have you taken leave of your senses?" Lord Revington demanded. "You can't be going off to Scotland before he gets home."

"Can't I just!" Adam said. "I am no longer your heir, so I am not going to resign my commission. It's peacetime, so you can hardly have any objection."

"Well, I suppose not," Lord Revington said grudgingly.

"Marian, you must write to Isabella at once," Adam said.

"To . . . Isabella?" she asked, all at sea.

"So she can come here and take charge of Jamie," he said. "You are going with me to Scotland, and who better to stay with the boy than his precious Aunt Isabella? It will not be as exciting as being at war, I am afraid, my love, but you will find quite as many broken skulls to keep you busy in Scotland as you did bullet holes in Spain, I promise you. The Scots are prestigious brawlers, as are my fellows when they're spoiling for a bit of action."

"Adam, I *forbid* you to—"

Adam took his father's shoulders and kissed him on both cheeks.

"Father, you have made me a very happy man," Adam said. "Give Philip our best regards! Come, wife. We have packing to do."